"Olivia," Sebastia[...] stop fighting me. We have to go in the house."

Her blue eyes still held the hollow look of fear. Olivia wasn't there; she was still lost. "I can't...I can't breathe in there." Her voice was a whisper. "I need to breathe."

He'd thought he could keep the truth from her. That he could hold her in the safety of the house while he tracked down the stalker. He saw now that that was impossible. To keep her safe, he would have to confess the truth.

"I know you do, sweetheart. But there's someone out there who wants to hurt you. And he'll go through anyone and anything to destroy what I care for the most."

Dear Harlequin Intrigue Reader,

Those April showers go hand in hand with a welcome downpour of gripping romantic suspense in the Harlequin Intrigue line this month!

Reader-favorite Rebecca York returns to the legendary 43 LIGHT STREET with *Out of Nowhere*—an entrancing tale about a beautiful blond amnesiac who proves downright lethal to a hard-edged detective's heart. Then take a detour to New Mexico for *Shotgun Daddy* by Harper Allen—the conclusion in the MEN OF THE DOUBLE B RANCH trilogy. In this story a Navajo protector must safeguard the woman from his past who is nurturing a ticking time bomb of a secret.

The momentum keeps building as Sylvie Kurtz launches her brand-new miniseries—THE SEEKERS—about men dedicated to truth, justice…and protecting the women they love. But at what cost? Don't miss the debut book, *Heart of a Hunter*, where the search for a killer just might culminate in rekindled love. Passion and peril go hand in hand in *Agent Cowboy* by Debra Webb, when COLBY AGENCY investigator Trent Tucker races against time to crack a case of triple murder!

Rounding off a month of addictive romantic thrillers, watch for the continuation of two new thematic promotions. A handsome sheriff saves the day in *Restless Spirit* by Cassie Miles, which is part of COWBOY COPS. *Sudden Recall* by Jean Barrett is the latest in our DEAD BOLT series about silent memories that unlock simmering passions.

Enjoy all of our great offerings.

Sincerely,

Denise O'Sullivan
Senior Editor
Harlequin Intrigue

HEART OF A HUNTER

SYLVIE KURTZ

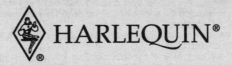

HARLEQUIN®

TORONTO • NEW YORK • LONDON
AMSTERDAM • PARIS • SYDNEY • HAMBURG
STOCKHOLM • ATHENS • TOKYO • MILAN • MADRID
PRAGUE • WARSAW • BUDAPEST • AUCKLAND

To my family whose continued support
means the world to me.

AUTHOR'S NOTE

Even a mild traumatic brain injury
can alter a person for a lifetime. Becuase of the short time frame
of this story and because it is a romance,
I downplayed the pain and the expected physical symptoms
someone with Olivia's injuries would feel.
Her recovery is an ongoing process that
will require her to adapt and will probably
last the rest of her life.

ISBN 0-373-22767-1

HEART OF A HUNTER

Printed in U.S.A.

ABOUT THE AUTHOR

Flying an eight-hour solo cross-country in a Piper Arrow with only the airplane's crackling radio and a large bag of M&M's for company, Sylvie Kurtz realized a pilot's life wasn't for her. The stories zooming in and out of her mind proved more entertaining than the flight itself. Not a quitter, she finished her pilot's course and earned her commercial license and instrument rating.

Since then, she has traded in her wings for a keyboard where she lets her imagination soar to create fictional adventures that explore the power of love and the thrill of suspense. When not writing, she enjoys the outdoors with her husband and two children, quilt making, photography and reading whatever catches her interest.

You can write to Sylvie at
P.O. Box 702, Milford, NH 03055.
And visit her Web site at www.sylviekurtz.com.

Books by Sylvie Kurtz

HARLEQUIN INTRIGUE
527—ONE TEXAS NIGHT
575—BLACKMAILED BRIDE
600—ALYSSA AGAIN
653—REMEMBERING RED THUNDER*
657—RED THUNDER RECKONING*
712—UNDER LOCK AND KEY
767—HEART OF A HUNTER†

*Flesh and Blood
†The Seekers

SILHOUETTE SPECIAL EDITION
1438—A LITTLE CHRISTMAS MAGIC

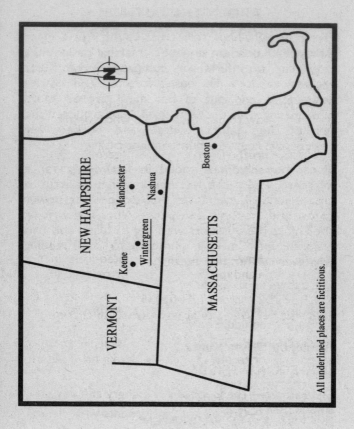

VERMONT

NEW HAMPSHIRE

Keene

Wintergreen

Manchester

Nashua

Boston

MASSACHUSETTS

All underlined places are fictitious.

CAST OF CHARACTERS

Sebastian Falconer—He's a U.S. Marshal caught between duty to the service and love for his wife, his haven.

Olivia Falconer—She's an artist who doesn't remember how to paint, and a wife who doesn't remember her love for her husband.

Paula Woodruff—Olivia's sister is determined to save her sister from her husband's domination.

Cari Woodruff—Paula's daughter wants someone to take responsibility for her father's death.

Edwin Sutton—Sebastian's boss is on a fast track to success and won't let anything stain his perfect image.

Bernie Kershaw—The fugitive is wanted for armed robbery, rape and murder. He's out for revenge for being caged.

Nathan Kershaw—Bernie's brother is tired of playing second fiddle.

Mario Menard—The Aerie's groundskeeper keeps an eye out for trouble. But did he have a hand in the security break?

Sean Greco—The U.S. Marshal is angry and dirty.

Allan Verani—Greco's roommate wants what he was promised.

Nelson Weld—The small-time thief is ready to sing to keep his freedom.

Kiki Bates—Weld's girlfriend has pinned all her hopes on the wrong man.

OLIVIA'S CHOCOLATE ORANGE
SNACK CAKE

1 2/3 cups flour
1 cup packed brown sugar
1/4 cup cocoa
1 tsp baking soda
1/2 tsp salt
1 cup orange juice
1 tsp vinegar
1/2 tsp orange extract
1/2 cup semisweet mini chocolate chips

Heat oven to 350°F. Mix flour, brown sugar, cocoa, baking soda and salt with fork in ungreased square pan, 8"8"2". Mix in remaining ingredients except chocolate chips. Sprinkle with chocolate chips. Bake 35 to 40 minutes or until toothpick inserted in center comes out clean. Makes 9 servings.

Chapter One

The hunter had returned. Decompressing, he called the time he needed alone after coming home from an assignment. But Olivia knew it went deeper. He was trying to shake off the mind-set of the man he'd hunted for the past month. He'd told her once it was like spending time in a sewer and he didn't want to poison her with the stench.

Was it wrong of her to want him to share his world?

She descended the stone stairs that led to the basement of their mountaintop home and the room she referred to as Sebastian's "cave." She'd called it so affectionately at first. Now there was a trace of resentment that left a bitter taste at the back of her throat. At the door she hesitated.

Bent over his paperwork, he was surrounded by all sorts of electronic gadgets that could have come from a science fiction movie set. His mind was focused, laser-sharp on his task. The lean muscles of his tracker's body were controlled. She'd seen this stance often enough to recognize he was detaching himself from one world and trying to reconnect with another. Why did that passage make her so sad?

She'd lived with him for ten years. She knew everything about him. The way he brushed his teeth. The way he peppered his corn. The way he checked the oil in her car before he left on assignment. But she didn't know his heart. After all these years, he still kept it to himself, its contents as secret as his operations.

He loved her. She had no doubt about that. But she wanted it all—the bad *and* the good. Not just the castle in the air he'd provided for her. To keep her safe, he'd said. But here in the rarified air she didn't know what she was capable of. And the longing for flight—for something more—grew every day. Especially when he was gone, and she was left alone with her thoughts.

Her heart—always so open—had lately closed a little. She found herself keeping things from him—thoughts she knew would upset him, musings he would take the wrong way, feelings he wouldn't understand. She didn't like that extra barrier between them, didn't like the way they were growing apart. Her fault. Sebastian hadn't changed. He was the same driven man she'd met at one of her father's business functions eleven years ago. She was the one with the curl of anxiety gnawing at her.

She loved him. She always would. Just watching him and all his intense self-assurance made her soul sing like nothing else could. But where was the answering melody? She'd signed on for a duet and lately had become aware she was singing a solo.

He looked up from his work and smiled. The brightness of it caught her breath just as it had the first time. One touch. That was all it would take to evaporate her resolve. She slid her gaze from his. If she looked into his eyes, she would stay and she needed to go.

"I'm almost done," he said, turning back to his work.

She hugged herself and leaned against the door frame. "Take your time. I just wanted to say good-night."

He glanced at his watch and frowned. "So early?"

"I'm leaving, Sebastian." The hard thud of her heart nearly drowned out her words.

"Leaving? I don't understand."

No, he wouldn't. He could see through the eyes of evil, but the working of his own wife's mind was alien. "I'm going to my sister's for a while." As much as Paula wanted her to leave Sebastian, she would not approve of her plan, either.

"I just got home."

"I know. I waited for you." And that, she realized, had been a mistake. She should have taken the coward's way out and left while he was gone. "I didn't want you coming home to a note."

After all the years they'd shared, she'd owed him that much. She'd thought hearing of her departure from her would hurt less than words scribbled on paper. She hadn't counted on seeing the ridges of fatigue drooping the corners of his eyes and bracketing his mouth. She hadn't known the pain in his eyes would arrow straight to her gut. And in the past month, she'd talked herself out of the power of his magnetism.

"I've missed you," he said. "Can't this wait?"

"No, I…" She knitted her fingers and breathed in courage. "I need to get away for a bit." She needed to prove to him she could fit in his world, and she thought the course in criminal justice at the community college in Nashua would give her a start—a point from which to connect. But if she told him, he would talk her out of it. Where would that leave them? Right where they were, and she couldn't go on like this.

He closed his eyes and blew out a huff of frustration. "Olivia, I'm tired. Can't we talk this over in the morning?"

By morning, she'd have melted into him and it would be too late. "No, I need to do this."

He went predator-still. Never a good sign. "This isn't just a vacation." His dark gaze bored into her, making her feel caught in a trap. Was that how his prey felt when he closed in on them? "You're leaving me."

She shifted to the outside of the door frame. "I'm not leaving *you*." How could she explain? How could she make him understand? "I'm going to myself, not away from you."

"That doesn't make sense." He gave her a puzzled look and rose from his black ergonomic office chair. He took one slow step. She had to hurry while she still could.

Looking down at her hands so primly knotted in front of her, she licked her dry lips and focused on her goal. Everything else she'd tried to dissolve the barrier between them had failed. "You're a contained man, Sebastian, and I need to spill over. For a little while. Until I figure out where you end and where I start."

"I don't understand." The pain slashing his features twisted inside her. He took another step forward. Though she wanted to flee, she held her ground.

"I've known you since I was seventeen. We were married when I was eighteen. You have five years on me. You knew what you wanted out of life. This." She arched her arm to encompass not only the room, but all of the house. "You. It's all I've known for the past ten years."

"I thought you loved the house." Another step. She stiffened.

"I do." She'd helped design it herself. The way the light played with the shadows, the way it fit snugly into the rocky New Hampshire landscape as if it belonged, the way each room was a restful den, made it a home, not merely a house. "It's not the house."

''The village then.'' His gun hand flexed. He wouldn't let her go. ''You feel isolated.''

''No, it's not Wintergreen.'' How could she resent a place where everyone knew her and treated her like a friend? If she wanted a taste of the city, Keene, Nashua, Manchester weren't that far. Even Boston was only a few hours away. She straightened against the stone wall and hugged herself tighter.

He stopped, let his head drop to his chest, then blazed her with a look of such sadness she nearly closed the distance between them to comfort him. ''I'm sorry I can't give you the baby you want.''

That was a tiny bit closer to the truth. Without that common goal, the wall between them seemed to get thicker. But a baby wouldn't fix the hollowness growing inside her. Until Sebastian trusted her with all of himself, a baby would only complicate the situation. ''It's not the baby.''

He took another step. They stood close enough for breath to mix with breath. He knew her weakness and was going to use it against her. ''Then what is it, Olivia?'' The reverberation of his voice was cat smooth and cougar dangerous. ''Help me out here. I don't understand.''

Then she made her second mistake. She touched him. Just a whisper of finger against the roughness of his beard. The heat of it shivered through her. The want, the need. His. Hers. ''It's the waiting and the worrying. It's killing me.''

''It's my job.''

''I know.'' And she did. She understood how his parents' murder at the hands of an escaped convict had driven him into the U.S. Marshals Service. She understood his need to hunt criminals and put them back in jail where they couldn't hurt anyone but themselves. She understood his need to leave her for long periods of time to do his work. He was the best manhunter in the Service, and his duty to the Service always came first.

And that simple little jealousy made her feel petty. How could she ask him to stay when what he did was so important? Why did he insist on shutting her out of the most important part of his life?

"But I want to share it."

He frowned. "We've been through this before."

"I know." And gotten nowhere. She wanted him in her life, of that she was sure. But she needed the balance to shift. She didn't want to simply be his haven. She wanted to be his partner. This course was the first concrete step to that partnership. "You're so strong. And I'm…" She shook her head. "I need to find my strength."

"You *are* my strength, Olivia. Don't leave. Not tonight."

He reached for her, eyes bright with that potent mixture of desire and danger that never failed to arouse her, and a small helpless cry escaped her. *No, don't touch me. I'll give in.* She could feel her body responding to his before he'd even finished wrapping his arms around her. He held her tight. She tried to push him back, but when it came to Sebastian, she was weak.

He was passionate about everything he did. And that passion, she was loathe to admit, was part of her attraction to him. The aura of intensity around him acted as an aphrodisiac for someone unsure of her place in the world. The bad-boy looks on a man who hunted for justice had made her believe that, at his side, she could find herself. And each time he touched her, she believed it again—until he left.

His chin snuggled against the top of her head. The strong beat of his heart drummed beneath her hands. His heat seemed to fuse her to him. She could start a day late.

She could leave tomorrow—after this storm of return. Maybe he'd understand then. Maybe she could tell him that her need to leave was like his need to decompress before he came to her when he returned from a hunt. Something that was temporary, but necessary.

"I love you, Olivia."

"I know." And the slow melting started. It shimmered from her heart towards her limbs and left her limp. She twined her arms around his neck to hold herself up and accepted the brand of his kiss. The searing heat of it, the desperate need in it, erased the boundaries between them. The savage taste of him filled her. The scent of him, so primal, so *Sebastian,* dissolved her will. She could feel herself slipping away, and her desire suddenly tasted salty with tears. "Let me go, Sebastian. For a little while."

"Stay. I'll take some time off. We'll go away somewhere together. No beeper. No phone. No computer. I promise."

"Until the next prisoner escapes."

He opened his mouth to answer. She covered his lips with a finger. He took the offending digit into his mouth and gently sucked.

"It's not you." As his hands slid up her sides, she tried to catch her breath and put some space between them and found her hands mirroring his, seeking the firm skin beneath his shirt. "It's me. I need…"

"What?" His thumb skimmed a nipple, drawing a gasp from her.

"Sebastian…"

As he continued his exquisite torture of her flesh with his hands, his mouth found the tender spot behind her ear, clouding her mind. "What do you need?"

"More. I need more." She crushed herself against him to gain focus, only to lose it again when his fingers rounded her waist and stroked the sensitive hollow at the base of her spine. "Let me go, Sebastian."

The sudden stillness in him was more frightening than the seduction she couldn't resist. But before he could say anything, the beeper on his desk shrilled.

"Answer it," she said, as the invisible web making them one separated strand by strand. "You know you have to." When they stood apart, an aching cold made her shiver. Why had she done this? Why had she hurt him? Why was she risking the love of the one person who made her feel secure?

Because the next time that phone rang, she wanted him to talk to her about the coming hunt and not shut her out. She wanted him to know she truly understood his job, him.

He stalked to the phone and ripped the receiver off the cradle. Punching in numbers, he stared pointedly at her. She memorized the lines of his face—the sharp jaw, the thin nose, the full lower lip, the cleft in his chin, the up-side-down V his work had creased between his eyes, the dark shadow of beard that he could never quite seem to get rid of no matter how often he shaved, the clean cut of his straight black hair. She closed her eyes and breathed in his scent. She licked her lips and imprinted his taste.

"Falconer," he barked into the phone.

She opened her eyes, blinked as if taking a last picture, then turned toward the steps. She wanted to stay. She had to go. Her heart suddenly weighed heavily with the contradiction of her needs.

"Olivia! Wait."

But she couldn't. She was leaving because she'd nearly lost herself in him again. When she was stronger, when she was his equal, when she could stand solidly beside him without forgetting herself...then she'd return.

"HOLD FOR MR. SUTTON," the voice on the other end of the line ordered in a clipped voice.

Sebastian put a hand over the speaker and called, "Olivia!"

But she wasn't waiting. She was running up those stone steps as if the devil were on her heels.

Maybe he was. In the past year, he'd felt himself grow colder, harder. Had his work seeped into his home life? Olivia was so sensitive that his dark moods were bound to frighten her. Decompressing took longer and longer. Would he one day get stuck in the mind of the scum he chased?

Tethered to the phone and his boss, Sebastian watched helplessly as the ten best years of his life walked out the door. Maybe if he'd been able to give her the child she so desperately wanted. But no, he realized, the slowly widening rift between them went deeper than that. Something had been bothering Olivia for months now, and he'd gone against his habit of facing unpleasant things head-on and chosen to believe the closeting he saw in her eyes was temporary. Winter blues. She had them every year. Should he have suggested adoption? Would that have calmed the sadness in the summer sky of her eyes? A vacation. They needed a vacation. Somewhere sunny.

He strained the length of the telephone cord. "Olivia!"

She wasn't really leaving. She couldn't. He needed her. Did she know he watched her sleep? That he took comfort in the slow rise of her chest, in her simply being there, alive, beside him? That she was the reason he could keep doing what he had to do and still stay sane?

Finding her was always his first objective when an assignment was over. Getting back to Olivia. The beat of that need pulsed in him from the second he ratcheted cuffs on a fugitive. And then, when the long ride home was finally over and he saw her, alive and breathing, he could let the tension slip, let his breath out, let his heart feel again. With the first hug came a silent prayer of thankfulness. She was safe. He was home. And for now the world was right.

But not tonight. Tonight the mountain smoked from the unseasonable sweat of the day. Every year in February, winter seemed to grow weary of blowing blue and mean. For a day or two, it teased New Englanders with the false hope of spring. Temperatures rose. The sun blazed. Snow melted. And that brief flirting with spring seemed to have the same effect as a full moon, making everyone a little crazy.

Cabin fever. That was it. She'd be back. He'd give her a day, then he'd show up at Paula's and take Olivia home where she belonged. Better still, he'd take her for that long-promised vacation and they would talk—really talk.

"Falconer," Edwin Sutton barked into the phone. Sutton was the executive in charge of a thirty-man, seven-state, ongoing Fugitive Investigative Strike Team covering the northeast. He liked for operations to run smooth, for the felon arrest numbers to run high, and he liked to play those successes to the press. With no wife, no kids, not even a dog, the Service was his life and ambitious couldn't even begin to describe him. "Head for Connecticut. We just lost two of our men."

A personnel loss wouldn't look good on Sutton's scorecard. He'd want closure and fast. "Who?"

"Sean Greco and Robert Carmichael. They were on transport. There was a fire. Two prisoners are dead. Three escaped. Somehow they cornered Greco and Carmichael outside the building, had them drive getaway, and cut the hell out of them under an overpass on I-95. This is going to get us blowback. I want it contained, and fast."

Bad PR would tarnish Sutton's record. With D.C. his next planned step up the ladder, he had to keep the stain from spreading. "Any leads?"

"We're working on IDing the three pukes on the run. Two more turned to toast in the fire. We gotta sort them out. I want you on this full time till they're back in their pen. And Falconer, the Feebs are involved. Crossed state lines and all that bull."

"Great." That meant the case was officially the FBI's, but protocol allowed participation of the slain officers' agency. He didn't want to work with the Feebs. They couldn't pass wind without permission and tended to mess up investigations. Not to mention their tendency to let the Service do the work, then steal their glory. This was *not* going to be fun. And it would mean putting Olivia on hold. Again.

No wonder she'd left him.

"One more thing, Falconer. The mutt slated for transport was Kershaw."

Sebastian went cold. "Is he one of the missing?"

"Yeah."

"Dead?"

"Won't know till the toast are IDed."

One life deserves another. Don't turn your back on that pretty wife of yours, Falconer. I'll take from you what you took from me. Kershaw had made that promise five years ago and the cold determination in the snake-yellow eyes had matched Sebastian's determination to put him behind bars. That's why he still checked on Kershaw's welfare once a month. "When were Greco and Carmichael killed?"

"We found them a few hours ago."

"*When* were they killed?"

"As best as the M.E. can make out, about four hours ago."

Four hours. Enough to get from Connecticut to New Hampshire. With time to spare. He dropped the phone and raced up the stairs, taking them three by three. "Olivia!"

She jokingly called this place "Falconer's Aerie." He'd built it for her high on the mountain. To keep her safe. He'd vowed to her father on their wedding day that his work would never touch her. This house, this mountain, was a haven. For her. For him. And now she was out of his reach on the road on a dark night with a madman licking at her heels.

THE NIGHT WAS EERILY CALM, making the car's engine sound as if it roared. Thick and white, fog rose from the road and made the mountainside seem to smoke. To her right, the dark fronds of pines and winter-bare limbs of oaks and maples poked through the mist, reminding Olivia of ancient druids in ceremony. To her left, the meager shoulder dipped into a black abyss, making the scaly snake of road appear too narrow for her car. At odd intervals, runs of wet snow slipped from the mountain's flank to slide under her wheels, making the steering feel sluggish. Each curve on the winding road flashed jagged arms of trees, points of rocky outcroppings or dizzying flirtations with the edge of the road. Olivia had never liked carnival fun rides, and this nightmare was no exception.

Turn back, her weak side urged. No, not this time. This time she was going to be strong. "Stick to the plan."

Trying to stay on the road, she hunched over the steering wheel and peered through the wavering curtain of fog.

The tears weren't helping.

Why was she crying when she was the one who'd chosen to leave? And this short separation was to strengthen their future. "For once in your life grow a backbone, Olivia."

She swiped at her eyes with the back of one gloved hand. She hadn't known it would be this hard to walk away from him. That she would miss him so much in so little time. That the emptiness in her would feel as dirty and as desperate as the fugitives Sebastian chased.

"You're a fool, Olivia," she told the haggard reflection haunting her on the windshield. She had a great home. She had work she loved and didn't have to worry about making money from it to survive. She had a man who loved her and supported her. Security. "You have everything a woman could want."

But all of these chains of overprotection were sucking the juice from her creativity. She hadn't painted in a month. Hadn't felt the drive or the pleasure. Her next memory trunk still sat in her studio with only its priming coat on.

And the last thing she wanted was to resent the only man she'd ever loved because she'd lost herself inside his strength. This quarter apart would give them both the needed distance to view their relationship more clearly.

As she followed a curve, the slope of the mountain angled less sharply than before. The turn for the main road was only half a mile away. She eased her grip on the steering wheel and blew a small puff of relief.

A deer jumped onto the road. Olivia gasped, jerked the wheel to the left and stomped on the brakes to avoid the animal. Mistake. The slush on the road became as slippery as oil. Her wheels churned. The car slid sideways. She lifted her foot off the brake, spun the wheel in the opposite direction and fishtailed.

Smoke billowed up from the dashboard. The acrid smell made her choke. The black cloud blinded her. She tried to straighten, but the back end of the sedan kept going, then dipped over the edge of the road. There the car paused.

Holding her breath, Olivia leaned forward as if her weight could counterbalance the downward pull and tried not to cough on the toxic smoke. The engine whined. The headlights swirled in the mix of black haze and white fog. The undercarriage creaked beneath her as the car sought its fulcrum.

Please, don't let me die. I promise I'll go back. I promise I'll try harder. I won't complain. I promise—

Gravity sucked the car down. Olivia screamed as she scratched at the dashboard as if she could escape her fate through the windshield. The car careened down the rocky slope, gathering speed. Boulders and trees didn't slow the metal skeleton. It simply bounced from the obstacles in pinball madness, up and over, side to side, tossing her painfully around the safety harness. Wrenching metal screeched. The air bag deployed, burning her face and suffocating her for a desperate moment. As a branch thrust through the windshield on the passenger's side, glass cracked and the blanket of crazed glass wrapped around the sprung mushroom of air bag.

Then the right rear quarter panel smashed into a granite monolith, grinding the car to a sudden halt, canting it sideways, and sending her head crashing through the side window. She saw stars and a bright pinprick of light. A warm rush flowed over her brain, turning everything blood red, then black.

Panting, she swiped at her eyes. If she couldn't see, how could she work? How could she paint? How would she fill the endless emptiness of Sebastian's absences?

The car slipped again. A foot. Two. She stilled and bit back the scream clawing at her throat. *Please…*

The car came to rest with the small bump of a landing

elevator, bobbing her head. That gentle slap of her temple against the metal frame was the final insult.

Like a light winking out, she fell backwards into the inky chasm fracturing her conscious mind. *I don't want to die! I don't want to be alone.* Panic made her fight the pull of darkness. Her arms reached forward. Her mouth opened for one last desperate cry, "Sebastian!"

Chapter Two

The red lights of the rescue squad turned the fog a bloody red. The slam of the closing ambulance doors cracked like a shotgun and thundered over the mountain. As the ambulance sped away, Olivia's blood-streaked face colored Sebastian's vision. Her closed eyes, her pale skin, the rip in her scalp, were a punch to the gut. The fading whine of the siren was a cry that swept him back too many years and pooled old dread into his boots like cement.

He swallowed hard and shook his head. *Don't go there. It's not going to get you anything. You have a job to do. Do it.*

Olivia was in good hands. Once at the hospital, he couldn't see her right away anyway. Doctors would need to examine her and patch her up. What good would he do her pacing the hall? Here he could get a jump on Kershaw. He flexed his fists. She would be okay. But not Kershaw. Kershaw would pay. Sebastian cranked his gaze away from the disappearing red lights in the fog to the scars in the slush made by Olivia's tires.

Resolutely, he pushed Olivia from his focus. She crept back in on the next breath. He crouched by the side of the road. *Read the facts, damn it. Pukes always leave a trace. If you let him get away, Olivia's the one who'll pay.*

He should be at the hospital with her. But in these weather conditions evidence would disappear fast. His gaze followed the run of the tire marks over the edge, and with each breath he got himself into Kershaw's head. Kershaw had vowed revenge. Kershaw had escaped from a maximum-security facility. Olivia was hurt. Too much of a coincidence and he'd never liked coincidence.

Concentrate. Feel what he feels. Fear what he fears. Trust what he trusts.

Sebastian turned off the emotional switch and went into hunter mode. *Catch the scum, then get back to Olivia.*

That was the plan.

Always.

With effort, he rose and strode toward Victor Denley, Wintergreen's chief of police. Both the mustache, waxed Western-villain style, and the weapon, cocked at an odd angle from the chief's belt, seemed out of place on the six-foot, barrel-shaped man. He looked more like a caricature of a cop than a figure of authority. But the accident had taken place in his jurisdiction and this was his scene. The Service prided itself on interagency cooperation.

"How soon can you get the car out?" Sebastian asked.

Denley snorted and shook his head. "I'm not sending anyone down there till daylight."

Sebastian bit back his temper. He needed answers *now*. "When you do, I want it gone over with a fine tooth comb. Anything and everything that might be out of place, I want to know."

"I don't have that kind of manpower or budget. You know that, Falconer."

"Tow the car to Cyril's and send me the bill." Sutton was going to bust an artery over his next expense report, but screw him. He'd given his all for the Service. His job was never supposed to touch Olivia. They owed her.

He hiked down the tailgate of his SUV and took a flashlight from his gear bag. "I forwarded a bulletin to your desk. I want your men—" All four point five of them. Cripes! This was a mess. "—aware of Kershaw."

"How serious is this guy?"

"He's armed and dangerous." Sebastian clicked on a utility belt. "And he wants payback."

"Wish you hadn't brought that kind of trouble to my neck of the woods."

In a town where the day's highlight was a free cup of coffee at McGee's General Store and writing a traffic ticket to an out-of-towner who strayed a mile over the speed limit, a cop's edge dulled in proportion to the spread of gut over belt. Kershaw was way over Denley's experience. "Trust me. That wasn't the plan. He's after Olivia. I want a guard posted by her hospital room."

"Budget—"

"Frank'll be glad for the overtime." Frank Brandt was young and eager, even if inexperienced. He liked to relax at the local martial arts dojo and his edge wasn't yet donut dimmed. Denley opened his mouth, but before a word could spit out, Sebastian repeated, "Send me the bill." Let Sutton choke. Danger wouldn't flirt any closer to Olivia than it already had.

Sebastian strode toward the edge of the road.

"Hey," Denley called, "where do you think you're going?"

"Looking for evidence."

"You'll mess up the scene."

Like that was going to make a difference with the way the EMTs had trampled it to rescue Olivia. "He already has a warrant out on him for the murder of two marshals. Whatever evidence I find here won't change anything." Cutting down the timeline was more important than preserving this scene—a scene that would melt away before morning. Sebastian headed into the fog that covered the black hole where Olivia's car had plunged.

Denley shone his flashlight at him. "You should get to your wife."

"If I don't catch this puke, he'll go after her again."

"He might not have anything to do with this. There's deer tracks. The road's slippery. On a night like this, could be just an accident."

No, Sebastian didn't believe in coincidence. Not with someone as determined as Kershaw. "What if he did? You don't want that on your conscience. To get what he wants, he'll go through anything and anyone. He's armed. He's motivated. He has nothing to lose."

"Getting aggressive and imaginative at this time of the night won't help you collar your mutt."

Aggressive and imaginative—cop-talk for breaking the law. This was for Olivia. He'd get as aggressive and as imaginative as it took to bring down Kershaw.

IGNORING THE BEEPER vibrating at his belt, Sebastian placed a call. Working alone, he'd woven a wide network of contacts. The best way to information was knowing who to tap.

"Felicia?" a sleepy voice greeted Sebastian on the other end of the line as he paced the hospital's emergency-room waiting area.

Officially, Aurora Cates was a librarian. But her real persona was information specialist. Why she hid her true calling was a mystery—one that was none of his business. Five years ago, he'd accidentally discovered that if he needed a fact, any fact—obtained legally—Rory Cates could dig it up. Best of all, she could do it efficiently and discreetly.

"Sebastian Falconer."

"Falconer?" He heard the rustling of bed sheets. "Do you know what time it is?"

He glanced at his watch. Where had the time gone?

"It's one-thirty in the morning," Rory informed him. "What could be so important at this time of the night?"

"I need information."

"I figured that much."

Sebastian swallowed around the knot in his throat. "Information on coma."

"Coma?"

His strictest rule was to never mix business and pleasure. That's why he'd never asked Rory why she was hiding in a library when her skills were better suited elsewhere. Business took place on one level; personal life on another. Few people knew where he lived, that he was married or anything about his background. Safer that way, he'd thought. Kershaw had proved him wrong. "My wife was in an accident."

"Wife? You're married? How long?"

"Ten years."

"And I'm just finding out now?" Her laugh was a birdsong. "If I need a secret kept, I know where to go."

Mixing both planes of his life was as awkward as doing surveillance in a snake pit, but Kershaw had smashed those boundaries. "Who's Felicia?"

"My sister." Rory sighed, and Sebastian heard the frazzled threads of a knotted relationship. "I haven't heard from her in a while and I'm worried."

"She'd call you this early?"

"This late. Yeah. I'd take her call anytime, though." The click of a pen. The shredding of a sheet of paper. Change of subject. Just as well, chitchat wasn't his forte. "What do you need?"

"Anything you can dig up on coma and brain damage. Recovery." The word tasted dry and made him wince.

"Jeez, Falconer," Rory said as she scribbled down what he'd told her. "I'm really sorry. I hope she's all right. She has to be a saint to put up with someone like you." She gave a mirthless chuckle. "I'll see what I can find for you."

Not a saint, but his angel. "Thanks, I'll owe you."

"I'll hold you to that."

As SEBASTIAN WAS disconnecting, the emergency-entrance doors burst open and his sister-in-law strode in like a witch riding a twig broom. Her ICBM-like gaze zeroed in on him. He didn't stand a chance, so he braced for the blow.

"Why wasn't I called immediately?" Her question screeched across the room, making the nurses at the desk look up. Her bottle blond hair bobbed with every laser-sure step in his direction.

"I'm just coming up for air myself."

One of Paula's hands beat the air like a conductor gone mad. "For hours no one answered the blasted phone. I was going out of my mind. Then I had to find out about Olivia from *that* man."

That man being Mario Menard, the Aerie's groundskeeper and handyman. That man was even now installing another layer of protection to keep Paula's baby sister safe. Sebastian couldn't figure out if she treated Mario like a nonentity because he was the hired help or because he was always polite to her even when she was giving him her best impression of a third-degree black belt witch. The situation only seemed to get worse after the bankruptcy and suicide of Paula's husband and Paula had to get a job.

"You were next on my list, Paula," he said gently. After all, Paula had raised Olivia. Paula had been more of a mother to Olivia than their own mother, who hadn't wanted the burden of a menopause baby.

"Next? I should have been first. What happened? How is she? When can I take her home?"

"Whoa, there." He put up both hands against her verbal assault. "She's coming home with me where she belongs."

Paula's eyes narrowed to barbed slits. "She's coming home with me. We both know she was leaving you. That's where she was going at that ungodly hour. To *my* home. Away from *you*. I figured you were giving her a hard time and that's why she was so late. I never thought you'd actually hurt her."

"I would never hurt her. The hour wasn't ungodly. She left before seven."

Both of her hands exploded upward. "Seven? That was almost six hours ago!"

"I had other things on my mind—like Olivia and her welfare."

Paula's hands hitched to her bony hips. "Her welfare? When have you ever bothered with her welfare? She wasn't happy with you. You should have seen that years ago. But no, not Mr. Important Deputy Marshal." She pecked her fingernail into his chest. "You were too busy doing your important job to see that she was dying inside. If you'd once bothered to ask her what *she* wanted instead of assuming she wanted whatever *you* wanted, then we wouldn't be in this situation right now."

"Paula—"

"No, don't Paula me. Your selfishness almost killed her." Rusty mascaraed tears dripped from Paula's pale blue eyes. Her voice cracked. "I want to see her."

"She's not allowed visitors yet."

Hand at her throat, she gulped. "How bad is it?"

"We won't know until she wakes up."

"Coma?" One hand covered her trembling lips; the other wrapped around her waist. The drips of tears turned to a stream. "Oh, God, no."

"I have another neurologist scheduled to see her first thing in the morning."

Paula keened. "Neurologist? There's brain damage?"

Sebastian tentatively reached for his sister-in-law and patted a shoulder. "She's going to be okay, Paula."

Paula's eyes narrowed and skewered him with pure hatred. "She'd better."

Sebastian backed away. Knowing what to push was only part of an investigation; you also had to know when to let things slide. This was a slider. He headed toward the entrance.

"Where are you going?" Paula called after him.

"Home to shower and change. I'll be back."

Paula's gaze rested on his shirt and traced the pattern of Olivia's blood staining the white cotton. "What if she wakes up while you're gone?"

"You'll be there to make your final bid for her to leave me. That's what you want, isn't it?"

Her shoulders bowed and she wrapped both arms around her stick figure. "I want what's best for Olivia."

"Then we agree on one thing."

EVEN AT EIGHT in the morning, the lights in the hallway outside Olivia's room seemed unnaturally bright. Such a dazzle should have cheered Sebastian, made him expect the best. But as the doctor exited the room, the brilliant islands of light only served to rush all that could go wrong at him in a giant black wave. *Olivia, you can't die. You can't leave me this way. We never got to talk.*

"How is she?" Sebastian asked, hands fisted deep in

the pockets of his pants. He'd demanded the best neurologist available and been told this beat-up dog was it.

Dr. Iverson crossed both arms over his chest like a shield. Fatigue seemed to sag his aging features into bloodhound droopiness. "Prediction of improvement is difficult at this stage."

Sebastian closed his eyes for a second. Patience, he reminded himself. "When will you know?"

"Again, making predictions at this stage is impossible." Dr. Iverson shrugged. "There are many factors involved in your wife's recovery. A loving, stable relationship is a great asset and will do more for your wife than anything we can offer her."

Stable relationship. A ticking like a time bomb settled in Sebastian's gut. Would she want to come home? Would she let him help her? He frowned. "What does that mean?"

"It means time is the best healer, and she'll need all the support you can give her. As soon as she wakes up, we'll know the extent of the damage."

Damage. He swallowed hard. Trying to ignore the mad ticking, he grasped on to "wakes up." "She'll be okay then."

Dr. Iverson's forehead wrinkled more deeply. "We're optimistic, but we're dealing with an acceleration/deceleration head injury and you should be prepared."

The ticking flared, started to burn. *That could mean anything. Let him explain.* "For what?"

"In this type of injury, the head, which was moving forward, came to a sudden stop when it hit a stationary object. In your wife's case, the driver's side window. When this happens, we often find bruising of the frontal and/or temporal lobes. Your wife may not be the person she was before."

"What do you mean?"

Dr. Iverson turned sideways. The good doctor would scram if he got half a chance, Sebastian thought, and blocked the doctor's route of escape. *You're not going anywhere until I have answers.*

"The injury is located on the left hemisphere," Dr. Iverson said. "She may have changes in thinking, behavior and personality. Problems with motor skills—"

"Like painting?" God, no. Olivia came alive when she painted. She created magic with her colors and brushes. If she couldn't paint, there would be nothing to hold her home. And he needed her. Why hadn't he told her so before? Why had he let her go? Because he'd never been good with words—at least the out loud kind.

"Painting. Writing. Organizing," Dr. Iverson said. "With the temporal lobe involved, she may also have problems with memory. But it's really too early to tell."

The ticking stopped and something seemed to implode. "Memory? As in amnesia?"

Dr. Iverson shrugged. "Amnesia. Short term memory."

"Temporary?" His fists curled. What if she couldn't remember him? Their life together? She would remember. She had to.

"We'll hope for the best."

Hope? Doctors were supposed to do more than hope. They were supposed to have answers. There was always some other trail to sniff, some other trigger to follow, some other fact to unearth. "Can't you run some tests? There must be *something* you can do."

"We've done everything we can for now. When she wakes up, we'll do a full neurological workup designed to tell us problems with reasoning, memory and other brain functions—"

"When will that be?"

"There's no way to tell. The sooner the better."

A squawky announcement over the P.A. system had the doctor cocking his head. Was it standard procedure? Give the doctor two minutes with the family, then page him to save him from their stupid questions? "I want to see her."

Dr. Iverson nodded. Without a goodbye, he spun on his heels and squeaked his way down the green hall and through the beige swinging double doors.

Sebastian fought the urge to follow him, grab him by the collar and shake him until he had answers. But the doctor couldn't give him answers he didn't have.

Amnesia. Brain damage. He did *not* want to go there. She'd be okay. She had to.

His beeper vibrated against his hip. He didn't bother glancing at it. Sutton was probably three shades of purple by now. But he'd have to wait. Kershaw was after Olivia. He had to make sure Olivia was safe before he focused on Kershaw.

What if he isn't after Olivia? What if you read him wrong because of your fear for her? Then Kershaw's timeline was getting bigger by the minute. Sebastian dragged a hand over his face. *Don't go there.* Olivia's accident on the heels of Kershaw's escape was too much of a coincidence.

The beeper's renewed massage centered him. *What do you know? You know Kershaw wants to hurt you through Olivia. You know he means to keep his promise. You know he's on his way.*

Don't you?

He took his handheld computer from his pocket and punched in numbers. He was letting his fear for Olivia screw up basics. First things first. Check to see if the fugitives were back into custody.

Not as of five minutes ago. That would be too easy.

Kershaw's transfer was to the new federal prison in Berlin, and he had a mother who lived in Nashua. She'd been vocal in her demands for a closer incarceration so she could visit. Cruel and unusual punishment having her boy so far away, she'd claimed. As if sonny's kidnappings, rapes, armed robberies, felony assaults and murders were nothing more than school-yard scuffles. She'd abet her worthless spawn in a second and lie through her false teeth about it. He made a note to put a check on her telephone records and tack on some surveillance.

The safest thing for Kershaw to do was to hunker down. Hunkering down meant getting outside help. But Kershaw also had an agenda. He'd keep moving. Moving, he made a target. All Sebastian had to do was connect the dots.

And protect Olivia.

He swore. One was never supposed to touch the other. That was the agreement. That was the plan. How could he be two places at once? How could he stay by Olivia's side and stalk Kershaw?

He had to find a way or else all he'd built over the last twenty years was worth nothing.

"Bing!" Up popped the instant-message window asking if he wanted to accept a message. He clicked yes when he saw Okie's name highlighted on his buddy list.

Okie: Hey, I think something's gone wrong.
Sk8Thor: No slip, sliding?
Okie: Slip, slide all right. Slip slide right into a coma.
Sk8Thor: Him?
Okie: Her. U said it'd B ok.
Sk8Thor: He's hurting, isn't he?
Okie: Yes.

Sk8Thor: That's what you wanted, wasn't it?
Okie: Yes.
Sk8Thor: Then what's wrong?

He could feel the hesitation and cursed it. That's what came of counting on someone else. But this required finesse, and one trick he'd learned long ago was how to make the best of any hand he was dealt. This one was too sweet to pass up.

Sk8Thor: He wouldn't help u when u needed it. He had to pay, didn't he?
Okie: Yes, but, she's nice, u know. I didn't want 2 c her hurt so bad.
Sk8Thor: This way he's hurting more. You're not gonna quit on me, are u?
Okie: 2 late now.

That's right. Too late now. You're my hands and eyes, and you're my fall guy. One by one he was going to breach each of Falconer's defenses. Then he'd pull the last pin and watch while all Falconer stood for caved in around him. How far did you have to push a man to betray his ideals? Not as far as most people thought. Affluence made people cream cheese soft. Falconer thought he knew it all, thought he could shed one skin and slip into another without the fat at the seams showing. But Sk8Thor saw through the stitches. A man's heart never changed. And Falconer's heart was as black as his. Sk8Thor was lean and mean and hungry. And Falconer, even wearing his hunter skin, couldn't compete with a lifetime of surviving in the sewers.

Falconer didn't stand a chance.

"Time to set up for show-and-tell." He typed one last note to Okie and pressed the send button. Laughing, he asked the screen, "Who do you trust, Falconer? Who do you trust?"

Chapter Three

When Sebastian could no longer put off Sutton, he stepped out of Olivia's room and got out his phone. Leaning against the hallway wall, he tried to blink away the image of Olivia's too-still body, but it was etched into his brain. Every detail of angry bruises on chalky skin became a horrid scene filled with accusations. As he punched in Sutton's number, he started to stride. The only way to stay ahead of the nightmare was to move.

"Where the hell are you?" Sutton barked.

"Hospital." Sebastian paced the outside of Olivia's room as if it were a cage.

Sutton swore more colorfully than a seasoned sailor. "What happened?"

"Kershaw got to Olivia."

Sebastian wished for static over the clean phone line. Anything to break the density of Sutton's silence.

"Are you sure?" Sutton asked.

Sutton liked black and white, but Sutton hadn't worked the field in a long time. And the field was nothing but shades of gray.

At Sebastian's silence, Sutton cursed again. "Not the gut thing."

Never mind that gut was often the thing that broke a

case wide open. "Kershaw swore he'd get back at me through Olivia. The fact Olivia was hurt the same day as Kershaw's escape can't be coincidence."

"Got anything to back you up?"

"Soon," Sebastian said, thinking of Olivia's car. Cyril Granger should be done with the automotive autopsy by the end of the day.

"How soon? I need results."

No doubt because the prison riot, the murder of his men and the escape of three dangerous felons had become a media circus. Wiser to say nothing.

"I'm sending in a team," Sutton said, his words tight and sharp.

"No."

A fist banged on wood. "Listen, Falconer, that lone-eagle crap isn't going to fly this time."

"You're glad enough for it when you need clean-up."

"This situation is raking in too much media. It needs containment *now*."

Sebastian stilled. "Kershaw's here. He's after Olivia. I'll get him."

"I'm pulling you off duty. Take some personal time."

"Kershaw's mine."

"You're too emotionally involved."

What no one realized was that he always got emotionally involved. All he had to do was think of the victim and he couldn't help it. He couldn't walk away from Kershaw. Not when he was after Olivia. "I can—"

"Bull! If it comes to choosing between Kershaw and your wife, you'll pick your wife. Why do you think I don't have any ties?"

It wasn't a question, but a simple statement of fact. For Sutton, the Service and life were one and the same.

"I know Kershaw." Sebastian bit his words to contain

the temper swirling like a hurricane about to beach. "I know how his mind works—"

"How are you going to handle this?"

"Solo."

Sutton swore again.

"I want *carte blanche*," Sebastian pushed on as a plan formed in his mind. "I want a clear path in the field. I don't want roadblocks from the locals. But if I need something, I don't want to have to ask twice."

"That's not how we operate."

"I've never let you down."

"This isn't the time to go for glory."

Sebastian sneered. This was a bust that would garner attention, and Sutton wanted it—preferably before the Feebs beat him to it. "If it was glory I wanted, I could've had it years ago. I've let you take the credit for every one of my collars. I made my bones a long time ago. I don't have anything to prove."

"What about Olivia?"

The mention of Olivia brought back the image of her bruised face in 3-D color. He resumed his pacing. "What about her?"

"Who's going to watch over her while you're out enforcing the law?"

No, not the law. Justice.

And there was the pinch.

Hunter and husband. Duty and love. And in the middle, justice and obligation. He owed both to Olivia.

The lone eagle. The clean-up guy. The guy who got the job done. People thought he worked alone because he didn't trust anyone. That wasn't the reason. He worked alone because he didn't want the responsibility of someone else's life on his shoulders. If he got himself killed, then it was his tough luck. He already had three souls on his conscience; he didn't want any more.

But he had a shoulderful of responsibility now. Olivia was here, in this hospital bed, in a coma, because of him, because of what he did, because of his need to rid the world of scum. Marrying her ten years ago was an act of selfishness. He knew it then; he knew it now. He'd tried to protect her.

And failed.

She was his strength. She was the one weakness he wasn't able to resist. And she was paying for his flaw. He'd gambled with her safety—and lost.

He closed his eyes and up popped the image of that purple-black bruise marring the left side of her too-white face. For once, he had to make her his priority. He had to stay by her side until she was well. And when she was, they would have to redraw the boundaries of their relationship.

How could he live without hunting? It was in his blood. Yet how could he live without Olivia? She was his soul.

When in doubt, act. If he couldn't physically leave, then he'd have to figure out a different way to track.

"Give me a team," Sebastian said. Teamwork wasn't his strength, but for now he was grounded. Someone else would have to do the flying. If he couldn't do the hunting, then he wanted to head the team that would. "I'll find him."

"A team?"

"Four men." With four men, he could cover his target. If he had to operate with a team, he wanted men he could trust. "Grayson Reed. Noah Kingsley. Dominic Skyralov. Sabriel Mercer."

Sutton whistled. "The best of the best."

"Do you want this circus over or not?"

A heartbeat. Two. "I'll set it up."

Sebastian punched out. The win should have felt good. It didn't.

Kershaw was on the loose. Olivia was his target. And he'd have to depend on others to catch his prey.

SHE AWOKE THIS TIME to a view of night through a window. Clouds raced across the moon, leaving a moving trail of patchy light on the gray linoleum floor. The metallic click of an artificial pulse kept her own company. The strong smell of sickness and floor wax twitched her nose. The blanket covering her right arm was strangely heavy.

When she moved her head to look at the warm weight, pain shrieked like a banshee and zigzagged through her brain with a lightning burn. The room spun around her. Her vision dimmed. Nausea rose and fell with roller coaster sharpness.

What's happening? Where am I?

Suddenly a hard and warm wall caught her. She fought against the strangling hold until a calming murmur penetrated through the roar in her mind. "Olivia, shh, it's okay. I'm here."

Olivia? Who was Olivia? Limbs shaking, she clung to the solidness of the man holding her to steady herself. Who was he? Why was he here? Did she know him?

"Do you want me to call a nurse?"

Nurse? "No," she croaked.

"Are you dizzy? The doctor said that was normal."

Doctor. A vague image like a thousand-piece jigsaw puzzle reassembled itself in the black of her mind. Real? It seemed so opaque—as if the glue holding the pieces together wasn't quite dry. Yesterday? Today? Brown hair streaked with white. Droopy face. Hospital. Someone—the man holding her?—answering a myriad of questions whose answers didn't mean a thing to her. Was she making up the impatience that throbbed from him like the boom of a drum? Accident. She was in an accident. At least that's what the man said. Car, he'd said. And the scarecrow woman, too. Her voice, thin and sharp like her body, had mixed words into a whirl until none made sense.

Then the doctor had poked and prodded, asking her to do all sorts of things—smile, chew, swallow, follow his fingertips, walk, stand on one foot—until all she could feel was layer upon layer of pain.

Just when she thought she could return to the security of her bed, someone had rolled in a wheelchair. Then they'd dragged her from machine to machine until fatigue took over. Finally, they'd left her alone, and she'd slipped into the welcoming blankness of sleep.

She saw all this in her mind as if it were happening to someone else, making her feel as if she had no more substance than a ghost.

"I should call a nurse," the man said. His worry was crushing, and all she wanted was distance.

"No." She didn't want any more poking and prodding. She wanted to be alone. Struggling out of his hold, she slipped to the other side of the bed and hung on to the side of the mattress with fists curled around the stiff sheet. A wave of nausea surged, then ebbed. The throb in her head steadied. The room stabilized.

"Olivia?"

"I have to…" The words were in her head. She could feel them there, pinging like flies against a lightbulb in the dark. They stumbled across her tongue like stinging bees and spit out already half spent. "…go bathroom." She slid one foot to the coldness of the linoleum floor and held her breath while the room wavered around her.

"Let me help you."

"No." *Don't touch me.* But she got tangled in the wires connecting her to machines.

He came around the bed, unhooked the clothespin-like device biting her finger and untangled the white cord that had wrapped itself around her forearm. Dark eyes stared down at her, their intensity unnerving. Who was he? Why was he here? Her skin crawled with an electric buzz when he wrapped an arm around her waist and helped her up.

"I fine." She shrank away from the too close contact of his body against hers.

His hand reached for her chin and gently forced her to look into his eyes. "Olivia…"

She saw pain flash bright in the near blackness of his eyes, felt an unasked question float between them, sensed a fear that echoed along her nerves, sending them jangling like alarms. "I have…to go."

"Okay." He looked away. She swallowed hard. A hollow keening rang inside her. The sense of loss was so deep she nearly buckled beneath it.

"I've got you." He tightened his hold on her.

"No. I'm. Fine."

"Let me…"

Pain again. In his voice. In the pinching of his forehead. In the downward arch of his eyes. She tried to relax in his grip, but tasted tears with each step.

She walked stiffly, grateful when they arrived at the bathroom. He turned on the light. "Do you…?" He shifted his weight and glanced at the toilet against the beige tile wall. "Do you…um…need—"

"No." She pushed away his supporting hand. The thought of him watching her while she emptied her bladder was too embarrassing. "I'm fine."

"I'm right outside if you need help."

She nodded, then regretted the move when it set the

room in motion once more. Holding on to the sink with one hand and the wall with the other, she held her breath until the man was no longer blurry.

Forehead rucked like a V of geese, he nodded and closed the door.

Once alone, she let her breath out in one long swoop. Turning, she braced both hands against the sink and caught a reflection in the mirror. Long strands of dark hair hung limply around a pale face streaked with blotches of purpling black on the left. A row of stitches crimped the hairline from temple to ear. The eyes, with their eerie ring of blue around too-wide pupils, lent the image an air of panic—as if the woman in the mirror would take off at any second. Was that what the man had seen? This panic? Was that what scared him?

Me? she wondered, searching every corner of the face. No, how could it be? She would know herself, wouldn't she? Nothing looked familiar.

"Olivia." She tasted the name and swallowed it all wrong. It didn't fit.

"Olivia." She tried again, straining for a scrap of recognition. She bit her lower lip with her upper teeth and watched helplessly as the image before her started to shake and tears to race a shiny run over the pale cheeks.

"Mrs. Falconer," she sobbed. The echo of the name they'd called her as they'd probed and poked grated like a door needing oil. "Olivia Falconer."

They'd called the man with the intense eyes and the serious face her husband. *Safe,* they'd told her. *He'll keep you safe.* A quiver of cold prickled down her spine, raising goose bumps along her arms. Married. She was married. To him. Then why did he feel like a stranger? As if she'd never seen him before? Shouldn't she feel something more than panic when he held her, when he looked at her?

She peered deep into the eerie blue eyes, tried to climb into the dark pupils to find the answers hidden beneath the shell of skull. And saw nothing. Her breath came in short bursts. Sweat, cold and clammy, slipped her hands along the edge of the white sink. And all she could hear was the thud of her heart.

She reached a hand to the image of the woman she did not recognize in the mirror. "Who are you?"

The knock on the door made her gasp. "Olivia? Are you all right? Should I get the nurse?"

"No. I'm...fine." Closing her eyes against the reflection taunting her, she backed to the toilet and took care of nature's call. Then she sat elbows on knees, head in hands, eyes closed, trying to glimpse into the deep velvet blackness of her mind. When he called to her again, she reluctantly stood and opened the door.

He helped her back into bed. She slid as far away from him as she could. He took the open mattress space as an invitation and climbed in beside her. The solidness of his body against her side, the furnace of heat he generated, stiffened her.

Go away. Leave me alone, she wanted to say, but the words stuck in her dry throat. An ill feeling crawled across her skin like a long-legged spider. She did not want to anger this man. Was he dangerous? Did a part of her know that? She rolled onto her side and stared at the restless chase of clouds over the moon. What was happening to her? Why was there nothing in her mind? What would become of her?

"The doctor said you could come home today," the man said, startling her with his ability to read her mind.

Home? Her heart thudded hard in her chest. Where was home? Why could she draw no pictures of the place where she'd lived with this man? For how long? The ache in her head started to burn again. Her throat tightened. She couldn't go to a strange place with a strange man. But if not with him, then where?

She drew the blanket tight under her chin. ''Am I losing my mind?''

''No, SWEETHEART. You're not going crazy.'' Sebastian leaned in closer, wanting so badly to hold her. She bit her lower lip and curled her legs up to her chest, rounding her shoulders away from him like a baby in the security of a womb. Even though the doctor had warned him that the amnesia would cause anxiety, he hadn't expected this rejection. Needing some sort of connection, he touched her shoulder. She rounded away from his touch and nestled her head deeper into the pillow, closing him out.

Swallowing hard against her withdrawal, he rolled onto his back. *She doesn't know me.* Hands behind his head, he stared at the ceiling. *Where do we go from here?*

How could this person who wore Olivia's skin, spoke with Olivia's voice, moved with Olivia's grace, not be Olivia? Medical explanation aside, reality was hard to take. How could one moment erase ten years, a lifetime? *Don't dwell on it. She'll be back. This is just temporary.*

''You were in a car accident.'' He tried to reach her on the level of facts, if not on the physical one that grounded him. ''And your brain was a little shaken up. The doctor said it might take a while for you to get your memory back. Headaches, anxiety, dizziness. They're all normal. They should all go away. And we're going to do everything we can to help you.''

The information Aurora had faxed him earlier in the day wasn't reassuring. Given the location of the damage to Olivia's brain, permanent memory impairment was a possibility. What if Olivia never remembered the life they'd shared? What if she never loved him again? What if *this* Olivia left him for good?

He gave a sharp shake of the head. No, he couldn't accept that. "Dr. Iverson recommended a rehabilitation therapist who specializes in traumatic brain injuries. She'll help you improve your motor skills and give you techniques to improve your concentration and manage the pain." And if he was lucky, she'd perform a miracle and give him his Olivia back—the way she was before. "I've arranged for her to meet us at the house."

He turned his head toward Olivia. She wasn't asleep. Her muscles were wound too tight; her breath came too fast and shallow to be restful. "Olivia?"

She didn't answer. The force of her fear stole his breath. And all he was doing was adding to it. His touch had once calmed her, aroused her, made her melt. Now, it sharpened her fear.

As she'd slept earlier, he'd tried to get into her head. What would it be like to remember nothing? The depth of the dark emptiness had almost swallowed him whole. No shared past. No trust. No love. Only fear. Getting into the most evil of criminal minds couldn't compare to the terror of having a lifetime erased.

If he believed in prayer, he would pray now. But he didn't. Hadn't in a long time. The future—their future—had always seemed so bright. But now, caught between an Olivia who wasn't Olivia and Kershaw's need for vengeance, he couldn't conjure up any of the dreams that usually saw him through his trips through the sewers of society for the scum that thrived there.

Catch the scum. Get back to Olivia. That was the plan. Always.

But the rules had changed and this was a whole new game.

Sebastian ran a hand over his face. He was stuck here, waiting, just waiting like a paralyzed slug. The trail was getting cold. He couldn't look for Kershaw. He couldn't find the information he needed. He couldn't seek the triggers to bring the whole damn thing to an end.

And in the panic-stricken eyes of the woman who looked like Olivia, he could not find the wife who'd been his haven.

Kershaw was God-knows-where. The team he'd requested was on its way, giving Kershaw time to do whatever evil his rotten mind plotted. Olivia wasn't safe here— not even with him watching over her, not even with the guard outside the door. Every doctor, every nurse, every aide who walked through that door was a possible threat. He needed to get Olivia to the safety of the Aerie. And for that, he needed to earn a slice of her trust.

He slid out of her bed and into the hard chair beside it. She would come back to him. She had to. In the meantime, she needed him even if she didn't know him. He leaned forward, dangling his hands between his knees. Closing his eyes, he touched her the only way he could—with his voice. "Let me tell you about home…"

THE NURSE HAD SHOOED Sebastian out of Olivia's room while they got Olivia ready to go home. Leaving the stiff stranger in the bed was a relief, and he hated that it was. She was his wife; she deserved his understanding. How was he going to get through the weeks, maybe months, before she was well again without going crazy?

Paula had dropped off a bag of clothes the night before and threatened to return early enough to spirit Olivia to Nashua rather than let her return to the Aerie. Sebastian hadn't told Paula about Kershaw yet, but he would have to, and he dreaded the blowback that would create.

First he had to get Olivia home, then he'd worry about Paula.

Needing to do something other than dwell on Olivia or Paula or the way his life was crumbling like slag on the side of a mountain, he snagged the phone out of his pocket and checked messages. Three from Sutton—the reason why he'd turned off the ringer. And one from Cyril Granger. He checked his watch and bit back a grumble, then punched in the garage's number anyway. At the sound of Cyril's cigar-gruff voice, Sebastian gave silent thanks for early risers. "Sebastian Falconer."

"Falconer! I got the results you wanted."

Hand in pocket, Sebastian braced. "Shoot."

"Lucky your wife had all that metal around her or she'd a been dead."

He'd made sure she had the safest car on the market— that was no accident. "What happened?"

"As far as I can tell, she probably hit the brakes for some reason. Maybe deer. Maybe snow. Maybe something else. Skidded and went over the embankment."

Sebastian couldn't wrap his mind around the information. He'd been sure Kershaw had tampered with the car. "An accident?"

"Looks that way."

"No tampering?"

"Here's the interesting part. I couldn't get the taste of smoke out of my mouth."

Sebastian frowned. "Smoke? From the crash?"

"No, that's just it. It didn't taste like engine smoke. It was more electrical. So I followed my nose and, sure enough, I found something."

"What?" Sebastian prodded as he ground tight steps the length of Olivia's room.

"Someone swapped the brake switch fuse from a 5 amp to a 40 amp."

Sebastian stilled. "What does that mean?"

"Means that if she woulda gone five more minutes down the road, smoke woulda billowed up and blinded her. She woulda choked on it. Her eyes woulda watered. Then you coulda blamed the accident on tampering."

Five more minutes would have put her on Mountain Road—close enough to run into a sheer wall of granite or into Trotter's Pond if she lost sight of the road.

Kershaw.

"Can you tell when the swap was made?" Sebastian asked.

"No way to tell for sure. Anytime between the last time she used the car and got into it again. It'd take about ten minutes for the wiring harness to catch fire."

And there was no way to ask Olivia when she'd used the car last. No way to ask her if she'd had any visitors. No way to put Kershaw at the scene, with the melting snow making any trace of him vanish. Because of the time limit on the wiring fire, the tampering had to have happened at the Aerie. And that was impossible. Not with all the security he had in place. "Thanks, Cyril. I'll need a written report."

Cyril humphed. "Well, I got a busy day ahead'a me. It's gonna be a coupla days."

"I'll need pictures of the brake switch fuse and the burnt harness."

"Anson's got himself a new digital camera. I'll get him to take the pics."

Anson was Cyril's college-aged son. "Great. Have him e-mail me the file." He gave Cyril his e-mail address and punched out.

The connection had barely closed before he entered another number.

"Menard," a sleepy voice said.

"Falconer," Sebastian said as he started pacing again. "When was the last time Olivia used her car?"

"Three days ago when she got groceries."

"Anybody come by for a visit?"

"Only Paula and her daughter."

Sebastian's steps got shorter, faster. "Meter reader? UPS delivery? Anything else?"

"Special delivery from the post office two days ago. Propane yesterday."

That gave him some place to start. "Did you make sure the security system was on at all times?"

"That's what you pay me for," Mario said, voice sore as if Sebastian had poked a bruise. Mario's hawks squawked in the background.

Things weren't stacking up right. Sebastian rubbed a hand over his chin. Could someone who'd just escaped a prison riot, killed two marshals and traveled four hours from a murder scene have been careful enough to leave no trace?

Kershaw wasn't into finesse. He was into results. Leaving evidence would mean nothing to someone bent on revenge. He'd have wanted Sebastian to know he was the cause of his grief.

Sebastian spun on his heels and faced the closed door of Olivia's room. If not Kershaw, then who? Who would want Olivia dead?

Chapter Four

As the nurse left with the wheelchair, Sebastian guided Olivia out the glass front doors of the hospital toward the parking lot.

"I will wait," she said, tugging her arm free from his grasp.

Standing still she made too big of a target, but he couldn't explain that to her without frightening her. "I can't leave you here by yourself."

Her hands knotted in front of her, and she shrank back toward the hospital entrance. "I will be fine."

She was afraid, and he didn't know how to make her feel safe. "I won't."

Her blue eyes searched his and made him feel like a heel for manipulating her cooperation. *I'm not your captor,* he wanted to say. But that wasn't really the truth. The Aerie would become a prison of sorts until Kershaw was caught. For her own good. With a sad nod, her gaze slid away and she stepped beside him.

Sebastian had almost made it to the SUV when the shriek of brakes had him instinctively putting Olivia behind the shield of his body and drawing his weapon.

The driver wasn't Kershaw or some other unknown piece of scum bent on mowing them down; it was Paula shooting visual daggers at him through the windshield of her ancient Volvo. While he holstered his weapon, he thought he'd rather deal with Kershaw.

"Oh, no you don't!" Paula stormed from her car and blocked the path to his vehicle. "She's coming home with me."

"You can't protect her."

"From what?"

He didn't answer. Couldn't. Paula more than anyone would relish his failure and throw it back in his face.

A small wounded sound came from Paula. She half sank to the asphalt, then sprang up. "I knew it. This is all your fault."

"It's no more my fault than Roger's leaving you penniless." Below the belt, but she was pecking at him as if she was a vulture, and he couldn't just lie there like carrion. He needed to get Olivia out of this open space and into the safety of their home.

The second Paula's face hardened, he regretted the flash of temper. Roger was dead; Olivia was still alive. Paula wasn't a fugitive. Fighting her dirty wasn't fair.

With a skinny hand, Paula slapped his cheek with all her might. The sound echoed across the parking lot like a shot. The mark burned and throbbed. "You bastard."

Contrite, he reached for her arm. "Paula—"

She twisted from his grasp. "No, you stay away from me. And from Olivia. I'm taking her home."

He grabbed her as she tried to go around him. Turning them both away from Olivia, he whispered, "You can't."

Her pale blue eyes searched his face and disgust narrowed them. "*What* have you done?"

He swallowed hard around the lump of his failure. "Someone I put in prison escaped. He wants to kill Olivia to hurt me."

Paula mewled.

"The Aerie is protected," Sebastian insisted, scouring the parking lot for hidden dangers.

"A lot of good that did her." She waved toward the hospital building with her free hand. "Look where she ended up."

"This isn't the time or place to discuss this."

"You're right. I'm taking her home where I can look after her. You—" She jabbed him in the chest. "—should do what you do best. Leave her alone while you hunt your fugitives. I can't believe you've done this!"

He maneuvered to keep Olivia safe between the shield of parked cars and his body. "If I thought leaving with you was the best thing for Olivia, I'd do it in a heartbeat. This guy has nothing to lose, Paula. He'll go through you, through Cari, to get to her. Do you really want to put your daughter in danger just to win this point?"

Paula shook her head. "No, you're lying. You want to keep Olivia to yourself. She was leaving you, and you're too selfish to admit she wanted out of your life."

Olivia's leaving had nothing to do with this hardheadedness. He *had* to keep her safe. It was his duty and his obligation. He reached behind him and found the softness of Olivia's coat. "Do you want to look at his rap sheet? Kidnapping, rape, felony assaults. He murdered two marshals to get here. Tortured them. Cut them up like bait. He doesn't want to go back to jail. He'd rather die. He has nothing to lose, Paula. And he wants to hurt me by killing your sister. Look what he's already managed."

He scanned the lot, took in the duo of nurses chattering to his left, the orderly with hunched shoulders hurrying to his right and the traffic getting heavier on the road. He needed to get Olivia out of there now.

Paula sniffed, shaking her head. "I can't let her go with

you. I have to protect her from you. She was leaving you, Sebastian. *She was leaving you.* You don't deserve another chance to change her mind.''

Because Paula was half right, Sebastian offered her the white flag of a promise. ''When Kershaw's back where he belongs, then Olivia can make her own choice. Until then I will protect her with everything I have.''

He didn't deserve this second chance, but he would take it. He'd never told Olivia how much her serene presence meant to him when he returned from the chaos of the ''real'' world. He'd never told her just how deeply he loved her. He owed a debt to Olivia for all the times he'd kept her waiting and worrying for him, for all the times he'd assumed she would always be there when his job was done. And the thought that he would fail Olivia scared him more than any special operation he'd ever worked. He felt her shift behind him and blocked her in.

''I'll fight you in court if I have to,'' Paula said.

Because he needed her as an ally and not an enemy, he tendered an olive branch. ''Olivia's confused now. She'll need a woman to talk to. Stay with us. She needs you.''

The shimmer of tears in Paula's pale blue eyes, the trembling of her lower lip and the press of her fist against her heart told him he'd finally said the words she'd wanted to hear all along.

SHE WATCHED THEM, the hard man and the stick woman, a breath away from her. They stood like gunslingers, exchanging barbs as hot as flying bullets. Anger rose from them in writhing snakes, and all she wanted to do was leave. But where would she go?

Standing here between the solid body of the man and the cold steel of a truck's tailgate, for a moment, she was disoriented. The sky was so wide and so blue, it spun around her and she was the eye of a hurricane. The pale yellow sun was so bright, its light washed everything in glittery white and, for a heartbeat, she was blind.

The odors were different, too. The crisp air smelled like ironed sheets and the coldness of it shrank her lungs so that she had to open her mouth to breathe. She wrapped both arms around her middle, wishing for the comfort of the four walls of the room she had just left.

She'd followed him because she'd had to. *He's your husband,* they'd said. *He'll keep you safe.* This hot anger didn't feel safe.

They were talking about her as if she weren't there, and she didn't like it. Though her insides felt as empty as eternity, she was still here and solid. *Hey, you idiots, can't you see I'm here, that I can hear every word, that I'm not deaf?* But the words were playing hide-and-seek in her mind again. Fisting her hands at her side, she forced them out of her throat. But the best she could do was to cannonball, "Stop!"

Both swiveled their heads in her direction. "Olivia," they said at once. But she wasn't done and while the words were sliding down her throat like snowmelt, she poured them out. "I do not want…to go anywhere…with either of you."

Heels digging into the hard asphalt, she spun around. Both hands went out to steady the world for a step. Then she focused on the glass doors of the building and headed toward them.

"Olivia!" Panic filled the word, made it roar, and the next moment, she was falling, and something big and black blurred a wall of hot exhaust and revving motor beside her.

Instead of bouncing on the hard asphalt, her head nested in the warm shoulder of the man. His body cushioned hers.

The drum of his heart was loud and hummingbird fast against her ear. And when she looked into his dark eyes, something sweet melted inside her, then shook like the tail of a rattlesnake. This man she didn't know, this man whose name she couldn't bring herself to say, this man who was taking her to a home she couldn't remember, he would willingly die for her.

No, she wanted to say, *you can't do that.* She didn't know why the thought of his death frightened her so much. Because she would be the cause? Because she didn't want to sever the narrow tie that somehow held a place for her in this strange world? Because some part of her still remembered him?

Staring into his mesmerizing eyes, she knew, and the knowing was icy hot. He was the key to the hole in her mind.

Beside them the woman jumped around and sounded as if she were a cat who'd had its tail stepped on. "Are you all right? Oh, my God! Are you all right?" she kept asking.

"You almost got hit by a car," the man said, smiling as he helped her up. The smile was a mask that was dry and cracking at the edges. "You have to watch where you're going." He tried to make the words light, but they weighed like stones. His gaze never wavered from hers as he dusted melted snow and grains of sand from the sleeve of her coat. "Are you hurt?"

Only in places that don't show. As much as she wanted to hide in the familiarity of the hospital room, to find herself, she would have to step into that wide unknown. She would have to trust him. "I will go with you."

He nodded and squeezed her hand. "I'll keep you safe."

Because he expected it, she nodded. But the truth came rushing at her as fast as the truck that had nearly hit her. If she went with him, if she let him fill the dark inside her with the missing memories, it was up to her to make sure he didn't die for her.

He waited for their arrival from a safe distance. Camouflaged as he was, even Falconer with his eagle eyes couldn't see him. Lifting the high-powered binoculars he'd taken from an Army Navy store, he followed the progress of the two cars up the long drive. A man and a woman got out of the SUV, another woman out of the Volvo. Two women? He zoomed in to focus on the thin one.

Ah, yes. He smiled. *That makes it even sweeter.* Pain before and after and all around—just as he'd had to bear for all these years. As he watched, the warmth stolen from him five years ago started to come back. He followed their track to the lovely nest perched on the side of the mountain. Their dance of return was an odd ballet of anger and fear, and he wore their discomfort like a quilt. "How does it feel, Falconer, to have your own home turned into a prison?"

Time was splitting him in half. Sebastian needed to trace the plate of the truck that had almost run over Olivia. He needed to go through the evidence and order his thoughts on Kershaw. Something about the timing niggled at him. But if not Kershaw, then who?

What he needed to calm the sea of unrest in him was facts. But he also needed to stay with Olivia to try to make her comfortable in her own home. She looked so lost, it tore at him. He would do anything to have been the one hurt in her place.

They were inside her studio now, and Olivia was looking at her own work as if it belonged to someone else. They'd toured the house she'd helped design. He'd pointed out all the touches she'd added to make it a home—the welcoming light in the foyer, the plants in the living room, the afghan in the den. He'd seen her frown as she touched—willing remembrance? Nothing seemed to leave a mark of recognition. When she spoke, her voice held a curious flatness. When she moved, her actions told of a blackness inside that Sebastian could do nothing to color.

He almost wished Paula were here. Then he wouldn't have to deal with the awkwardness of showing Olivia to herself on his own. But Paula had gone back to Nashua to collect her daughter and a suitcase of clothes. "If the Aerie's safe for Olivia, then it's safe for us, too," she'd said. His sister-in-law and his niece's presence in the space he'd never liked to share with anyone but Olivia was going to feel like an invasion. But he could not handle this Olivia alone.

Greenhouse windows overlooked westerly views of Mount Monadnock. Light flooded the tile floor and danced at Olivia's feet. It kissed her skin with soft gold and teased her hair with gilt. In that moment, from that angle, she looked like his Olivia.

But she wasn't.

Remembering that simple fact was so hard.

"You painted that trunk," he said when she ran a finger along the edge of a pine chest on a wrought-iron stand. He remembered the day it had come to life. "You sat with the client. She'd brought pictures, and you talked to her for hours. By the time she left, you'd made a dozen sketches." *And I'd been jealous as hell of the time this woman had stolen from me.* He jerked his chin toward the chest. "That's the one she picked."

The scene depicted a lifetime—children, grandchildren, homes, important moments—and was meant as a fiftieth-anniversary present. He'd have to look through Olivia's files and make sure it was delivered when expected.

The irony wasn't lost on him. Olivia had once painted treasures to preserve other people's pasts and now couldn't recall her own.

"Small lines." She traced the intricate details decorating the painted house.

"You like to get the details right."

She moved three steps back, taking the trunk in as a whole. "It looks…alive."

Sebastian drew in a quick breath. Olivia had never realized that the light she brought to her work was anything special. "It's just dabbling, Sebastian," she'd said, dismissing his comment with a shy wave of her hand when he'd tried to explain the appeal of her work. She seemed so surprised anytime someone phoned to commission a memory trunk from her.

"It gives people joy."

She'd shrugged. "It's still not art."

He'd let it go because he didn't want conflict to stand between them. Olivia was home, and home was comfort. But now something worse than a difference of opinion put bars between them. The loss of the past they'd shared was a wall harder and thicker than the mountain on which their home was built.

"Yes," he said to this Olivia, "your touch brings life." And he missed that touch, that smile, that warmth, missed the life this woman brought to his. *You're being selfish,* he told himself, biting back the bitter taste of self-pity. *She needs you. Be there for her.*

When the front-gate buzzer rang, he was pathetically thankful for the interruption. He led her to the garden bench by the window and sat her down as if she were an antique doll. The blankness in her eyes firmed the impression of a breakable figurine. "I'll be right back."

At the monitor, he checked the driver. She identified

herself as Cecilia Okindo and offered her hospital badge as proof. He'd already done a background check on the therapist and buzzed her in.

Her skin was caramel. Her smile brought sunshine into the gloom settling over the house. Her big-boned body seemed capable of handling anything as she shook his hand firmly.

"I am Cecilia Okindo." Her voice made him think of surf and sand and soft breezes.

"Sebastian Falconer."

"And where is my lady?"

"This way." He led Cecilia to the studio where he found Olivia just as he'd left her. Something in him had half believed he'd find her sitting on the large canvas cushion on the floor, paintbrush in hand—as he had so many times before. He could almost see the love in her smile, the crinkles of happiness near her eyes and hear the sweet lilt of her voice as she took him in. *You're home!* The memory burst like a soap bubble, leaving behind rings of disappointment. "I'll leave you alone."

Cecilia smiled. "Oh, no, it's best you stay."

"I have work—"

"And this beautiful lady, she needs for you to understand the changes in her."

He nodded, wishing he could ignore the changes in Olivia. Despite the sunshine in Cecilia's voice, the litany of expectations was even gloomier than the ones he'd heard at the hospital. In some ways, dealing with Olivia would be like dealing with a child. Repetition, Cecilia said, would create new paths in Olivia's brain. The old ones wouldn't reconnect, but the creation of new ones would give her a future—and, eventually, a past.

Fatigue, headaches, dizziness, pain pills, Dramamine,

coping mechanisms to deal with her motor problems—they were going to be part of her reality now. Part of his.

When Cecilia brought up the possible loss of desire, altered sensations and physiological problems with sex, Sebastian wanted to groan. Up until now, he'd avoided thinking that far ahead. All that had mattered was getting Olivia home and safe. Sex with Olivia…well, it was as calming as a lullaby, as satisfying as winning a lottery, as important as breathing. Having her so close without touching her was going to be pure hell.

He was caged in his own home. Grounded, he felt as if he was no longer master of his own fate. And to make things worse, he didn't even have the pleasure of his Olivia.

Kershaw spent the last five years planning his vengeance. So far, it was working perfectly.

NIGHT BROUGHT A DIFFERENT flavor to his frustration. Sebastian walked Olivia to their room. In this room, they'd made love. In this room they'd shared bits of their souls. In this room, they were safe and secure, cocooned. He stood there awkwardly as she looked around at all the things that should be familiar—the ash bureau she'd picked, the sleigh bed she'd fallen in love with and just had to have, the shades of blue from carpet to comforter to sheets that just a few days ago he'd thought of as a nest.

He reached into the second drawer of the dresser and pulled out one of the flannel pajamas she loved and he hated. He much preferred to pile on quilts against the cold and feel her skin to skin. But tonight, she would need the softness and warmth of that flannel. "Here."

She took the navy plaid bottoms and navy fleece top from him and held them to her chest.

He drew the curtains shut.

"No," she said. "Leave them open."

Bright stars on deep purple sky. A thumbprint moon that kissed the tops of the mountains. He couldn't blame her. The view was spectacular.

He strode to the bathroom and flicked on the light. "There's everything you need here. Soap, lotions, toothpaste."

She looked at him with wide eyes and nodded.

"I need to look at your stitches."

She stiffened.

"For signs of infection."

She nodded.

He folded down the top to the toilet and gestured her to sit. She did, folding her hands one on top of the other over the pajamas in her lap.

Gently, he pushed aside a strand of hair. She sat ramrod straight, staring at the escape of the door over his shoulder.

"No sign of infection," he said, and backed away, giving her breathing space. *Only of how I've hurt you.* He took the three prescription bottles from the pharmacy bag, read the labels and shook a pill from each. "Here, swallow these. They'll help with the pain and nausea."

She took the pills in one hand, the glass in the other, and did as he asked. With a bit of a shake, she handed him the glass.

"Do you need help?" He gestured at the pajamas in her lap. Not that he relished the thought of her flinching away from his touch as if he were a stranger. "Should I call Paula?"

Olivia shook her head. "I'm fine."

He wanted to believe her, so he pretended she was. "If you need anything, just press this button." He pointed to the intercom system. "It rings in my office. There's one beside the bed, too. Just hit talk, and I'll hear you."

Pressing the pajamas to her chest, she nodded. "I'm fine."

He hesitated at the door. "Anything at all."

She gave him a small smile. "Thank you."

Silently, he closed the door and escaped to his office.

Connecting to the outside world with his computer eased the feeling of confinement, of helplessness. He spent hours tracking the possible triggers Kershaw had left behind, hours putting himself in Kershaw's mind. And all those hours did was confirm his belief that Kershaw was close, that Olivia was still in danger.

BY THE TIME HIS TEAM arrived in the morning, Sebastian had regained a piece of his lost control.

The four men whose presence he'd requested sat in his office, munching on the take-out cinnamon rolls and coffee he'd dispatched Mario to get. Ordinarily, Olivia would have taken care of these details and have had fresh coffee, a plate of fruit and home-baked muffins waiting. He'd seen her do that when she hosted a client or a committee. She'd have charmed each man, making him feel at home, and she'd have had each man wishing he were Sebastian. He'd seen her do that with the old men who played chess on the porch or around the potbellied stove at the general store.

But Olivia wasn't Olivia, and he'd never brought his business home before.

He'd have to get over it.

Somehow.

He'd worked with each of these men before and trusted them. As Sutton had said, they were the best of the best.

Dominic Skyralov was out of Texas. A former football player, he was the resident knight-errant. Jeans and T-shirts were his favorite uniform. He was fluent in L.L.

Bean and could spend hours leafing through sportsmen's magazines. He fancied opera and Elvis and dabbled in short stories and fly-fishing. The Cowboy appeared to be mild mannered in an oh-shucks-ma'am type of way, but you didn't want to get on his wrong side.

Grayson Reed, out of San Diego, was Hollywood personified. He looked as if he were off to pose for a GQ shoot. Yet he could fit in anywhere, talk to anybody and make him believe he was his best friend. Day or night, inside or out, he always wore shades. He claimed it was because of his sensitive silver eyes, but Sebastian knew it was because every thought and emotion showed in them—not a good thing in this business.

Noah Kingsley was known as the Boy Scout because of his clean good looks and because he was always prepared. Electronics were his specialty, and he usually holed up in the El Paso Intelligence Center. He wore red suspenders for style—sometimes Sebastian thought it was just to make sure he was seen—and a belt to hold his holster and weapon. Because of his slight build, people tended to dismiss him easily. And that was always a mistake. He had a wolf's heart in a sheep's skin.

Sabriel Mercer wasn't long on words, but he was the model of principles and economy. He was a skilled rifleman, currently working out of Boston. He was a contemplative man with a deep appreciation of Oriental thought and took his martial arts seriously—hell, took everything seriously. Sebastian didn't think he'd ever heard the man laugh. Unlike the others, he looked dark and dangerous—and was. But if Sebastian had to follow anyone to the gates of hell and expect to come back alive, it would be Mercer.

Sebastian handed each man a packet of information and it felt as if he were airing his dirty laundry. Olivia was his responsibility and, to protect her, he had to expose her, expose himself and his failings. "The prison toasts were IDed. Kershaw is definitely one of the felons on the run. A witness saw an argument between Greco and Carmichael an hour before they were due at Allenwood. The Feebs are looking into that. As you know, they've got the scene. One of their techs went over the car and found nothing. They're putting down the slice-and-dice as a demand for respect."

The heels of his Gore-Tex hiking boots resting on the lip of Sebastian's desk, Skyralov chuckled. "Really went out on a limb on that one. Hatred as motive. When has a fugitive ever loved the sight of us?"

Disbelieving shakes of agreement all around.

"I have a problem with the public nature of the murders," Sebastian continued.

"Why's that?" Reed asked, foot on the seat of a chair, elbow on his raised knee, other hand on hip as if posing to show off the three-piece charcoal suit that somehow sported no wrinkle despite his red-eye flight.

"They're on the run," Sebastian said. "They know the cops are looking for them. Why kill our guys out in the open when they could've done it in private and put us off their scent for longer?"

Skyralov chose a roll from the box. "Mutts aren't known for their brains."

"Mutts, no, but Kershaw's on a mission. He'd want to scramble the timeline for as long as he could."

Reed adjusted his shades. "Unless he was throwing this in our face."

"Got IDs on the other fugitives?" Kingsley asked, pen poised over his reporter's notebook—he never left home without it.

"Harvey Rand and John Cupp. Looks like they scattered after they killed our guys. Rand was picked up after he robbed a bar just over the Massachusetts border. Cupp was spotted in Vermont. Looks like he's trying to make the border. The BOLO's been altered to show the capture. The Feebs have agents out talking to the usual sources, but so far all their leads are getting us nowhere.'' Not that Be-On-the-Look-Out bulletins ever got the fast and full distribution they needed.

Kingsley hooked the thumb of his left hand around a red suspender. "I don't suppose Rand is talking."

"Says he was just along for the ride. Pins Kershaw for the murders."

Skyralov licked icing off his fingers. "Real surprise there."

"What do you need?" Mercer asked, cutting to the chase. Finding him among the shadows of the wall of shelves filled with electronics took Sebastian a moment.

"Kingsley's going to be your tech support. He's going to run the computers. You need surveillance equipment. You need information. You need support. Kingsley's your man. I'll trade off manning the command center with him."

Kingsley nodded as he scribbled. "I'll need—"

"Make a list and I'll get it for you."

Looking at Reed, Sebastian said, "I want you to pay a little visit to this address." He handed Reed a piece of paper, holding on for a second longer than necessary. He should be the one going out there. He should be the one hunting. He should be the one cranking cuffs on Kershaw. "The kid nearly ran us over yesterday morning in the hospital parking lot. I couldn't find any ties to Kershaw, but that doesn't mean there aren't any. Charm him out of his secrets."

"No sweat." Never any sweat for Reed, not even after a five-mile run.

"Skyralov, I want you on the mother." Sebastian tamped down the twin curls of frustration and envy, and concentrated on dispatching the plan he'd spent all night perfecting. "Flip her if you can. Kershaw has to have some help. Behind the felon, there's usually a woman. And this one's been vocal about the cruel and unusual punishment we've pushed on her poor defenseless boy." That brought a round of chuckles. "Check on the rest of his family, too. He has a brother and a sister."

"You got some flash?"

Flash money helped to grease the way to information. For a twenty, neighbor would rat on neighbor. For the cost of a fix, a junkie brother might sell out his kin. For the price of a john, a sister who worked the streets might let her tongue flap. "I'll get you some."

He turned to the man melding with the shadows of the room. "Mercer, I want you to check out who's been put in lockup for drugs in the last few days and see if we can get a lead that way. Kershaw has a hard time getting laid without a little pharmaceutical help. After five years behind bars, he'll want a little tail before he nails me."

"What about Cupp?" Reed asked.

"Let the Feebs get him. It'll make them feel good."

Rough barks of laughter erupted.

"You want Kershaw brought in or smoked?" Mercer asked. No emotion colored his tone. There was something unnerving about this man's unflappable evenness. And if the question had come from anyone but Mercer, he'd have wondered at his choice. But Mercer prided himself on his ability to work a case without drawing his weapon.

Cop killers had a hard time making it safely into custody. No one would blame Sebastian for choosing a permanent resolution to this problem. No one but him. If he chose to gun Kershaw down, then he would be no better than that piece of scum, no better than the creep who'd shot his parents for the seventy-six dollars in their wallets.

But he also understood Kershaw. Kershaw didn't want to go back to the hell of prison. This was his goodbye, and he was going to make sure it made fireworks worthy of a Fourth of July celebration.

For Kershaw, death was the only acceptable outcome.

And somehow Sebastian had to make sure Olivia was left out of the equation.

"The choice is up to him."

Chapter Five

Being in the kitchen with the woman who called herself her sister and the girl she was told was her niece was like being trapped in a beehive. The thin woman flitted from the granite counter to the mammoth stainless-steel stove to the walk-in pantry as if she were pollinating flowers. The buzz of her voice was as dizzying as her crooked flight path. Olivia hung on to her teacup with both hands, trying to keep the room steady. What was her sister trying to outrun?

Every touch of her sister's hand felt like a slap, every word like a piercing whine. Steam from the stove fogged the windows, blocking the steadying view of the mountains she'd so loved yesterday, and closed her throat. A part of her wished for her husband's solid presence—except that having him look at her and wish for someone else was even more painful than this fretful whir of activity.

The strange creature across the table from her kept staring at her as if she were a monkey in a cage. Red and purple streaks spiked her niece's short blond hair. A thick line of kohl raccooned her pale blue eyes. Tiny silver revolvers hung from the lobes of her ears. A black dog collar studded with silver diamonds circled her neck. Her clunky shoes seemed to weigh more than she did. The screaming red of her tartan flannel pants and the black leather jacket did nothing to complement her snow-pale skin.

"Eat." Paula plopped down a bowl of fruit salad next to the plate heaping with scrambled eggs that were an anemic white and sausage links she was told were soy. Had she eaten this way before?

The creature leaned toward her. "Just eat. She'll nag you to death if you don't."

"I heard that, Cari." Paula put a hand on Olivia's shoulder. "You've been through a trauma. You need to build your strength."

Maybe she was right, Olivia thought. A strange weakness coursed through her limbs, making them move as if they were made of cement about to set. She picked up the fork and ate a bite of eggs. It went down like crumpled paper. Letting go of the fork, she reached for the warmth of the teacup and thought of the man who was her husband.

She'd half feared he'd climb into the big bed with her last night; she was half disappointed he hadn't. The dark room had felt like a tomb. She wanted to be left by herself to tiptoe her way through all this strangeness. All their expectant stares made her skin crawl. Yet being alone made her feel like an unwanted baby abandoned on a doorstep.

You can't have it both ways. Make up your mind. A short, sharp laugh escaped her. *Yeah, if you can find it.*

"Where is he?" she asked, unable still to make her mouth form any of their names. Was her husband avoiding the alien who now lived in his wife's body? She couldn't really blame him. She didn't much care for the alien body she now inhabited.

"Sebastian?" Paula asked, stilling the spatula above the skillet.

Olivia nodded, holding her breath, afraid suddenly of the answer she might hear.

Paula attacked the eggs in the pan as if she were wielding a bayonet in enemy territory. "Umph! He's where he always is—doing business. It's no wonder you were leaving him. You'd finally come to your senses and decided to come live with me."

Leaving him? She inhaled sharply. Olivia had meant to leave him? Why, when she was sure he would have moved a mountain if Olivia had so desired?

Cari slammed the cereal box on the table. A dozen flakes flew out, peppering the red-birch tabletop with small plinks. "Mom, she doesn't need that right now."

"She needs the truth." Paula dumped the eggs on a plate.

Cari sniffed at the milk container, then poured some on the cereal in her bowl. "Yeah, right, like you're so big on truth all of a sudden."

"What do you mean?" Paula jammed the plate in front of her daughter.

"Never mind." Cari dismissed her mother with a wave of her hand.

What was she missing between mother and daughter? The spaces between the words were snakes looking for a chance to strike. Had Olivia known about the tension that clung to her family? Her gaze drifted to the foggy window and, suddenly, she wanted the steadiness of those mountains. "I'm going out." She started to get up.

"You can't." Paula whirled around, sinking both hands into Olivia's tender shoulders and sliding Olivia back into the chair. She winced.

"Why can't she?" Cari asked, frowning.

"Because she can't." Paula's features pinched, but her eyes danced with fear. Was she afraid Olivia wouldn't remember the way home?

Cari snorted. "So much for the truth."

"I won't go far, sister." Olivia tried to pull Paula's claws from her shoulders.

"My name is Paula." Paula leaned into her so closely, Olivia could see the thin lines spidering the corners of her eyes. Her sister mouthed her name louder and more drawn out, as if Olivia were deaf. "Pau-la."

Snapping her gaze away from her sister's, Olivia ground her teeth. *What am I? A stupid child?* "I know what your name is."

Paula brightened, retracted her claws, clapping her hands close to her chest. "You do? Oh, that's wonderful!"

"You told me yesterday. And the day before."

"Oh, yes. I did." The busy bee took off again, skittering along the tiled floor of the kitchen, displacing pots, pans and dishes as she went.

"Mom," Cari said in a voice dripping with ennui. "Leave her alone."

Shoving a spoonful of cereal in her mouth, Cari winked at Olivia. Olivia hid her smile in her cup of tea. Why did this one, who by all outward looks should give her most cause to feel terror, instead put her at ease?

"Here." Paula dumped a trio of pills in front of Olivia on the table. "Take these."

"Mo-om."

"Cari, please. This is important." Paula bent down and whispered, "She can't remember things, so we have to do it for her."

"I think she can handle things just fine," Cari whispered back.

"Why can't you take anything seriously?" Paula's face

fractured like the shell of an overcooked hard-boiled egg. Turning toward Olivia, Paula snapped her chin at the pills rolling toward the woven place mat. "Take them."

"I take things seriously, mother. You just see what you want to see. And you're going to smother her just like you smother me. I don't see why I have to be here."

"Because I said so. It's for your own good."

"If it's for my own good, then I should know why. I'm eighteen and technically on my own."

"That's why you're still living at home, eating the food I buy. Where's that famous job you were supposed to get?"

"I've got feelers out."

In the past two days, Olivia had discovered that her skin felt things with sharpness. This morning, she'd had to change twice before she found something that didn't scrape her skin. Though her sister and her niece's words were couched in forced smiles and underlined with care, each was like a stab with a dull fork. The closer the magnet of their friction brought them, the sharper the stab pierced her skin.

Break the spell, she thought as she swallowed the pills. *Make them snap apart.* "What do I do?"

Paula spun on her heels and stared at her, blinking like an owl. "What do you mean?"

"What do I do?" She tried to find the words in her mind and stumbled. "Before. What did I do all day?"

"Oh." Paula sank to a chair, twisting the green-and-white dishtowel she held. "Well, you did all sorts of things. You, you—"

"Tried to avoid your nagging sister's phone calls," Cari chimed in.

"Cari! I'm trying to help her."

"Then treat her like the adult she is." Cari turned to

Olivia. "What you did, Olivia, was make everybody try to feel good. And sometimes, you forgot yourself."

"Cari, that's enough."

Cari pushed the half-finished cereal bowl to the center of the table. "Yeah, Mom, the truth hits too close to home, doesn't it?" She turned to Olivia. "The truth is that your sister and your husband both wanted you for themselves and stuck you in the middle because you love them both."

Earlier, Olivia had felt the tug of anger between Paula and her husband. Was that why she'd wanted to leave this home? Had the tension made living here impossible? Was that why she had, as Cari said, forgotten herself? She stared at the smooth mirror of tea in her cup, but there was no answer there—only the reflection of her too-wide eyes. And if she'd wanted to get away from the tug between her husband and her sister, why had she headed toward her sister's home when she'd left her husband?

Paula stood. "We'll continue this conversation later."

"That's right. The ostrich wins the day. If you pretend it isn't there, then it can't be real. Well, some things are real, even if you pretend they aren't. Like what happened to Dad."

Paula flitted back to the busyness of the counter. Olivia looked around at the red-birch cabinets, at the sunny yellow of the walls, at the green accents that seemed to wrap around her like vines, and swallowed hard. She was missing something in the thick undercurrent eddying all around the house. But what? She looked at the hands knotted around the mug of tea. Had she been happy here once?

Cari leaned across the table and cupped a hand around her mouth. "Want to blow this pop stand?"

A zing of eagerness flashed through her. The kitchen that a moment ago had seemed to tighten around her like a boa constrictor now loosened its hold. Freedom, she thought, as she pictured the wideness of the sky, the solid strength of the mountain. Olivia nodded and scuttled back the chair.

''Where are you going?'' Paula asked, hands on her hips.

''To Olivia's closet. I'm going to play dress up,'' her niece lied.

Paula frowned. ''I don't think that's appropriate.''

''Why not? Afraid she'll feel like a normal person for a change?''

Paula sighed.

''Want to come?'' Olivia asked. Cari kicked her and mouthed, ''No!''

Eyebrows scrunched like pirate hats on stick figures, Paula stared from daughter to sister and finally sighed again and turned back to the sink. ''You go ahead. I'll be up in a while.''

Taking Olivia's hand, Cari slid through the kitchen door. ''This way.''

In the mudroom, Cari slipped on a black down coat and Olivia reached for the navy wool coat she'd worn home from the hospital.

''The light-blue one.'' Cari pointed her chin to a marshmallowlike parka. ''Warmer. And those boots.'' She pointed to a pair of leather boots that laced up the front and were lined with lamblike fleece. ''Here.'' Cari launched a dark blue hat and a pair of gloves her way, then opened the door and stuck her head outside. ''All clear.''

The coldness of the outside air hit Olivia's lungs like a broom and swept out all the staleness of the house. Cari crept along the foundation. Olivia followed.

''Where are we going?'' Olivia whispered.

''The sugar house.'' Cari pointed to a stand of trees over

a rise to her left, but Olivia could see no structure there. "I used to go there all the time when I was a kid. No one's going to bother us there." She chanced a look around the corner of the house, then started to cut a diagonal toward the trees. "You have watch out for my mom. She latches on and then it's impossible for her to let go."

Olivia giggled as the image of a leech wearing Paula's face popped into her mind. "Why are we sneaking?"

"So Uncle S. won't see us."

"You don't like him." Olivia thought of the sliding warmth and shrilling alarm that fired through her every time he was near. Did Olivia fear her husband? Was her sister right when she'd said Olivia wanted to leave him? Why?

"I like him fine. Most of the time anyway. It's just that sometimes he's hard, you know."

"How?" The solid sureness of him had felt good. Was she wrong to think so?

"Don't worry," Cari said. "He's hard on everybody but you. He loves you."

"Oh." And another snake of uncertainty slithered inside her as her feet sunk through the hard skin of snow, glittering in the sun. Had she loved him in return? She searched the dark corners of her mind and kept tripping over the black hole of her amnesia. If she had loved him, then that love, where had it gone?

Don't think of it. The past doesn't matter. Only the future. And she could make anything of the future she wanted. The thought cheered her. She was an artist, they'd told her. She would paint a bright new tomorrow for herself.

Halfway up the rise, Olivia pointed at the tracks in the snow that looked like two half-moons closing in to kiss. "Deer tracks."

"That's right." Cari smiled, as proud as a mother.

Olivia hung on to that smile. And on the wings of that little triumph, her heart flew straight into that wide open blue of sky and soared.

She had not forgotten everything.

"SHE'S GONE." Paula crashed through the door to his office like a thunderstorm and burst. She grabbed at him and the force of her despair pulled Sebastian out of his chair. "She's gone. She's not in the bedroom. She's not in the studio. She's not anywhere."

"Calm down, Paula. Cari has a talent for disappearing." Why did the woman have to be so hysterical about everything? Why had he invited Olivia's family here to complicate his life? Stuck in rebellion mode since her father's death, Cari had gone out of her way to make life difficult for everyone around her. The last thing he needed was one more problem. "She'll be back. You told her not to go out without—"

"Not just Cari." Paula's nails dug into his forearms. "Olivia, too."

No, not Olivia. Not with Kershaw out there. As his heart pounded, he swore. In one breath, the air in the office went from relaxed to action ready. He'd asked Paula for one thing. One damn thing. Keep an eye on Olivia. He couldn't be at her side every minute of the day. Flexing his hands, he shook off Paula's hold. "Stay here. We'll find them."

Before Paula could open her mouth, he was racing up the stairs, his team close behind. "Kingsley, take the upstairs. Reed, the downstairs." The two men branched off. Sebastian went by the front door and saw it was still locked, so he continued to the mudroom off the kitchen. Both Olivia's and Cari's parkas were missing. Outside, tracks on the ice-crusted snow wound around the edge of the house. "Mercer, cover the back. Skyralov, the front."

His leather shoes slipping now and then on the icy crust of snow, wind biting through the cotton of his shirt, Sebastian followed the tracks and soon spotted them. They bobbed like children as they weaved through some sort of game. Sun bounded off the snow, making them look as if they shone. Their laughter echoed over the mountain like crystal bells, clear and melodic. And for a second, the sound froze Sebastian. Playing like that with Cari, she was Olivia, and something in his heart sighed with relief. He knew that smile. He knew that laugh. He knew that unselfconscious grace of movement. She was back.

He whistled, calling to Mercer and Skyralov to cover him and swept down on Olivia and Cari who'd frozen like ice sculptures at the sound of his arrival. Left arm wound protectively around Olivia to shield her, he scanned the nearby shadows of trees. "Let's go."

"No!" Olivia fought his hold, stuttering his concentration. Olivia never opposed him.

Cari got into the action and tried to pull Olivia from his arms. "Let her go!"

"It's dangerous out here." Kershaw could be anywhere. On the limb of a tree, the rifle he'd stolen from the marshals pointed right at them. How could Cari lead Olivia into danger like this? "Your mother warned you—"

Cari snorted. "My mother's not too big on truth."

"Let me spell it out for you, then," he said, holding on to the squirming Olivia. "Out here, you're a target. Get back to the house. *Now.*"

"Why?" Hand on hip, she copped a pose that reminded him too much of Paula on one of her rampages against him.

"Now's not the time, Cari." He tried to force Olivia forward, but she dug in her heels.

"No, let me go."

She wriggled out of his hold and raced away from him toward the trees. He whirled after her. "Olivia!"

A white cloud scuttled over the sun, deepening the shadows along the ridge Olivia climbed. The writhing casts of limbs seemed to snatch at her. The wave of wind surfing through the trees seemed to carry her name on its moan, Kershaw's laugh in its wake. Cari's shouts behind them added a macabre counterpoint. "Olivia!"

He grabbed at her coat, unbalanced her. With the cry of caught prey, she twisted, leaving him holding the empty shell of her parka. Damn it! Why was she fighting him so hard? What was wrong with her? Couldn't she see he was trying to protect her?

Of course not. She couldn't remember him. She didn't know about Kershaw. She wasn't herself.

He lunged at her, slamming them both to the ground. The skin of ice on the snow cracked. Her cry of anguish echoed all around them, silencing the creatures in the woods. "Olivia," he said gently, "stop fighting me."

But she didn't. She writhed and kicked. A punch connected with his face, radiating pain through his jaw. The soft wool of her navy sweater slipped in his grip. They moved over and under each other in an awkward dance as he tried to still her without hurting her. Finally, he pinned her beneath him.

He captured her chin and forced her to look at him. He knew then that what he'd seen earlier was an illusion. The blue of her eyes still held that hollow look of fear. Olivia wasn't back; she was still lost. "We have to go in."

"I can't...breathe in there." Her voice was a whisper, brittle and thready. Her hands fisted into the material of his shirt. Her tear-bright eyes widened as if to take in the sky. "I need to breathe."

Because he couldn't help himself, he kissed the top of her head and hugged her close. He'd thought he could keep the truth from her, that he could hold her in the safety of the house while he took care of the problem and never add the burden of his failure to her recovery. He saw now that that was impossible. To keep her safe, he would have to confess his sins. "I know, sweetheart, but right now, there's someone out there who wants to hurt you."

"Oh, that's just great," Cari said, panting behind him. "And I was just supposed to guess?"

"Your mother was supposed to tell you." He helped Olivia up, holding her securely against another burst of flight. "This guy's dangerous. He'll go through anyone and anything to destroy what I care for the most. Do you understand, Cari?"

Mutely, she nodded, then handed the discarded parka to Olivia. "He's ruined the fun anyway. Let's just go back."

Meeting his gaze as she draped the parka around her shoulders, Olivia asked, "When do I get to breathe again?"

And through the mirror of her eyes, he could feel the straw-thin constriction of her chest, feel the skintight closing of the walls of the house around her, feel the ocean-deep pull of her fear.

What had he done to her?

"Soon." He tucked her in the shield of his body. He hoped this wasn't another promise he'd have to break. Scanning their path, he led her toward the house. Mercer and Skyralov joined the odd formation, flanking them.

When they reached the house, Skyralov pulled him aside. "There's something you have to see."

Reluctantly, he surrendered Olivia to a weeping Paula's care and followed Skyralov to the front gates. There, hanging backwards on the iron lances, was a dried funeral wreath with a wind-shredded ribbon. Probably stolen from the cemetery on Mountain Road. Gold lettering spelled out, "We'll miss you, Sam." And beneath, letters cut out of magazines and glued to the ribbon said, "Welcome home, Falconer."

Kershaw was here, and he was playing with him.

"Have Kingsley go over the security tapes." After unlocking the security box, Sebastian entered a code and the gates opened. He took down the wreath and handed it to Skyralov.

Crouching, he searched the hard pack of snow for evidence of footprints or tire prints he didn't recognize. He was about to close the gates again when Skyralov handed him the wreath. "I'll handle that. You're needed at the house. Your wife, she'll want an explanation."

She'd want more than that. And he had no idea how to lay out the whole wicked story so she would understand and not hate him.

The shiver that wracked through him had nothing to do with the cold and everything to do with letting someone else do his work. He needed to be out here. He needed to hunt. But he also needed to protect Olivia.

Reluctantly, he took the wreath and headed back toward the house. Why did it feel as if cuffs jangled between his wrists?

Chapter Six

Cecilia Okindo's arrival that afternoon was a welcome break from her sister's hawklike supervision of her every move. Olivia gladly closed the door to the studio and let out a sigh as she took in the view of the mountains through the wall of windows. Shapes defined themselves in the granite. Space between mountain and clouds engaged. Colors mixed in a palette in her mind. And the stir of something known pulsed through her until her fingers tingled.

"I want to paint," she said before the therapist, who smelled like brown sugar and cinnamon and spoke with the slow heat of summer, could open the case she carried.

"Well, now, love, that sounds like a terrific idea. Today, we will work on small motor skills."

Olivia strode to the shelf unit packed with art palettes, paints and paper. Where to start?

"Where is that handsome husband of yours today?" Cecilia asked, joining her.

The choices on the shelf before her blurred and the image of Sebastian's face floated there for a moment. The deep frown when he'd returned to the house had held an equal measure of anger and determination. He'd stalked past them like a man with a purpose and disappeared in the dark bowels of the house. Because of her? Because she'd gone out? Because she'd wanted to breathe? "I don't know."

"Ah, well, maybe he'll join us later. Let's start with a sketch." Cecilia reached for a large pad bound with a silver coil. She snatched a pencil from a cup with a cracked lip and a fat wad of gray eraser from a blue ceramic tray.

Olivia sat cross-legged on the large canvas cushion on the floor and propped the pad of paper against her knees. Closing her eyes, she visualized the picture she wanted to draw. As she saw the elements of design drift apart and come together, she smiled. This, she remembered.

Drawing in a long breath, she opened her eyes and poised the pencil over the clean, white page. The first line swished across the page, not in a straight road, but in one filled with ruts. She frowned and tried again. She could see each tiny detail in her mind, understood how to form each one with the pencil, but her fingers were acting like toddlers just learning to walk. With a roar, she pitched the pencil across the room.

"Um," Cecilia said, eyebrows scrunched pensively over the page. "Look at all these tiny lines. I need a magnifying glass to see them." She walked over to the shelf and picked up a brass looking glass. With a grin, she telescoped it out and put the large end to Olivia's eye. "This is what you're trying to do."

Through the glass, Olivia saw a row of mountains as tiny and as rough as the flakes of cereal Cari had dropped on the kitchen table this morning.

"Now," Cecilia said, turning the glass around to the narrow end. "This is what I want you to try."

This time, one mountain loomed large, each rock and tree a wide brushstroke. Smiling, Cecilia turned the page and handed Olivia another pencil. Cecilia was not looking for what Olivia could not do, but rather sought to bring out what she could. There was no judgment in her midnight eyes—only encouragement. Olivia accepted the pencil and tried again.

The elements of the design slowly fell into place, giving her a sense of strength for the first time since she'd arrived here.

Some time later, the door to the studio opened. Looking up, she saw Sebastian hesitate, one hand on the curved brass handle. Wanting to make up for running from him earlier, she beamed a smile at him and held up the sketchpad. Instinct told her she wanted—needed?—to please this man. What better way to do that than to give him a part of Olivia he remembered? "Look."

She liked the sureness in his stride, the power of it, as he came toward her. Had that confidence pleased the old Olivia, too? The heat of anticipation warmed her skin as he crouched beside her and took the sketch pad. She held her breath. *Please let this be right.* The scent of him, fresh like winter, wrapped a secure arm around her. And for a moment, she let herself believe everything *was* right.

"That's the mountain right outside the window," he said. His approval glowed a fuzzy warmth inside her.

Then the tiny seed of fear took root again as his gaze shifted to the trunk sitting on the black iron holder and back to her crude drawing. Was that disappointment shuttering his eyes?

Blackness erased every trace of warmth. She took the sketch pad from him. "I have a headache."

"Tension." Cecilia directed Sebastian to move behind Olivia. "Sit here. I will show you how to work the knots from her shoulders."

He did as he was told, and Olivia was glad she couldn't see his eyes. She couldn't bear the sadness in them, the soul-deep sorrow of wanting one woman and being stuck with another. Did the aura of strength around him draw her simply because he was the key to her past?

With Cecilia's instruction, his sure fingers unknotted the hard gnarls of tension in her nape and shoulders. His touch didn't feel like a slap as Paula's had...it felt somehow soothing. Her neck, her spine, her knees, jellied. Fear again? Would it be a constant companion from now on? Except that this fear didn't have a cold edge. It was warm and sweet and made her lick her lips with longing.

The spin of yearning reminded her of the picture on the bureau in the bedroom. Sebastian and Olivia on their wedding day. Would his eyes ever shine for her the way they had for that Olivia? She could still feel the sharp bite of jealousy as she'd looked at herself and him and not been able to recall how love had felt between them. A knot formed in her chest and the sting of tears burned her eyes.

She turned her head to look at him over her shoulder and tried to explain the turmoil roiling inside her. "I'm not Olivia."

He kissed her temple and it tasted of regret. "Give it time."

She leaned into the warm strength of him. *Please let me remember. Let me be the Olivia he wants. I promise, I'll never ask for anything again.*

AFTER MIDNIGHT, THE FAMILIAR bing of online companionship chimed. Under the cover of ether, all needs were answered. He smiled and greeted Okie.

Sk8Thor: Hi!
Okie: I'm in.
Sk8Thor: Good going!
Okie: U owe me.
Sk8Thor: I'll take care of u.

Okie: Darn right u will.

Sk8Thor: I need the security blueprints.

Okie: It's going to be tough. There's always someone there.

Sk8Thor: Distract.

Okie: Got anything on the skinny guy? He's holed in there like a mole.

Sk8Thor: Blind him with your wit.

Okie: Ha, ha! No guarantees.

Sk8Thor: Just do it.

Okie: Can't u just hack yr way thru?

Sk8Thor: It's all about finesse.

Okie: I thought it was about revenge.

This was more than revenge. This was proof. You could bully your way through the world or you could finesse. He'd show them all that he was worth more than the animal who'd stolen everything from him. He wouldn't do it with muscle and brute force. He'd do it like he'd done everything else—with brains and style.

Sk8Thor: Revenge and more.

He thought for a moment then added:

Sk8Thor: Here's how to give 'em something to think about.

SEBASTIAN WAS COMING TO HATE the inside of his own office. The space had once seemed large, a cocoon to shift from hunter to husband. Now Kingsley had crammed the electronic instruments of his trade over every surface. Even with Skyralov still on surveillance, the three remaining men on his team made the room appear too small.

Stale coffee perfumed the air as heavily as the frustration steaming from his own skin. He wanted a drink—Glenlivet straight from the bottle. Hell, even Old Smuggler would do. But he had to keep a clear head. Punching his handheld computer, Sebastian brought up his notes. He forced himself to concentrate on the situation at hand and not on wishing for the impossible. "Reed, what'd you find on the van driver?"

Jacket off, but still styling, Reed posed in the epitome of relaxation. "Just a kid. Nineteen. Got scared when he thought he'd hit the two of you and punched the gas instead of the brakes. Then he kept going because this citation would've put him over on points and the state would've yanked his license."

"You believe him?"

"Everything checked out. He's got a baby and a wife to support. Losing his license would've meant no transportation, and he'd have lost his job. He's trying to do the right thing and screwing up at every turn."

That, Sebastian could empathize with. "No ties to Kershaw?"

"None that I could see. Kid's been to Nashua only a handful of times and most of those at the mall."

"That doesn't prove no ties."

"The responsibility for that baby's got him too scared to have time for the likes of Kershaw. He's been home or at work for the past six months. It checks out, Falconer."

Reed bit out the words with his customary smile, but they bore a hard edge. *If you don't trust me, why am I here?* they seemed to ask. Sebastian nodded. Letting go was like handing out little pieces of himself. "Mercer."

Mercer's voice floated from somewhere in the shadows of the room. "I'm following a lead."

Sebastian ground his back teeth. "I need more details."

The feral green of Mercer's eyes seemed to glow in the shadows where he stood. "Found a city cop, tinned him and got a scoop on the local drug scene. Took less than ten minutes to spot a street vendor. Swapped a C-note for ten names. Paid the local jail a visit."

Imagination. Sebastian had always liked that in a cop. Mercer could have gotten the same information from the local authorities, but official channels would have taken longer. He'd picked someone in jail for leverage. Junkies in jail were always dying to help. "What'd you get?"

"The brother's in a transitional-living facility in Nashua. Nathan Kershaw was in-pocket at the time of the escape."

Transitional-living program translated to a halfway house for paroled drug addicts seeking recovery.

No suspect. No lead.

Sutton wanted daily updates. He wasn't going to like this one. Sebastian massaged the back of his neck and the feeling of Olivia's skin this afternoon steamrolled over him. So smooth. So soft. So warm. He'd wanted her then, wanted the woman wearing Olivia's skin, wanted the illusion he could have the past again. He shook his head and tore the unfaithful desire to shreds.

"He was released two days ago," Mercer said. "I'm working the triggers."

Maybe all wasn't lost after all.

"I want a look at Greco's Blazer," Reed said, hand in pocket at an angle that couldn't possibly feel as relaxed as it looked.

"Any particular reason?"

Reed cocked a boy-next-door smile. "Well, now, seeing

as how they're all specialists down there at the Bureau, I want to be sure they didn't miss something. You know how those obvious places aren't a challenge enough to warrant a thorough inspection.''

Rocky laughter peppered the room. ''Search your heart out.''

''The special agent-in-charge okayed it,'' Reed said, ''but the Bureau's regional crime specialist turned me down flat.''

''Did he give you a reason?''

Reed shook his head and not a hair moved. ''No, but the SAC's willing if you could find a way to skip the chain of command.''

Sebastian nodded. ''I'll have Sutton call his Bureau counterpart.''

''Let's talk security,'' Kingsley said, flipping the cover of his reporter's pad open and hooking his left thumb around a red suspender. ''This here's a nice place, but it's full of holes.''

Sebastian crossed his arms over his chest. ''It wasn't meant as a prison.''

''Maybe not, but we'll have to turn it into a fortress to keep Olivia safe. Those windows—''

''I can't ask her to stay in the dark. She's already too afraid.''

''A couple of days of fear are better than ending up dead.''

Was watching the light in her slowly fade from the inside out any better? He wanted Olivia back, not to drive her deeper into the shadows of her mind. Sebastian closed his eyes and tried to pinch the fatigue thumping between his eyebrows. ''Find a way to work around her. I don't want to take more away from her than she's already lost.''

Through his wire-rimmed glasses, Kingsley shot him a speculative glance. "How long have you been up?"

Too long. Not long enough. He remained silent.

"That's what I thought. I'll take first shift tonight. Get a few hours of sleep."

Sleep was the last thing he wanted, but Kingsley was right. To be competent, he needed a well-rested brain. "Mercer, find the brother and squeeze him. Reed, I'll get permission for you for that search by morning." He turned to Kingsley. "Skyralov check in?"

"So far, the mother's not giving anything away. I pulled her phone records for him. She got a couple of calls from Allenwood. Got a couple more from pay phones in the area. Want me to have him pour on the charm?"

He nodded, wanting to be the one out there asking the questions. Skyralov knew the drill. But trust had never come easily. "Let's hope she's into cowboys."

THERE WAS NO PLACE LEFT to be alone in the house, Sebastian thought, as he climbed the steps to the upper part of the house. Kingsley had taken over his office. Someone occupied every bedroom. The studio held too many memories of Olivia. Cari wandered the halls at all hours like a ghost dragging chains, bemoaning her fate. Paula claimed the kitchen as her territory, asking him what he wanted every time he walked in. He couldn't even pour his own cup of coffee anymore, and his favorite mug had gone missing.

What he wanted was his home back—the peace, the quiet, the healing of it. Paula couldn't give that back to him. No one could.

That left the bathroom. He flipped on the switch and sat on the closed lid of the toilet, elbows on knees, chin resting on his upturned palms. Then he spied the counter with its double sink and swore silently.

No escape.

The Olivia he remembered was here, too, in bottles and tubes lined up like sailors in the blue and cream basket that served as their boat. He rose and picked up a bottle of lotion. Sniffing the thick light pink cream brought Olivia back—the summer freshness of her, and the smile that went all the way to her eyes and lit up her whole face.

What he'd loved best about her was the way she was still awed by simple things—the flight of a hawk on a cold winter morning, the feel of thick sweaters on the first crisp day of fall, the scent of maple sugaring in the spring, the taste of summer sun-warmed tomatoes right off the vine. She could make him see the beauty of this world even when evil lurked right around the corner. She was his balance, and without her, he was afraid he would get stuck on the wrong side of the hunt.

The bottle suddenly weighed a ton. He put it back in the basket and weariness settled deep in his bones. He was losing control of his life, and there was nothing he could do about it.

Standing in the glare of the bathroom light, he looked toward the bathtub. No, he wasn't sleeping there. The sofa in the living room was too short. He was tired. He needed sleep. He was not going to be pushed out of his own bed. Olivia would just have to deal with it.

"Olivia?"

She turned her head toward him.

"There are no beds left. I need sleep. I won't touch you. I just need some rest."

She nodded and dropped her head back to the pillow.

He undressed in the dark and slipped between the flannel sheets. Having her curl away from him was an insult sharper than a blade.

He reached for the extra quilt folded at the foot of the bed and rolled it. He tucked the roll between their bodies and pulled the blankets up again. Turning his back to her, he closed his eyes and willed sleep. Perverse creature that it was, it refused his command.

"Tell me about Olivia," his wife's voice whispered in the dark.

Having her ask about herself brought the truth too close to home. He thought of all Olivia was, of the artist, of the lover, of the friend, and could think of only one way to describe all she meant to him. Olivia was home. Would this woman who wore Olivia's skin understand?

He wondered at the use of the past. Had he already accepted Olivia was gone? No, he decided as he punched the pillow. There was still hope. He had to believe that. "I'm really tired, Olivia."

"Why did she want to leave?"

He wished Paula wouldn't have mentioned that fact first chance she got. Now he was going to have to explain his shortcomings, justify them, and that itched like raw wool. "My work takes me away from home a lot. Waiting was hard on Olivia. She wanted…"

What had she wanted? Had he ever asked her? Had he ever tried to slip into her skin, the way he did with the fugitives he pursued, and see his work from her eyes? He'd expected so much from her. What had she wanted from him? He tugged the blanket tighter around his shoulders. "She wanted a baby, and I couldn't give her one."

Another shortcoming. Stress, the doctor had told them, had affected his sperm count. But he couldn't give up his job. He had to hunt. He had to put scum back in the prison where they belonged. He had to make the world safe. It was his reason for living. Olivia was a selfish indulgence. One he couldn't give up, either.

"If she doesn't come back," she said, "what will you do?"

Having her voice his fear that the Olivia he knew might never come back, that all his hope might be just that—vain hope—made the possibility too real.

Emptiness whistled through him as the past flashed back in living snapshots. Olivia's shy smile the first time he'd seen her. Olivia's laugh when he'd taken her sailing on Trotter's Pond while they were dating and they'd ended up in the water. Olivia's pleasure when he'd held her in his arms as he carried her over the threshold of the Aerie. The hundreds of memories they'd created here echoed against the walls and clamored for his attention, choking him.

Looking ahead, the future was nothing but a hunt in the night with no light. Strength, control, had gotten him where he was in life. They were of no use to him now. His hand fisted around the corner of the pillow. He swallowed hard. No, he wasn't ready to give up yet. "We'll work it out."

He could not admit she was his weakness and that her departure would kill what little was left of his heart. He would not beg her to stay. He could not tell her that the sight of her worked better than drugs to relax him, that the scent of her was more soothing than his favorite scotch, that touching her kept him sane and centered.

"You would let her go?"

He closed his eyes and heard the thunder of his heart slap against his ribs, felt pain stab at his chest. "I would do anything for her."

"You would let her stay?"

He tried to swallow the knot at his throat, to breathe around the bubble of hope. "Yes."

"Even if she couldn't be the person you wanted her to be?"

He had tracked thousands of fugitives. He had cuffed thousands of felons. He had faced evil a thousand times and won. Nothing had ever cost him as much as answering this one question. "Yes."

Silence had a weight, he discovered, as he waited for her to lift it, waited for some sort of reassurance. But if he didn't know exactly what he expected, how could she give it to him?

"I don't know how to be myself."

"We'll work it out." Air gushed from his lungs as if they'd collapsed. That was the best he could do right now. He had no easy solutions. She had become someone different than the wife he knew. Everything, including him, was new to her.

Soon the tension eased from her body and her breathing shallowed. Sleep still escaped him.

Even in the dead of night there was no pure quiet. Sounds crept through the double panes of the window— the drone of an airplane flying overhead, the moan of wind as it wrapped itself around the house, the brittle bone clack of dry oak leaves still clinging to a branch.

And somewhere out there was Kershaw.

In her sleep, she turned. Her body and the roll of blanket separating them curved to spoon around his body. Her hand—as it had a thousand times—cupped the space above his heart possessively. He was still hers. Always would be. Placing his hand on top of hers, he tucked her in closer. He floated on the wave of his exhaustion and her warmth. The gravity pull of their ebb dragged him toward sleep.

The screech of alarm crashed over him in a breaker of noise, jarring him wide awake. A red light blinked on a panel of steady green on his bedside table.

Someone had breached security at the front door.

Chapter Seven

The Harris's Hawk posed on the Aerie's front step was dead. Its black-and-brown wings were spread as if it was in flight. Its yellow eyes—once piercing, now glazed—were open. Its gray beak held a tiny brass vial like the ones once carried by messenger pigeons. Bells adorned its legs. Sebastian recognized the bird as Orion, one of Mario's hunting companions. He'd seen Orion soar through the sky and bring down a pheasant in the woods. To see him dead like that on his doorstep made him want to wring Kershaw's neck just as he'd done to the bird.

Sebastian ground his back teeth as Kingsley snapped photographs of the hawk against the snow. The bursts of flash made every gory detail too stark.

Patience, once a strength, had all but frittered away over the past week. *Do something. Get it over with.* The beat of that need gunned like a revving engine as his life fell apart around him. And here he was standing, waiting. Again.

Once Kingsley was done, Sebastian carefully extracted the metal vial with tweezers from the Swiss Army knife he carried in his pocket. Using the tweezers and the tip of the knife, he unrolled the tiny scroll. The message, printed in Old English script, read, "Who's afraid of the big bad manhunter? Not me. Not me."

He could practically hear Kershaw's laughter on the wind. The icy bite of it slashed at his chest. He scanned the area, but could see nothing in the shifting darkness of night.

Kershaw was out there, watching. His presence prickled Sebastian's skin with the intuition hunter had for prey. "Find him."

Mercer nodded and started out the door.

"Hang on." Sebastian turned to Kingsley. "Did Mario open the gates for anyone?"

Kingsley shook his head.

Sebastian's gaze connected with Mercer. Kershaw would go through anyone to get to him, and Mario wasn't exactly in his prime. The master falconer wouldn't have let anyone get to his birds without a fight. And those damn birds were the reason Mario had refused to leave until Kershaw was caught. "Check out the gatehouse. Make sure he's okay."

Mercer nodded again, and Reed followed him out.

"Anything show up on the security cameras?" Sebastian asked Kingsley, focusing on the job at hand and not on the fact that he wasn't the one out doing the hunting.

Kingsley peered at the digital images frozen on the screen on the back of the camera. "Not a flicker."

"Run the tapes again. He couldn't have gotten past the sensors."

Kingsley nodded and left.

"What's going on?" Cari asked.

Sebastian turned and saw the three women huddled in the hallway and ran a hand over his face. He didn't need this right now.

Cari was dressed in flannel pajamas patterned like a sky.

With her tousled hair and her face free of ghoulish makeup, she looked like the vulnerable girl she was. Paula held on tight to the throat of her gray fleece zippered robe. Her eyes were owl-wide and her mouth hung open in a choked O. Olivia wore a navy sweatshirt over the pale lavender nightgown that skimmed her ankles—his sweatshirt. She looked lost in it. Her eyes were filled with questions. And he found he liked that expectant look better than the vacant one.

"Go back to bed." He closed the front door to hide the dead bird. "It's nothing."

"A dead bird is nothing?" Cari snorted. "Did you notice the thing's a hawk? Looks like a message to me, *Falconer*." She patted the pockets of her pajama bottoms. "I need a cigarette."

"Smoking's bad for you," he said, not quite sure how to deal with a scared teenager.

Cari glanced at the closed door. "Like living here's going to do much for my life expectancy."

"Go back to bed." If he'd had his way, he wouldn't have had to compromise and neither she nor Paula would be here to complicate the situation. "I'm handling it."

"Yeah, right." She rolled the scrunched pack of cigarettes between her palms. "You're doing a swell—"

"That's enough," Paula said, waking from her stupor. "Give me that." She snatched the cigarettes from Cari's hand and stuffed them in the pocket of her robe. Putting an arm around both Cari and Olivia, Paula herded them toward the kitchen. "I'll make some hot milk and we can all calm down."

"How about a drink?" Cari asked. "I saw some scotch in the living room."

"Carolina Woodruff!"

"Oh, mother, lighten up."

Olivia's gaze wouldn't let his go. She twisted away from Paula's grasp. "The man?"

He'd never found achieving the balance between truth and protection hard before. One answer would scare her; the other would anger her. Anger was easier to handle than vulnerability. "The bird probably just flew into a window. Happens all the time."

Cari snorted. "At night?"

Paula herded. "Hot milk. That's the ticket. We'll all feel better and get a good night's sleep."

Olivia frowned, fighting the tide of Paula's will. "Sebastian…"

It was the first time she'd used his name since the accident. He'd always liked the way it sounded wrapped in her voice.

They disappeared around the corner, and Sebastian let out a breath. Using the shovel he kept in the hall closet for spreading salt on winter ice, he scooped up the hawk and placed it in a paper bag. Maybe Kingsley could find some trace of evidence.

He headed down to his office. As he closed the door, pressure opposed him. He looked up, and Olivia's expectant eyes met his.

"I want to help," she said.

"The best way to help is to let me do my job."

"She waited," Olivia started to say, then her hand went up and plucked the air as if it would help bring the words she sought to her. "And she was leaving."

"It's not the same thing, Olivia."

"I don't want to just wait."

He shook his head. "Olivia—"

"The bird…it's from the man." She licked her lips and frowned. "The man who wants to hurt her to hurt you."

He was fighting to protect her. Why couldn't she just accept that and let him do his job? "That's a possibility."

"He wants to hurt *her,* but I'm not her."

"Olivia, you'll get better—"

"Tell him." She grabbed on to his shirt collar and tugged on it. "Tell him I'm not her. Tell him I can't hurt you."

He bowed his head. If she only knew how much power she had—memory or not—over him. "It won't work, Olivia. He knows I won't let any innocent person get hurt."

It had come out all wrong. The pain in her eyes cut him.

"She waited, and she left." She touched his cheek. Her forehead rucked. She shook her head. "I don't want to just wait."

He dragged her palm to his lips and pressed a kiss into it. Her staying was a small victory he wanted to have earned. "I have to keep you safe." He'd failed his parents. He'd failed his partner as a rookie cop. He'd already failed Olivia once. He couldn't let anymore harm come to her.

"The house? It's safe?" she asked.

"Yes," he said, trying not to think of the holes Kingsley had mentioned or of the frozen weight of the dead bird in the bag in his hand. He avoided looking at the accusing bruise glaring at him from the left side of her face.

"Then let me help. Here, in the house."

Olivia and work were separate. He had to keep them that way. If the lines blurred, how would he come back to himself? "There's nothing for you to do, except work on getting better." *And* be *here when it's all over.*

"They help," she said, jutting her chin in Kingsley's direction.

Only because he'd had no choice in the matter. "I have all the help I need."

Kingsley looked up from his monitor. "She can file."

Sebastian threw him his most deadly stare. Kingsley's eager-puppy eyes didn't flinch. He jerked up one shoulder. "What? I can't keep up with the paperwork. It'll give her something useful to do."

Sebastian didn't want her in his office. She belonged upstairs where the sky and sun lived. Not down here where the stench of evil made the air stale. His free hand flexed at his side. This was still his home. He was still in charge. He handed Kingsley the package with the dead bird, then took Olivia's elbow. "I'll walk you up."

She was silent as they climbed the stone steps. The sound of his shoes and her slippers scritched against the stone like whispers of ghosts.

She let him lead her through the hall, and she let him support her when her toe caught the edge of the hall runner. Their shadows crept ahead of them like phantoms in the backlight from the stairs.

At the entrance to the living room, she grabbed his sleeve and pulled him in. Letting go of his shirt, she paced the oval of carpet patterned with fall leaves with an agitation that sent up flags of warning.

"I don't know you," she said, not with accusation, but as a matter of fact. "I don't know myself."

"Olivia—"

"I can't paint. Paula won't let me cook. You won't let me leave the house. What am I supposed to *do?*"

He crossed his arms over his chest. "Work with Cecilia. Get better."

"Writing notes to myself so I won't forget?" She shook her head, then grabbed a white square of paper from the coffee table. One of the many such pieces scattered around the house. She scrunched it and pitched it toward the fireplace. "No, I need more."

"You were in an accident. You need to take it easy."

"For how long?" She flung the words at him over her shoulder. Her eyes held the same sad look she'd worn the night she'd left him. Was it only a few days ago?

"This isn't forever," he said, knowing instinctively she wasn't talking about her recovery but her imprisonment. The echo of her plea resonated in his mind. *You're a contained man, Sebastian, and I need to spill over.* Did this Olivia still feel the need to spill over, too?

She swiveled to face him, both fists hard at her sides. "How long?"

She was pushing him, and he didn't like to be pushed. His jaw tightened. "As long as it takes to put Kershaw back behind bars."

She came toward him one deliberate step at a time, eyed him straight and strong. "How long?"

I need to find my strength, she'd said.

Looks like you found it, sweetheart. And he didn't like the way it had him scrambling for the upper hand. "A day. A week."

"A month? A year?" She shook her head and lifted her arms. He could almost see the dead expectations he'd failed to meet rising around her. "And I'm supposed to just sit here and wait for you like she did?"

One Olivia superimposed herself on the other, making a dizzying mirage. *Let me go, Sebastian.*

No, I can't. "Be reasonable."

She stood there before him, so stiff and still he could feel the rumble of the volcano inside her waiting to erupt. "If she could help, would Olivia have just sat there?"

Why was she pushing him? "Olivia would have understood. She would have lost herself in a painting, and she would have left me to my work—no questions asked." He frowned at the hitch of confusion twisting in his thoughts.

A quarter turn. Her gaze scanned the rough-hewn maple mantel above the stone fireplace, resting for a brief moment on each framed photo. ''You'll get those pieces of your life back, Olivia. Give yourself a chance.''

Then her gaze settled on his favorite picture of her—all of her soft gentleness captured by his lens. *That's it, Olivia. Look at how I see you.* ''I took that picture in September when we hiked to the top of Monadnock.''

With a swipe of her hand, she tumbled the row of frames. He reached forward trying to catch the fall of the past before it shattered. He caught her wrist to stay the thrust of her unexpected anger. Too late. Frames and glass fractured on the stone hearth in splinters and shards.

Holding her securely in his arms, he turned her toward him. She glared at him with all the fury of that dormant volcano spewing to life. Each word was perfectly enunciated, blistering with heat, blazing with a passion he'd never seen in Olivia. ''If that's who she is, then I do *not* want to be Olivia.''

The air around her crackled. The sparks in her eyes challenged. The flush of her cheeks radiated the hot fire of her temper.

''Why are you being so difficult?'' How could she reject herself out of hand like that without even giving herself time to heal? Adrenaline flamed his blood. Breath jammed in his throat. Fingers sinking deeper into her soft flesh, he meant to push her away, but drew her closer. ''You *are* Olivia. Whether you remember or not, you'll always *be* Olivia.''

''No.''

If he could not reach her with logic, he would reach her in the silent language they spoke so well. He bent his head toward hers and crushed his mouth to hers. Rushing sea burst against hot lava. She was his. Always. The sizzling taste of her electrified him. The feel of her against him fed the hunger he'd had to leash since he'd returned. The way her curves molded to his angles was both well-known and strangely brand-new.

"I am not Olivia." She was breathless, but softening as she always did in his arms.

"She's you. You're her." He barely recognized the guttural noise scraping out of his throat as his own voice. He feasted on her mouth, her neck, her shoulder. He drank in new responses from familiar flesh. His hands claimed, possessed.

"She's gone." She met him kiss for kiss, caress for caress, need for need, and he found his lost self again in the woman who was his salvation.

"Olivia." It was a plea. It was a prayer.

He would not give up on all they'd built, on all they'd meant to each other. It was there still inside her. Had to be. How could it not when she responded to him like this? "I'll help you remember." If it took a thousand nights, a million kisses. "I won't let you forget."

Holding his jaw with both her palms, she held his gaze with her wide-opened pupils. The heat of her breath shimmered against his mouth. "She's gone, Sebastian. All gone."

"No, not all." He knotted her long hair in his fists. "You look like her." As if he were a dying man needing oxygen, he breathed in the flowery scent of her shampoo, the sweetness of her skin. "You smell like her." He tipped her head to one side and savored the pulsing heat at her neck, gorged on it as if it were nectar. "You taste like her." No, not like her. Different. Damn. Richer, rawer, sharper. Dazed by his discovery, the fever of his desire mutated, but didn't cool. He wanted her still.

"There is a woman wearing her skin and her hair and

her smell, but she isn't Olivia.'' Her voice was a choked whisper.

Melancholy fisted his gut. Breathing hard, eyes closed, he held her, heart drumming against heart, while he tried to recover his control.

If he could want the stranger in Olivia's skin so fiercely, what did that say about him? About the strength of his love for his wife? About his competence?

Biting back the strangled growl that tore through him, he ripped his body from her beguiling heat and left.

HE HAD NOT COME BACK to the bedroom they shared. She'd watched black night turn into purple dawn and still his side of the bed remained empty and cold. Olivia turned in the flannel sheets to face the sunny window. The peaks of mountains greeted her, strong and tall in the golden sunlight.

She heard him now on the other side of the bathroom door. All the little noises that made up the man—the scrape of razor over cheeks, the swish of brush over teeth, the rush of comb through wet hair. They all seemed so ordinary, so normal.

The steam from his shower carried his scent, bringing back the sensory overload of his kiss. Her sensitive skin still tingled from his touch. The taste of him had had a wild edge to it that she found she liked. The look of him, raw with need, had set off a chain reaction she hadn't wanted to stop. In his arms, she'd felt alive, not like the walking dead. Was that how it had been between her and him before, live wire crossing live wire, sparking?

She wanted that electrifying feeling again. She wanted more. But she wanted it for herself, not for the Olivia she couldn't remember.

She reached for the photo album on the night table. In

each of the photographs, she looked for herself in Olivia and saw only a stranger. For days now, Paula had walked her through the pictures of her past, and for days she'd looked through the pictures like an archaeologist and tried to put back the pieces of the life she'd once led.

With a snap, she pushed away the album, flung back the sheets and got up. She strolled through the room like a sleuth looking for a clue. She touched the teal-and-blue swirls in the glass vase that held no flowers. She could not remember why she'd chosen it, where she'd bought it or if she'd ever arranged flowers in it. Palms curved around the glass, she silently begged for a spark of recognition. When she got none, she banged it back into place. A chip broke off the base and skittered across the smooth surface of the dresser.

She fingered the earrings and pendants and bracelets with their shiny gold and precious gems in the teak jewelry box. She tried to remember wearing the pear-shaped amethyst, the oval sapphire, the square emerald, and could not recall their weight against her skin. Holding them now, she commanded a glimpse into their history. When she got none, she shoved the jewels back in the drawer.

She sat in the ash glider by the window and willed herself to remember being here. But the back and forth movement stirred nothing inside her, except the echo of tears she couldn't shed.

She rose and strode to the closet. Looking at Olivia's clothes hanging from padded hangers, folded neatly on shelves, organized by shades and styles, a small cloud of dizziness swirled around her. How could she expect to compete with that? As far as she could tell, Olivia was perfect while she barely had a fingerhold on the cusp of adequacy.

She slammed the closet door and marched out of the

room. She'd spoken the truth last night. She didn't want to be Olivia. Even if it meant she would have to leave after Sebastian's fugitive was caught. The woman she saw in the photo album, the woman Paula and Sebastian painted for her with their memories, was too soft, too forgettable. Something in her wanted releasing and she would start with color. At Cari's bedroom door, she stopped and knocked.

"Who is it?" a sleepy voice called.

"Oli—me. It's me."

The door opened and Cari blinked at her like a sun blinded mole. "Are you okay?"

"I'm fine. Can I look at your sweaters?"

Cari scrunched her forehead. "Are you sure you're okay?"

"I'm perfectly fine." She peeked in at the mess strewn around Cari's room. "So, can I?"

Cari stepped aside. "I guess."

Her niece sat at the foot of the bed while Olivia stepped through the minefield of clothes littering Cari's floor. She spotted a red sweater and scooped it up. There was not a drop of red in Olivia's closet. No bright green. No royal blue. Just navy and gray and pastels. As she held the sweater before her and looked at her reflection in the mirror, Olivia wondered why. Her skin and her soul were starving for color. And red seemed just right for the flame starting to flicker inside her. Cari liked to swim in her clothes, so the sweater should fit. "Is this clean?"

Cari jerked the sweater from her, sniffed it, then pitched it back. "Clean."

"Can I borrow it?"

"I guess."

Olivia slipped the soft lamb's wool over her nightgown and watched as a blush tinged her cheeks. She pulled on the hank of hair caught in the cowl neck. As she held the hair in her hand, a new Olivia appeared in the mirror. Not soft and smooth, but edgy and unruly like the new fire crackling inside her. Letting go of the hair, she spotted a pair of manicure scissors on top of the dresser. She snipped a six-inch coil of hair. The blaze in her surged.

Cari sprang up from the bed and snagged the scissors from her hand. "What are you doing?"

"Cutting my hair."

"Uncle S. loves your hair."

"He loves Olivia's hair. I am not Olivia."

Cari stared at her in the mirror and swallowed hard. She put the scissors on the dresser, then put an arm around Olivia. Her eyes brightened with tears. "There's a knot in your belly, right?"

Olivia nodded, rounding a fist on the hot, hard tangle no amount of massage could unlace.

"A hollow feeling inside?"

A hollow that now burned with a fervor that scared her as much as the cold void had. She nodded, swaying a bit on her feet. How did Cari know?

"Me, too." Cari let her go and leaned against the wall. "The counselor Mom sent me to after my dad died last year said it was from the grief I was holding in. I still miss him. Although I'm not supposed to say so. Mom can't take it. Mom can't handle things like that too well." She swiped the tears with the back of her hand. "It's like that for you, too, I bet. You lost yourself. That has to hurt." She pushed herself off the wall. "Mom, she won't understand. But I do. Wait here."

Cari stuck her head out her bedroom door, looked out, then slunk out. She returned a minute later. From her pajama pocket, she extracted a pair of scissors and snipped at the air. "If you're going to do this, might as well do it right."

She dragged a straight-backed chair before the dresser. "Sit." Their gazes met in the mirror. "You trust me?"

Olivia sat, looking Cari straight in the eye, and nodded.

"How short do you want it?"

Olivia gulped, suddenly unsure. How much would be too much for Sebastian to take? Would he understand this bid to find herself in the remnants of his wife?

"Okay." Cari raised the scissors level with the top of Olivia's head. "I'll do it in stages. You tell me when you look like you want."

Olivia smiled. She heard Cecilia's molasses voice, urging her on. *One step at a time, love. One step at a time.* A part of the hollowness filled with purpose and no longer felt so dark. "Okay."

PAULA'S SCREAM HAD SEBASTIAN streaking out of his room lightning fast. Dressed in only jeans, heart pounding, weapon drawn, he half expected to see Kershaw appear around the corner. But the crisis wasn't Kershaw. It was only Paula overreacting.

"What have you done?" Paula asked, marching into Cari's room to the dresser where Olivia sat surrounded by a puddle of her dark brown hair. She seized the scissors. *"What have you done?"* She glared at her daughter. "This is all your doing."

"She was going to hack it off herself." Cari fluffed up the short lengths of hair, giving Olivia a pert look that took him aback. "I offered to help."

Holding one hand in front on her mouth, the other arm wrapped around her waist, Paula shook her head. "Olivia..."

"Liv." Olivia stood and slowly turned around. Her gaze

sought Sebastian's and held it, not gently, as Olivia would have, but in a challenge that was both unyielding and uncertain. "Call me Liv."

More than the color of sin on her cheeks had him thinking of hot sex, more than the sassy cut of her hair had him thinking of wicked games, more than the invitation in those wide blue eyes had him thinking of getting lost in those deep canyons was a perfectly sensible thing to do. It was the energy. This Olivia vibrated with a life that stirred his blood. She disturbed him on a level as base as the one he descended into to hunt fugitives.

And he didn't like it.

He wanted the woman he'd fallen in love with. Olivia was the calm after the storm. Olivia was home. Olivia was where he came to find himself, not lose himself.

He hated himself for this weakness.

He crossed the room and stood before her. He ran a hand through the short curls that now almost hid the bruise on the left side of her face. The tips of his fingers connected to the rosy smear on her cheek and burned with a jolt of desire so sharp it hurt.

"You're beautiful," he said before he could stop himself.

When she beamed a smile at him, another punch hit him square in the solar plexus.

He wished all this mess with Kershaw, all these people invading his home, didn't stand between them. Because right now, right here, he wanted to show her she pleased him. Very much.

Call me Liv. She was asking for acceptance of this change. He didn't want to give it to her. He wanted things as they'd always been. But as her steady gaze held his, he knew that if he didn't yield a little, he'd lose what he had left of her. "Liv."

"Falconer." Kingsley's voice had everyone in the room turning toward the bedroom door. "They found him."

Chapter Eight

"Here's the situation," Sebastian said as he huddled with his team at the rendezvous point on the dirt road—only a few miles from the Aerie. Called back from surveillance, Skyralov stood with Mercer and Reed. "The cabin is a one-story building. Clapboard, cheaply made. There's only one door. One window out front and two out back. Three rooms—front general area, back bedroom on the right, back bathroom on the left. He's armed with the same gear we have, including the bulletproof vest he stole off our guys."

He checked the mike attached to an earpiece. "Kingsley?"

"Go ahead."

"When I tell you it's on, call the locals and let them know there's a police action taking place in town, but don't give them our location. I don't want any patrol cars coming around."

"What's the takedown plan?" Skyralov asked.

"We'll keep it as simple as possible." Elaborate plans, Sebastian had learned, increased the chances of something going wrong.

"Are we giving Kershaw a chance to come out?" Reed asked.

"We'll give him the opportunity, but I guarantee he won't take it." Sebastian jerked his chin towards the tailgate of his SUV where the rough sketch Mercer had drawn lay. "Mercer, you'll have the back. Reed, you'll carry the shotgun. I'll have the sledge and go through the front. Skyralov, you'll back us up." He looked up and eyed each of the men. "Any questions?"

They all shook their heads.

"Grab your gear."

The four men moved quickly, strapping on second-chance vests, checking weapons. They surrounded the small building that had once served as a fishing camp. Smoke curled from the chimney. The roof sagged. No light shone from the windows. In summer, the brown clapboard and green shutters camouflaged the building. In winter, the paint scheme stood out starkly against the white snow, making the house look like a sad old man.

The widower who owned this cottage died last year. His children lived out of state and had shown no interest in the aging building. Because of town zoning, each lot on the pond was at least two acres. A girl's summer camp resided on the piece of land to the east. In winter, no one lived there. The land to the west of the cottage saw its church group only on scattered weekends. To the north was the lake, and to the south, conservation land. There was no activity in the cottage now, but then felons rarely got up before noon. Each lot was heavily wooded, affording Kershaw all the privacy he wanted to concoct his plans to hurt Olivia.

Sebastian shook his head. Olivia had no place in his thoughts right now. Officer survival was his number one priority. *Get the job over and done with. Then get back to Olivia.* He chased away the chill at the thought that this drive to get back to his wife no longer held the same urgency. *Olivia's accident isn't her fault; it's yours. Stop blaming her for your shortcomings.*

A light snow had fallen overnight, capturing boot prints leading into and out of the house. Two pairs. Same tread. Different stride. "Be ready for company."

Adrenaline coursed through blood. Sweat poured under vests. Weapons were drawn. Everyone was breathing hard, waiting for the signal. Anytime you had to go in to grab a mutt, especially an armed one, the stress was high.

Sebastian shook off the bristling of the hairs on the nape of his neck and spoke into the mike. "Everyone in place?"

All the responses came in affirmative. "It's a go."

Backs to the wall, Skyralov stood to the right of the door—Sebastian to the left. They listened for several minutes, but heard nothing stir inside.

Sebastian banged on the door. "U.S. Marshals. Open up!"

No answer.

Sebastian sledged the door. Reed was the first one through, jacking a cartridge into the chamber of the twelve-gauge riot gun for effect as he stormed in. Sebastian and Skyralov burst in behind him. They all shouted as they moved. "U.S. Marshals…freeze…don't move…"

"Clear," Reed said as he bulldozed his way through the shared kitchen and living room space.

Skyralov moved right; Sebastian left.

"Clear," Sebastian called after he checked the bathroom.

"In here," Skyralov said, his weapon trained on the target. "Someone got to him before we did."

Inside the bedroom, they found a male lying on a cot. Everything about him looked peaceful, except for the raw mess where his face should be.

Sebastian slowly made his way to the cot and studied

the corpse. The size and build were right. The hair color—
what was left of it—matched. ''Kingsley?''

''Go ahead.''

''Pull up Kershaw's FPC number.'' The fingerprint clas-
sification number was a series of numbers and letters as-
signed to each digit. A suspect's prints were individually
classified, then the code was entered into the National
Crime Information Center computer. The loops, whorls
and arches by which the prints were coded could be read
in the field by a good investigator, saving time and aggra-
vation in identifying suspected fugitives on the scene. The
skill wasn't taught by the USMS, but Sebastian had picked
it up from his mentor during his first raid. It had come in
handy more than once.

Kingsley came back on. ''I'll make it easy for you. Left
index is an X.''

X meant a missing digit. Sebastian reached for the left
hand and the top portion of the left index finger was gone.
We've got him. Euphoria spiked his blood, but he tamped
down the rush of victory. *Can't make a mistake now.*
''Read me the rest.''

Sebastian compared and each matched. The M.E. would
confirm, but Sebastian didn't need the corroboration. ''Pull
up the case file. Read me the marks and tats.''

''Vertical scar across the left cheek.'' *Can't confirm
that. Not with his face blown off.* ''Teardrop tattoo between
thumb and index finger of both hands.'' Both were faded,
but there. Prison tattoos from his first visit to a state insti-
tution as a teenager. ''Scorpion on the left bicep. Eagle
with lightning bolts in its talons on the right.'' Each new
incarceration seemed to deserve a new tattoo.

Sebastian pulled down the rough brown blanket and
spotted the crude tattoos on both biceps. ''They match.''

It was over.

Why did it feel like a letdown?

Someone had saved him the trouble of killing Kershaw. They'd have to find the murderer, of course. But the danger to Olivia was gone.

The marshal had his man.

Olivia was safe.

Now things could go back to normal.

"'MORNING, MISS OLIVIA," Mario said, brown knit hat between his square hands. He stood at the mudroom door, his wiry body ballooned by his black parka. Above the zipper, a black-and-white flannel shirt and a red thermal Henley peeked through. His brown hair was shot with white and cut short and neat. His smile reached his dark brown eyes and made them shine. "I'm here for the grocery list."

When he turned to close the door behind him, Liv saw that a bandage covered the space above his right ear where he'd been hit trying to protect his birds. No one had told Liv that, but she'd overheard Kingsley talking downstairs. Someone had cuffed Mario on the head, disarmed the perimeter sensors, somehow fooled the camera and dropped the dead bird at the front door. Kingsley was not happy about missing the breach.

"Come in," Liv said, leading him into the kitchen. "The list isn't ready yet." Because no one had told her Mario would expect her to have a list ready. Or maybe Sebastian had told Paula yesterday before all the excitement broke out.

But Paula was taking a bath, and Liv had no intentions of disturbing her. She hoped that Paula would soak in the tub for at least an hour, and that Cari, who was at her computer—no doubt complaining about her horrid living conditions to friends—would stay closeted in her room all morning. Liv needed this time alone without her sister's constant chatter or her niece's dogging of her every step.

She could do this, she decided as she offered Mario a seat. She could put together a simple grocery list. She'd done this in the past—of that she was sure.

It seemed to her that Olivia was the kind of person who would have made sure that Sebastian's needs were filled before he quite felt them. She'd bet he'd never run out of toothpaste or shampoo, that he'd never had to worry about how low the milk or orange juice were running, that he'd never found his sock or underwear drawers empty. "Would you like some coffee?"

Mario sat at the edge of a chair. "That would be nice."

Liv smiled and poured him a mug. He nodded his thanks and wrapped his big hands around the green ceramic mug, dwarfing it. She scrounged around for some paper and found a pad and a pen in a drawer near the phone, then sat opposite Mario at the table. "How are you feeling?"

"Got a bit of a headache, but other than that, I'm right as rain."

"I'm sorry about your bird." Even in death, it had seemed such a noble creature—fierce and regal…like Sebastian.

Mario nodded and studied the contents of his cup, trying to hide his affection for the hawk. She wanted to do something to ease his sorrow, but could think of no words that would soothe.

She would bake, she decided. She would make him a cake. That seemed simple enough. "What's your favorite kind of cake?"

He looked startled, and Liv wondered how he'd gotten along with Olivia. "I like the chocolate orange snack cake you make."

"Okay, then, I'll bake you one." So she had baked for

him before. Now Liv just had to find the recipe. She rose and went to the row of cookbooks along the counter. She picked one and it fell open to a well-creased page. Chicken with Sage Corn Bread Crust. She tried another book and found a page with splatters. Fusilli with Peppers and Onions. Another book, another well-used page. Chunky Mediterranean-Style Soup. A small thrill sang through her.

Liv would bet anything these were the dishes Sebastian liked, the dishes Olivia had made most often for him. Before she knew it, Liv had constructed a menu and a list for Mario—including the mini chocolate chips she'd need for the snack cake.

Lists. Cecilia had told her lists were important for her at this stage of her recovery. She now saw the power in them as she tacked a copy of her menu for the week on the refrigerator with a magnet in the shape of a loon.

She was still floating on the cloud of that victory when the phone rang. Smiling, she grabbed the receiver and twirled the cord around her. "Hello."

"Olivia Falconer, please."

"Speaking."

"This is Susan Glass from the Nashua Community College. I'm calling in regards to your registration."

She frowned. "My registration?"

"For the winter quarter. You signed up for two classes. Introduction to Criminal Justice and Introduction to Psychology."

"I did?" Criminal Justice? Psychology?

"Classes started last Tuesday."

Tuesday. The day after the accident. She leaned against the wall and wrapped the phone cord around her middle finger. "I was in a car accident last week. I'm afraid I'd forgotten about the classes."

"I'm sorry to hear that. Are you planning on joining the

classes for the rest of the quarter? We have a waiting list for the psychology class.''

With the man who wanted to hurt Sebastian still on the loose and her motor skills not quite up to snuff, she didn't see how getting away for classes was possible. She rubbed her aching temple. Then why the wave of disappointment? ''Not at this time.''

Liv made arrangements to receive a refund for a portion of the tuition she'd already paid. Then she sat at the table, rolling over the conversation in her mind as she massaged the pulsing points of pain the way Cecilia had taught her.

Sebastian was wrong. Olivia had not waited. And she hadn't left him. She'd gone away to find an entry into his world. Criminal Justice. Psychology. It made sense. She wanted to understand him. She wanted to share his world. At least she could understand that much of Olivia. His job seemed the only way to Sebastian's heart.

Liv got up abruptly and started to pace. When the room began to spin, she grabbed the counter and stared through the window at the mountain. As she counted out the three pills she'd forgotten to take earlier, she thought about her situation. She was an artist who could no longer remember how to paint. She was a wife who could no longer remember her love for her husband. She was a woman who could no longer remember her hopes and dreams. The blank slate of her mind frightened her as much as the silent expectation in Sebastian's eyes.

If she forced him to see her as she was, as someone other than the Olivia he remembered, then things could be different. Then she could discover who she was, what she was good at, what she wanted. How she fit.

And as Olivia had discovered, the only way to reach him was through his job.

She raced down the stone steps to the office in the basement. She plowed through the door and skewered Kingsley's gaze. "Show me how to file."

Kingsley hesitated, tweaking a few dials to buy himself time. "Are you sure you want to?"

He wasn't referring to her desire, but to the consequences of her actions. Sebastian wouldn't be pleased. He'd made that clear enough. She couldn't understand why he wanted to separate the two halves of his life that way. But how else could she show him that she wasn't simply a part of the background, that she could be of use? She nodded.

Kingsley smiled. His dimples gave him the look of a mischievous boy. He showed her how to log the information scattered on pieces of paper all over his desk. He showed her how to put together a case file. He showed her how to draw a timeline. In a childish handwriting, she wrote copious reminders into a notebook, made checklists for each task and surprised herself by catching on quickly. The computer translated her handwriting to neat copy and her checklists to near works of art. And Kingsley's sense of humor, and Cecilia's encouragement during her afternoon visit, made the whole awkward task pleasant.

"You're a sweet man," she said as she worked the label maker for a new file. A fresh confidence thrummed through her from the tips of her fingers to the pulse point at her ankles.

"Yeah, that's me. Everybody's brother."

She cocked her head at his frown. "I meant it as a compliment."

"Yeah, that's always the way." He chuckled. At her puzzled expression, he continued. "The trouble with sweet is that women don't take you seriously. They tell you their problems. They tell you their deep, dark secrets. But when they want romance…'' He shrugged. ''Well, they go for guys like Hollywood or Cowboy or—''

''Sebastian.'' Hadn't she felt that fine net of attraction toward her husband? Because of his looks, as Kingsley suggested? Because of his size? She shifted her position on top of the spare desk where she sat and glanced at the eight piles of papers. It was more than looks, more than breadth, she decided. Something about Sebastian made her feel secure.

''You know what the worst part is?'' Kingsley said. ''Guys like Sebastian don't even notice when they're being hit on.''

Her head popped up from its task. The nail of her index finger toyed with the edge of the file balanced on her knees. ''Women hit on Sebastian?''

''All the time. You tell me what's so attractive about a guy who frowns so much.''

Liv thought of the steely competence that seemed to wrap around her like a bulletproof vest when Sebastian was around, of the strength yet gentleness of his touch, of the way he made her feel as if he would face an army of barbarians to protect her. ''A woman feels safe around him.''

''But not me?''

The security Sebastian offered came at a price, she realized. For him there was no yielding, no show of weakness, maybe not even any sharing. The things he gave and the things he took fell on separate sides of a line he'd drawn—a line she didn't quite understand. Kingsley offered an easy companionship that could disarm and not threaten. She laughed as she labeled another file. ''You're a different kind of safe.''

He laughed with her. ''Like I said, everybody's brother.''

''There's someone out there who'll appreciate that kind of honesty.''

He adjusted his glasses and bent toward the computer screen. ''Not with these hours.''

The office that this morning had looked as if it had been flattened by a tornado now looked neat and orderly. The order pleased Liv. She'd done something, and she'd done it well in spite of the holes in her memory or her uncooperative fingers.

The door suddenly arched open, and Sebastian stood like a slab of granite, hard and cross.

''What's going on here?'' he asked.

''It's called organization,'' Kingsley answered. ''And it's about time we got some around here. Now we know where everything is.''

Sebastian's gaze met hers. ''I'll see you upstairs in a minute.''

''I'm not done.'' Heart beating fast, she pointed at the three remaining piles of papers on the desk.

His fists curled at his sides. ''Olivia—''

''Liv. Call me Liv.''

''Liv,'' he said, swallowing hard as if her name was bitter. ''I'll talk to you upstairs.''

She did not want to surrender. She did not want to feel the helplessness of having someone else making all her decisions. Sliding from the desktop, she stood to face him. ''No, I can do this.''

''She's done a great job,'' Kingsley said. But Liv noticed he was suddenly much busier with the keyboard.

''It's not a matter of can,'' Sebastian said, slowly as if she were a dull child. ''It's a matter of—''

''She wasn't leaving you.''

SEBASTIAN GLANCED AT KINGSLEY who tactfully got up from his control chair. "Anyone for coffee?"

No one answered him. He grabbed his mug and swung close to Sebastian as he was leaving.

"She needs to hear you tell her she's done a good job," Kingsley said in a low whisper.

"This is none of your business."

"I know, but it seems to me that when someone tries so hard to—"

"Kingsley."

"Right. None of my business. She just wants to feel needed." Kingsley closed the door softly behind him.

Sebastian's gaze continued to study Liv's face. In the familiar curve of cheekbones, in the fullness of lips, in the flaring blue of her eyes, he saw a new determination that put up his guard. He didn't need this streak of stubborn independence. Not when he had so many loose ends to tie to wrap up this case. "Give me a day, and we'll sit down and talk."

"She wasn't leaving you," Liv said again. "She was going to find a way *to* you."

"That doesn't make sense." But then this new Olivia often spoke in riddles. He scrubbed a hand over his face as if it could wash off the fatigue seeping into his bones.

"Of course not. Because you're so busy trying to prove you don't need anyone." Sentences broke over each other in jagged waves as if her mind worked faster than her ability to translate thought into words. "You don't want to need them. You didn't want to need her. You don't need me because I'm not her."

"That's not—"

"I wish I could climb into the shower and scrub away the dead feel of this skin." She plucked at the shoulders of the red sweater she wore and he could feel the magma rising in her, hot and angry.

He crossed his arms over his chest, a shield against the coming assault, against the inappropriate arousal her fire caused. He wasn't concentrating on the right things and that was dangerous.

"I wish I could wipe away the mist on the mirror and say, 'Ah, there you are,' and smile at the reflection I see." Her hands strangled the air around close to her face. "But wish as I might, the face looking back at me is that of a stranger."

"Recovery takes time."

She pulled at her short hair and gave a growl of frustration. He had to curl his fingers against his ribs to keep himself from patting down the little horns of hair she'd lifted. "This isn't something to get over. It's a different atmosphere. I need to learn to breathe in it. If you shut me out, like you shut her out, if you cut off my oxygen, then how am I supposed to learn how to live here?"

He thought again how he wanted the old Olivia back. Not because he wanted her unflinching obedience, but because he was hurting, and he was tired, and she'd been the one steady thing in his life. He wanted to walk into the house and see her looking up at him as if he'd created the sun and the stars. He wanted the comfort he'd always found in her smile and in her arms. Seeing her in his office, with his work in her hands, with poise and pluck giving her eyes brightness and her cheeks color, made his footing unsure. "Liv—"

"I got a call this morning. She had registered to take a course in criminology—"

"Criminology?" A spike of pain hit him square in the gut. "Olivia?"

"Don't you get it? She wanted to understand what you do."

He got it all right. He suddenly understood the past year with a crystal quality that was blinding. Why hadn't he seen it before? The baby. They'd given up on conceiving eighteen months ago. Without that unified effort, their lives had started to drift. Guilt had made him bury himself even deeper in his work.

And she'd feared that slow deviation. He could see it now in all the little ways she'd tried to redirect the straying flow of their lives. The dancing lessons that were forgotten after he'd missed too many because he'd been called away unexpectedly time and again. The tour of bed-and-breakfast inns that was canceled halfway through when he'd had to leave. The collection of true crime books she'd read, then tried to engage him in discussion.

And each time he'd let her down, she'd grown a little more quiet, a little more reserved.

"I made a promise to your father when I married you. My work would never touch you." The promise had come easily. As a man, he'd believed he could do what he'd failed to do as a thirteen-year-old boy when he'd found his parents knifed to death in their own kitchen.

He'd been wrong.

"You always keep your promises."

Not a question, but faith. His jaw flinched. She stood close, close enough for him to smell the hint of rosemary and peppermint in her shampoo. It was the wrong scent, he thought. Too fragile for the strong woman she was becoming. "I try."

"You promised to love her in sickness and health." She cocked her head and the brown curls snaked across her cheek. He started to reach for one and wrap the silky ribbon around a finger, then jammed his hand into his pocket.

He nodded. Where was she going with this?

She touched his cheek tentatively and shook her head. "So love her and let her go. It takes more strength to let go than to hang on."

But if he did, where would that leave Liv? Where would that leave him?

KILLING BERNIE HAD BEEN a tactical error. But Bernie'd asked for it. Bernie could make him madder than a starved pit bull with just a look. The stupe had the nerve to laugh at him. Laugh! Then he'd asked him to run errands as if he was just another chump. Before he knew it, he'd pulled the trigger and Bernie was gone.

If Nadine wasn't always so busy bailing Bernie's ass out of trouble, then he could have had all he wanted and gotten out of the hellhole his life had become. But he was trapped here because of Bernie. It was always Bernie, Bernie, Bernie—as if the rest of the world didn't exist.

Now she'd gone and messed this up, too. Bitch. All her fault. If Bernie hadn't brought her up, if Bernie hadn't laughed, then everything would still be on track. Now he'd have to think this through.

Everything was so perfect before. Two more steps and he'd have been there. Bernie and Okie would've taken the fall, and he could have ridden off into the sunset to the life he deserved.

From his perch, he could see the blues and browns of law enforcement milling through the scene like cockroaches. A pair of blues stuffed the white body bag holding Bernie's body into the meat wagon. Good riddance!

He'd covered his tracks. All the pigs would find was what Bernie had left behind and their own man's gun.

Dead end. He laughed, patting the second pistol tucked at the small of his back.

Now he had to let them believe the danger was over because they still owed him that life. And he was going to take it.

Chapter Nine

Over the years, Sebastian had grown used to certain things done certain ways. Olivia kept this private world of theirs running smoothly. Mornings meant coffee in a quiet kitchen in the winter, and out on the deck in summer. There was an unspoken understanding that conversation came only after he'd downed his first cup of coffee and caffeine flowed freely through his veins.

What greeted him this morning was a face-off.

Liv was trying to bake something. Paula was attempting to do it for her. Cari was hiding behind the pages of an Iris Johansen hardcover, ignoring the whole scene while she stuffed forkfuls of French toast into her mouth. He almost turned back to head down to his office, but the picture Olivia—Liv—made had him staring at her like a pervert at a peep show.

Unruly curls framed her face, giving her sass. The kitchen's heat—or maybe the anger she was trying so hard to contain—gave her cheeks sinful color. The bright blue sweater she wore hugged her well-remembered curves as intimately as he itched to. She looked good. She looked great. And God help him, he wanted to peel that sweater off her body and put his hands all over her.

Totally inappropriate to feel this way.

"Let me do it." Liv elbowed her sister's helping hand away. Flour dribbled out of the cup and onto the green tiles of the floor.

"Your hand's shaking."

"I'm fine." Pebbles of frustration made her voice rocky, but she didn't back down from her sister. Sebastian silently cheered her on. He'd never liked the way Paula tried to keep Olivia dependent.

"I'm just trying to help." Paula's fingers knitted and reknitted so fast that if she'd had yarn in her hands, she'd have a scarf by now.

"This isn't rocket science, Paula. The recipe doesn't even call for a bowl." The orange juice container shook as she brought it up to measure out a cup.

Paula's hands reached out, then snapped back to her body. "You're spilling."

"Cecilia says I need to practice."

Paula gasped as Liv overstirred the batter in the pan, causing gobs of chocolate goo to plop onto the counter.

Liv was a valiant fighter. Had she always been like that? Hints of her determination peppered his thoughts—the baby, the trips, the books. Subtlety had underscored all her efforts, hiding her strength. Maybe in all those years she hadn't needed him as much as he'd needed her.

Time for a distraction.

"Good morning, ladies." Sebastian stepped into the kitchen and headed for the coffeepot on the counter. Paula beat him to it and poured a cup into his least favorite mug. The brown ceramic sported the face of a troll. He didn't know where it came from, but looking into those big, round eyes as he drank made him think of the Three Billy Goats Gruff of children's book fame. He'd never liked that story, and Cari had dragged that book with her on visits at the Aerie for years.

"It's safe now," he said as he helped himself to a grape-fruit half on the cutting board. "You can go back home."

As he'd hoped, Paula switched her attention from Liv to him. She retrieved a platter of French toast warming in the oven and plunked three on a plate in front of him. "I'm glad to hear you took care of the problem you created. But that still doesn't mean I'm leaving."

"Why not?" He stabbed the grapefruit too hard and juice spurted into his eye.

"Someone has to keep her safe from you."

"Liv is safe." He would see to that.

Paula glared at him, one hand on her hip, the other waving a spatula. "And I intend to make sure someone is watching out for her interests until her memory returns."

Paula had a way of disregarding evidence that didn't please her. She'd never accepted that her husband had appropriated her share of her parents' inheritance to shore up his failing business—even when she was shown her zeroed-out account. She'd never accepted that Roger had resorted to imaginative accounting to hide his failings—even when he was indicted. She'd never accepted that he'd committed suicide—even when she found his body in the bathtub, wrapped in a shower curtain for easy clean up. Pointing out that Olivia would most likely never return to her old self was useless. "I'm sure Cari's dying to get back to her friends."

"Actually, I'm fine. This is giving me time to think, you know. Decide what I'm going to do with my future and all."

"Olivia's offer to pay for college still stands."

"See, that's what I mean," Paula said. "You're awfully free with her money."

"If I said I'd pay for college, I will."

Why was Paula pushing away family money? "I don't

have access to her funds," he reminded his sister-in-law. "Olivia would still have to make the withdrawal herself."

"That's okay, Uncle S. I won't be needing college money for a while."

"What?" Paula's eyes rounded as wide as the troll's on his cup.

"I want to try out a few things before I settle down."

"That's a good idea." Liv slipped the cake into the oven. Her hands barely wobbled. She was getting stronger every day. "It won't hurt to find out who you are before you choose a career."

Paula glared at all three, then dropped into a chair as if she needed the force of gravity behind her weight to solidify her intentions. "We're staying."

He looked at Liv across the kitchen and found they could still have a conversation without speaking a word. They needed to get rid of all this interference for the chance to find out what else they still had in common.

But first he owed Sutton a call.

"WE'RE MISSING SOMETHING," Sebastian said to Sutton over the phone. He settled at his desk in his office. The quiet of the room was a balm. His report sat in front of him, and all he could see were the gaping holes that seemed to mutate into trenches before his eyes.

"Look, Falconer, don't make this more complicated than it is. The two fugitives are back in their pen. Kershaw is dead. Case closed."

For you. The pencil in his hand drew question marks across the report. "You want me to just forget that someone blew Kershaw's face off?"

"Not related."

"How can you say that?" Why was he trying so hard to bury this loose end?

"Every case has inconsistencies. That's just the nature of the beast."

"I know that." Sebastian frowned and pitched the pencil on the desktop. It rolled to the floor. Holes in logic he could accept. After all, the criminal mind wasn't a healthy one. But when the edges of these holes were filed to make theories line up, that didn't sit well with him. Justice shouldn't waver as if it stood in front of a fun house mirror.

"What's important here is that the mess is contained. No harm done."

"Except to my wife." As if thinking of her had conjured her up, Liv appeared at the door. His heart actually fluttered. After ten years of marriage, shouldn't he be used to the sight of her? Then he remembered. The last time he'd seen her standing like that, she'd left him. He plopped his boot heels on the desk and waved her in. Her smile glowed straight into his solar plexus, warming him.

"Kershaw's dead, Falconer," Sutton said. "Your wife is safe. There's no evidence Kershaw was responsible for her accident. The report you forwarded even says the electric short wasn't the cause."

"Which supports my theory that there's more to the situation than we're seeing." Sebastian's gaze tracked Olivia as she moved into the room.

"We're all on the same side here."

She sat in Kingsley's command-center chair and gathered the pieces of paper he'd left behind when he'd gone to bed. With a grace and efficiency Sebastian had seen in her when she painted, she filed and logged. He didn't understand why his heart should beat so fast or why his pulse should kick up a notch. It wasn't as if she were peeling off the bright blue sweater. She wasn't even trying to flirt, for pete's sake. She hadn't even said a word. She was just sitting. Filing.

Maybe that was the problem. She was here in his world.

And she fit.

Sebastian massaged the back of his neck. "There are holes."

"I don't see any," Sutton insisted. "The bad guys are where they belong, and they'll add time for murder to their sentences. They won't see the light of day again in this lifetime. The good guys win another round."

Not to mention that the press had played Sutton up to look like a hero for ending this threat to society. Too neat. "I don't want easy, Sutton. I want the truth. Something doesn't fit."

"Don't start with that crap."

"Blowing off a face is personal."

"So he pissed somebody off. That's not exactly big news."

"Whoever tampered with the car is still out there." And that was the biggest hole of all.

"He's the only one with motive for hurting you."

"In this business, every mutt we collar is a threat."

"You're looking for trouble where there isn't any."

Maybe Sutton was right. Maybe he was looking for trouble. Maybe he just needed to keep moving so he could stay ahead of the twisted snarl of his feelings for Liv. She caught him staring at her and smiled again. He frowned.

This went deeper than playing chicken with himself. Something about this case still gave him indigestion. Gut gave him direction, but he never let it rule. He backed it up with hard evidence and facts. Every time. He wasn't going to make an exception just because Sutton wanted neat.

"What about the jail break?"

"They took advantage of an unrelated situation. It was contained."

"What if Kershaw orchestrated the situation?"

Sutton barked like a seal. "He was a model prisoner."

One with a seething need for revenge. "What about Greco and Carmichael?"

"What about them?"

"Two trained, armed marshals couldn't handle unarmed prisoners?"

"They were desperate. Took our guys by surprise."

"And they didn't fight back?"

"They were cornered and disarmed. They didn't have a chance."

"Doesn't fit."

Sutton sighed. "Look, some people would rather you just let things stand as they are."

"Who? Why?"

"I'm ordering you to take some time off," Sutton said. "Send the team home."

"I need to see this to the finish."

"The last thing the Service needs, deputy, is a hot dog."

Sebastian heard the unspoken warning loud and clear.

Time off suddenly seemed like the perfect solution. Sutton's package was tied neat and pretty—even if the box was full of holes. As far as Sutton was concerned, the case was closed. If Sebastian didn't take the time off offered, he'd end up working another caseload in no time.

Someone had killed Kershaw. That someone was still out there. He needed to know who. He needed to know why. He needed to be sure Liv wasn't in anymore danger. And for that, he'd have to buy time.

When he had his answers, he could put this mess behind him and concentrate on what he was going to do next. He looked up at Liv and cursed the gnaw of hunger just seeing her could stir. He'd put Olivia on hold too many times and it had nearly cost him his marriage. He wanted another chance to make it right.

"The team's been working overtime for a week," he said as a plan formed. "They deserve some time off, too."

Sutton seemed relieved Sebastian had backed down. "I'll see what I can do."

Sebastian cut the connection. When he looked up, his gaze spliced with Liv's. Her sweater's color reflected in her eyes, making them bluer, brighter than usual. And there leaped that primitive urge to devour and possess again, leaving him heavy and aching. Not reaching for her took all he had. He crossed his arms over his chest and tried to twist his mind back to the plan.

"You're not going to let this go, are you?" she said. The file cabinet snicked shut behind her.

He shook his head. "I can't."

"Okay, then, I'm in."

"In?"

Her chin rose. Not much. Just enough to dare. Opposition. Olivia would have backed down with a look. Liv was already digging in her heels. "It concerns me, too. I want to help."

He was suddenly tired of fighting the whole world. Kershaw. Sutton. Paula. And now Liv. He needed someone on his side. And before, Olivia had always taken his side—on his terms, but his side. Keeping Liv close by didn't seem like such a bad idea. He'd be there. And if he was right and this case wasn't closed, this time he'd be able to protect her. So he gave in and opened the door he'd sworn would always keep the two halves of his world separate. "Get me Kershaw's file."

Her smile alone was worth the small yield of control. He'd always liked pleasing her. It didn't take much. Hot chocolate after skating. Blueberry picking after a paddle on the pond. A picnic on top of Mount Monadnock after the long hike up. Food and Olivia and passion. They were all mixed together. Was it any wonder he was always hungry when she was around?

She rolled Kingsley's chair next to his and spread the file before them. "Where do we start?"

He glanced at Liv's dark head bent over the file. The scent of her so close wrapped him in warmth. Home. Yearning unraveled. And when his arm touched hers, he let the contact stand. "At the beginning."

Always a good place to start.

THEY PUT IN A FEW HOURS of work when Liv suddenly looked up. The room spun a half circle before it steadied. Her muscles were as stiff as dried paint from sitting still so long. The air in the office was growing stale and a headache was starting to pound at her temple. She needed air. And Sebastian needed a distraction. "Let's run away."

"No time." Sebastian's fingers clicked keys so fast they made a melody. The computer's blue screen bleached his skin corpse gray in the low light.

When they'd squeezed all the information they could out of Kershaw's file, Sebastian had widened the net, looking for those elusive threads that would somehow connect him with the damage done to her car and Kershaw's death. On one hand, she'd found the logical track of his thought process fascinating. Hers seemed to run in spirals and loops, skipping and dipping. On the other hand, she saw him change as following those threads took him deeper and deeper into the dark web. Putting himself in Kershaw's mind, then in some other twisted mind, seemed to suck the life out of Sebastian, make him harder, grimmer. No wonder he frowned so much.

"Fresh air will do us both some good. Clear our heads." The lure of the mountain called to her. She wanted to feel wind flow through her hair and pinch her cheeks.

He looked up and gave her a speculative look. Calculating odds?

She leaned across the desk, putting her elbows on the top and her chin in her upturned hands. "Take me somewhere. Show me some place we both like."

He toyed with the mouse he otherwise had not used all day, then tented his hands above the keyboard. The corner of his mouth twitched up and, like a flag reaching out for the breeze, a smile unfurled. She sucked in a breath. "Do that again."

"What?"

"That thing you do with your mouth."

This time laughter spilled like the sputters from a rusty engine and its echo purred inside her. "Did we do that often...before?"

He reached for one of the curls brushing the edge of her face and twined it around his finger. "Your laugh was one of my favorite sounds."

"Show me." She tugged on the cuffs of his sleeves.

He let her haul him up to his feet. He skimmed a quick kiss across her forehead, then pushed her gently toward the door. "Go put on layers."

She craned her neck over her shoulder while a warm maple syrup kind of feeling slid through her. She hadn't known she'd been waiting for this until part of the thick wall around him cracked. "Where are we going?"

He smiled again as he shut down the computer. "Skating."

"WHAT DO I DO FIRST?" Olivia looked up at him expectantly. No, not Olivia. Liv. The woman in front of him was not the shy Olivia who'd charmed him with her softness all those years ago and made him believe he could follow two obsessions at once without getting burned. This was a woman brimming with curiosity and crackling with energy. He wasn't sure how to handle her, only that he couldn't let her go.

The specter of the unknown mutt out to hurt Olivia still clouded his mind. But the crime-scene team was still crawling around the cabin and the curious locals rolled through extra patrols of Mountain Road often during daylight. The pond should be safe enough to give Liv a half hour of sunshine to bloom.

As he took her gloved hand in his, a quilted calm came over him, and he knew everything would be all right. One step at a time. That's how he'd won her. That's how he would reach her once again. She might not be the Olivia he remembered, but she was still his, and he was still hers. For the first time in a long while, he let tension unwind, dropped his guard and gave Liv all of his attention.

"First, you separate your feet."

She giggled as she mimicked his widened stance on the ice of the pond. The sound teased him as gently as the breeze. She'd been a good skater. He had no doubt she would catch on fast.

"Skating is like walking. First, put your weight on one side. Like this." He stood next to her and glided forward a few feet on his right foot. "Then on the other. Like that."

Liv copied his every move. Her body remembered how to skate, even if her mind didn't remember she had. Her smile, her laughter, her pure pleasure tugged at his heartstrings, connecting her to him.

At that moment he wanted to believe in happy endings. When he sensed fatigue overtaking her, he led her to the big rock on the point of the island. The pond was shaped like an hourglass—two rounded ends with a cinched-in waist. Blueberry Island sat square in the middle like a showy belt buckle, leaving two narrow strips of water on each side to connect the two fat ends of the pond. The sun had melted the snow off the flat-topped rock at the west end of the island, making it perfect for sitting. He wished he had hot chocolate for her, but he hadn't dared go in the kitchen when Paula was there. He didn't need to debate the merits of wanting to spend time alone with his own wife.

He pointed to bare bushes along the rocky edge of the island. ''In the summer, we kayak over to this area and pick blueberries right from the boats.''

''Does anyone live there?''

''On the island? No. It's a wildlife preserve. There's a trail that goes all around it.''

''Let's go.'' She started to get up, but he pulled her back down.

''I need to rest for a couple of minutes.'' He wrapped an arm around her shoulders, and she leaned her head against his. They sat in companionable silence for a long time, and he wished he could bottle this moment.

''Can you hear it?'' Her breath tickled his ear.

''What?''

''The whisper of the wind in the trees. It's like a song.''

And it was. Soft like a lullaby, the breeze swished by.

Smiling, he tugged her up, drew her close and spun her in lazy circles over the rough surface of the ice. The navy of their gloves, clasped close to their chests, melded hand to hand and body to body so that he could barely figure out where he ended and where she began. For a moment, Kershaw, the unsolved puzzle of the tampered car, Paula's wish to pound in a wedge of mistrust between him and

Liv, faded, shrinking the world to only the woman in his arms. He sighed into her. "God, I've missed you."

She leaned back in his arms, trusting he would hold her. Her eyes glittered more brightly than the sapphire he'd given her for their last anniversary. "My heart remembers you."

His heart took a plunge down to his feet before it found its right rhythm.

She twined her hands around his neck, smiling as she pulled his face closer. "Kiss me, Sebastian. I want to know you all over again."

As always when it came to her, he could not resist. His gloved fingers tangled in her hair. His kiss opened her, and he breathed in her fire. It was like the first time all over again. The heat, the need, the slight edge of desperation as if parting would leave them both lost. She fit against him as she always had—perfectly. She followed his lead, then surprised him by asking for more.

"Liv." He breathed her name as if it were an incantation that could save him.

Eleven years ago, after their first kiss, he'd tried to let her go. He'd tried to pretend she didn't invade his dreams. He'd tried to use the danger he had to pursue to slice her out of his life. But he couldn't. He'd needed to find himself in her goodness as much as he'd needed to put evil behind bars. He'd given into his weakness, married her, and lived with the sweet hell of coming home to her only to have to leave her again.

"I can't." He gently pushed her away. He couldn't do it anymore. He couldn't pretend he could keep her safe as long as his work dragged him through the muck of evil. He couldn't stop hunting. But he didn't know how to let her go.

"Can't what?"

He shook his head. "We should head back."

She stiffened against him. "Don't shut me out."

Only their hands touched now and it felt like goodbye. "You're tired."

"My memories might be gone, but I still live in this body. I feel just fine."

He rammed his hands into the pockets of his jacket. "Your legs are shaking."

She planted the toe pick of one skate into the ice, spitting up shards. He thought of a bull pawing as it saw red and already felt the horn of her anger gore him between two ribs.

"You know what your problem is?" she asked, forehead rucked, eyes narrowed. "Your problem is that you're afraid, and you're afraid of being afraid."

"That doesn't make sense, Liv." He turned from her and took a step toward shore. He lived with fear day in and day out. He didn't fear fear. Fear kept him sharp, kept him strong.

She grabbed on to the tail of his jacket. "Then give, Sebastian. Share. Don't keep all your sewage bottled up inside of you. It just festers there."

"You don't want to go there." He skated forward. She didn't let go, and he tugged her along. If he tainted her with the stain of his job, then what would he have to come home to?

"If I didn't, I wouldn't ask."

"You have no idea how dark it is in here."

"How can I when you won't let me in?"

"It's safer."

"For you or for me?"

He stopped and spun to look at her. "For both of us."

She cocked her head and her eyes softened. "How did you know the ice was safe?"

"This time of the year, it's usually thick enough."

"What about the warm weather earlier this week?"

"Not warm enough for long enough to melt much of the ice. We've had cold days and nights since then." He pointed to tracks that looked as if a miniature tank had rumbled across the pond. "If it's strong enough to support a snowmobile, it's strong enough to hold us."

"But you didn't know for sure." She grabbed on to the collar of his jacket and jerked it impatiently. "There could be a soft spot somewhere."

"Not likely."

"What if there was?" Her fists tightened around the nylon of his jacket. "What if the ice just cracked, and we fell in?"

He closed his eyes against the intensity dancing in hers. But the dark gave him no solace. Instead, he saw them plunging into the ice-cold water, saw the dark swallow them, saw him desperately fighting…and coming up empty.

She touched his cheek gently. "What do you think is going to happen?"

He could feel the tear again. It ripped like a limb being torn from his body. He'd been able to come back to Olivia all those years because he'd known she was safe.

But she wasn't. The safety he'd forged was illusion.

He could build a fortress. He could fortify it with cannons. He could make her a prisoner in her home. But still he couldn't guarantee all these precautions would spare her harm. The only way he could keep her safe was to let her go.

"I'll lose you all over again."

She smiled at him. A big, brilliant smile that put the sun to shame. Then she skated backwards, gouging deep scars into the ice. She extended her hands to him, beckoning him with her fingers. "I'll leave a trail."

He couldn't help it; he threw his head back and laughed. He tasted the bitter edge of resignation. His muscles quivered, and he couldn't stop their weakness. She was right. He was doomed—had been since he'd first seen her. He would follow because he couldn't help himself. She was the one thing that kept him from becoming what he chased. He opened his arms, and she rushed toward him.

That left him one option. And he wasn't quite ready to look at it yet.

She stumbled over one of the gouges she'd made on the ice and tumbled them both into the snowbank at the edge of the pond. Still laughing, he brushed snow from her hair, then helped her up.

That's when he saw the tracks.

The same tracks that Skyralov had lifted at the cemetery when he'd found the wreath—a wreath that was stolen from a grave near his parents'. The same tracks that Kingsley had photographed in the snow by the Aerie's front door when the bird was found. The same tracks that had led into and out of the cabin where they'd found Kershaw with his face missing.

The hunt wasn't over yet. He had to get Olivia home.

THEY WERE SO CLOSE he could smell them. Their laughter drilled into him like a dental pick on a rotted tooth. He squeezed the pillowcase of supplies he'd taken closer to his chest and shrank behind the boulder guarded by thick pines.

Glancing across the stretch of ice, he could not see the camp he'd made on the island. Had they? He'd covered the fire. He'd stowed the sleeping bag. He'd taken his tie to her with him. There was no trace of him. Their laughter bored into him again. No, if they had seen anything, Falconer wouldn't be laughing.

Back against the cold stone, he made himself small and still—something he'd learned to do well a long time ago. The can of baked beans dug into his sternum, but he didn't move. Holding his breath, he tuned into them, latched on to their frequencies. He smelled the shift, smelled the sudden spurt of fear tainting the air. The instinct to run flooded him with pins and needles, but he didn't obey. Patience. It was the power of his survival.

Eyes closed, he heard them skate away. He followed them with his mind's eye. And when they reached the gates, he stood and headed in the opposite direction.

Time to move.

Chapter Ten

Fort Knox, Liv was sure, couldn't possibly have as many defenses as Sebastian could put up in the blink of an eye. One second, she'd been staring at his soul, willingly falling into him, the next, vault doors were slamming down and the locks bolting on. She'd held on to his hand as he'd hurriedly led her from the pond. She hadn't let go—not even when they'd reached the house—and he'd tried to shake her off as if she were a pesky puppy nipping at his heels.

"You might as well get used to me." She followed him down the stairs. "I'm not leaving."

He grumbled as he headed into his office, but he didn't shut the door in her face. Not that it would have stopped her.

As long as he insisted on shutting her out, they would get nowhere. So she had to let him see that her presence in his world would not cause it to crumble.

Trying to decipher the sudden change of mood, she unwound the navy scarf from around her neck. "What's wrong?"

"Nothing." Coat still on, he shuffled the papers on his desk faster than a collator on a photocopy machine. A brick wall. She'd have more luck getting through a brick wall.

"Is it the kiss?" The kiss that had melted all of her bones and was about to thaw the ice under their skates when he broke it off. She wanted to remember Olivia, give her back to him. But she didn't want to return to being merely decorative paper on the wall of his life. "Are you afraid of what you feel for me? Because I'm not her?"

He looked up at her and blinked. "It's not the kiss."

"Then what?" She wanted the closeness they'd shared at the pond back, the waltz to the music of the wind, the magic of his smile and his gaze that for a moment had made her feel as if she were the center of the universe. All of her fractured parts had come together, and she'd felt whole.

"I don't want you involved."

"Well, that's too bad. I *am* involved. You're my husband. Everything you do affects me." *The way you kiss me. The way you hold me. The way you turn your back on me...* She wanted to cry for the sheer stubbornness that made him stand alone like a mountain.

"This is work." He stepped to the desk Kingsley used and scattered the neat piles Kingsley had put together to make her filing task easier.

"It was work before we went skating." The warmth. She wanted that back, too. Wrapped in his arms, it could have been July. In this cold basement, she wondered if she'd ever feel spring again.

He turned his back to her and headed for the file cabinet.

Like a turtle, she curled into herself. "What changed?" Something had, in the space of a heartbeat.

"He's still here."

"Out at the pond. You saw something." Understanding

what he was looking for, she nudged him aside and pulled out a file from the cabinet.

Their gazes met and held. She saw it then, the small fissure in the wall he'd erected to keep her out. But he caulked it as soon as he noticed it and took the file from her hands.

"Tracks." He spread out a series of photos of boot prints on the oval worktable. "As long as he's out there, you're in danger."

She took her place at his side. "Then I'd say I was involved."

"Liv—"

"He took away my life."

He looked at her long and hard, then gave a small nod. And she couldn't help wondering who had hurt him so much that he'd needed to put up the wall in the first place.

SEBASTIAN WASN'T THE ONLY ONE who didn't like the way the pieces of this puzzle were being forced to fit. Even knowing the job was officially over, Reed had left for Connecticut that morning to check out Greco's Blazer. Mercer, Skyralov and Kingsley were notified they were on vacation, but not one of them had packed their bags. Skyralov elected to spend his time off attending Kershaw's funeral. Mercer didn't say where he was heading, but mumbled something about scum and tracks. And Kingsley was still yoked to his electronics, plowing through information as if it were soil.

Liv helped Sebastian check the whereabouts of escapees he'd put back behind bars. They found each one where he belonged, adding more gaps to their growing puzzle.

At the end of the day, the men returned. The remnants of a greasy pizza now sat on the corner of the oval worktable, congealing. Only a shred of lettuce remained in the teak salad bowl. Cookie crumbs snaked trails across the tabletop. The five men had consumed enough food to stave off world hunger for another week.

Enough testosterone floated in the air to fuel a small nuclear device. They spoke a language she could barely understand. Their logic glided down paths that left her lagging behind. Their sense of humor often tripped down macabre alleys. She should have felt out of place. But she didn't. Being here in this room with these men, adding to their bits of clues, made her feel as if she was finally sketching lines that made sense on the blank canvas of her life.

"He's close." Like smoke, Mercer detached from the shadows. His dark looks reminded her of a storm filled with lightning and thunder, but his eyes held an eerie calm that made her think she could trust him with her life. The tracks Sebastian had found at the pond had led Mercer to the island. There he'd found a sleeping bag, the remnants of a fire and the buried refuse of a week of stolen meals. The ice had given whoever camped there easy access to the island. The low winter occupancy gave him the privacy he needed. The freshest set of tracks led to the road and didn't return.

"I'll try again in the morning." With that, Mercer melted back into the shadows as if staying in the open would leave him too vulnerable.

Liv could empathize. Any minute now, Sebastian would ask her to leave. She'd seen the hint of it every time he glanced up from his work and saw her there. And every chance she got, she inoculated him to her presence with a touch, with the sound of her voice, with another scrap of information he needed and she'd filed away. If she left, she was afraid he wouldn't let her back in. Without him, the canvas that was her life would remain black and white.

She was lost enough without having to give up that small sense of belonging.

Skyralov reached for the last cold slice of pizza. "Kershaw's mother's all shook up. Nearly fell into the grave with grief. The priest had to pull her off so they could lower the coffin. She was the only one there. Neither the brother nor the sister showed up to pay their respects."

He chomped on the pizza and chewed. "I got curious and looked up the sister. Seems Mother Dearest didn't bother telling sis her brother was dead. Not that she'd have gone to the funeral anyway. Seems there's no love lost between them. She blames her glamorous life on him. Bernie got her hooked on heroin."

"Yeah, it's always somebody else's fault," Reed said. When he shook his head, not a hair moved.

"Sometimes you can't do anything about the circumstances you're in," Liv said. A second. That's all it had taken to change her life completely. She reached for her teacup and found it empty.

"Still." Kingsley leaned back in his chair and hooked both thumbs around his suspenders. "It's a decision. You can fall into circumstances, but you don't have to let them bury you alive."

"Heroin's a bitch of a mistress." Skyralov's easy face clouded over, making her wonder if he'd lost someone to that demanding mistress. "Once she's in you, it's hard to shake her off. This girl can't hear another tune."

"That's sad." Liv twirled the teacup round and round in her hands. What tune was *she* listening to? Her own or someone else's? Her fingers gave an odd spasm and knocked over the cup. Good thing it was empty.

"What about the brother?" Sebastian frowned as he stared at her hands. She picked up the teapot and carefully poured another cup. He was not going to use an act of everyday clumsiness to ditch her. *See,* she said silently as she raised her cup. *Everything is fine.*

"The brother's still M.I.A." Skyralov rose and stretched. The ease of his move seemed odd on such a big man. But then, she'd noticed that of all Sebastian's men. There was more to them than they allowed anyone to see. Something sad, she was sure, had led them to this life. "Hasn't shown up at the halfway house in Nashua for nearly a week. Broke parole conditions, so now he's officially a fugitive."

"How lucky for the state of New Hampshire that we're on the case!" Reed's smile was toothpaste-commercial bright. He craned his neck toward Kingsley. "Got anything on that number yet?"

Reed's search of Greco's car had earned him a credit-card receipt missed by the FBI's team of specialists. The wadded-up, water-stained receipt had taken Kingsley a while to decipher, and he was now letting the computer do its thing.

"Coming right up," Kingsley said, hitting the print command with a flourish. "Belongs to one Nelson Weld. His rap sheet is taller than he is. Finished serving eighteen months for fencing stolen goods. Got out early six months ago for good behavior. Guess where our ODC spent the night last Monday?"

"ODC?" she asked. Her hand spasmed again, so she tucked it into her lap.

"Ordinary Decent Criminal." Sebastian scrubbed a hand over his face. Five o'clock shadow gave a wild edge to his good looks. One she liked. "Connecticut?"

"Give the man a cigar." Kingsley tapped out a drumroll with two pencils on the desktop. "A quaint little place called the Doze Inn—right down the highway from where they found the wreck."

"Got an address on him?" Sebastian crossed his arms over his chest. His forehead furrowed and his eyebrows flattened. Like rock under pressure, he was squeezing the soft coal of frustration into a diamond-hard barrier.

Not just me, she thought, *he shuts out everyone.* She wanted to go over and uncross his arms, rub the furrow between his eyes and somehow make him understand that he didn't have to fight all alone. Instead, she settled for a hand on his shoulder and a squeeze as she passed by him to neaten the dinner mess.

"Nashua. French Hill section," Kingsley said. "Seems Weld and Kershaw were practically neighbors."

"Worth checking into," Mercer's voice floated from the shadows.

"Won't find him there. According to the history I pulled up on his credit card, he started heading west last Wednesday. There's a charge for the night at the Sleep Chalet outside of Cincinnati."

Skyralov reached across the table for the last of the chocolate chip cookies Paula had baked. "Don't you just love it when they make it easy?"

"Haven't been to Cincinnati in a while," Reed said. "How about you?"

"I hear the steaks are fine out that way," Skyralov said.

Reed cocked his head and adjusted his shades. "That's right, we're on vacation."

"Or is it the barbecue?"

"You're thinking of Kansas City."

"So I've got two for Cincinnati?" Kingsley typed. "Your flight leaves at 6:05 in the a.m."

Skyralov snatched the itinerary Kingsley handed him. "Good thing we're on vacation."

"Yeah, I'd hate to have to get up that early to go to work."

There was a rhythm here, an ease that seemed as smooth as watercolor flowing on paper. Not that these men would appreciate her thinking of their teamwork as art. And Sebastian, as artist-in-residence, watched them color the sketch he'd started. "Sutton gets wind of this and it could be your careers."

"Careers?" Skyralov laughed. "We ain't got no stinking careers. This is how we breathe."

One by one, they left, talking and laughing.

Sebastian shifted his attention to her. *This is my life,* his gaze seemed to say.

"I want to be a part of it."

"It never ends."

"That's why."

His gaze went from her hands cradling the teak salad bowl close to her belly to her eyes, and seemed to penetrate every corner of her brain. It was as if he'd taken an MRI and found that the lesions of her amnesia were too dark to allow her to add lines to this already well-sketched design. She would scratch a wayward mark and make him reach for an eraser.

He reached for the salad bowl. "Let me."

"No, I can do it."

She held his gaze without blinking. *Don't shut me out. Don't shut me out. I don't know where else I belong.* Any minute now she was going to start to lose her color again, and the thought brushed a streak of panic through her.

"I want to."

She let go of the bowl. He'd protected Olivia for ten years. *Give him a chance to adjust.*

"It gets dirty," he said, his eyes growing darker, the light in them getting farther as if she'd mixed too much water with the paint.

"I wash clean." There was a desperation to her words—

as if she couldn't draw fast enough to keep the picture whole.

Her answer was a weight he added to the burden on his shoulders. She hadn't meant for that to happen.

"Sebastian…"

"Shh. Let me sleep on it."

Silently, he took her hand and led her upstairs. He didn't say another word as they dropped off the dirty dishes in the kitchen or as he went through his nighttime routine. He didn't speak as he climbed between the flannel sheets of their bed. He didn't kiss her good-night. He simply spooned his body around hers.

"Sebastian?"

"Shh."

She didn't let herself fall asleep until his breath shallowed and his hand relaxed against her ribs—until she was sure he would stay pasted at her side.

THE FIRST THING SEBASTIAN did the next morning was try to leave Liv at home. That didn't work. Now that she was here in the SUV beside him, he might as well have painted a bull's-eye on the windshield. Every car that passed them suddenly seemed suspicious. Every pedestrian who glanced their way made him feel like a target. Every red light had him sensing the bead of a sniper's rifle.

Never before had he felt so vulnerable on the road. Always before it had been hunter and prey. Alone. Now his attention was divided and it took away the strong edge he needed to corner and capture.

The second thing he did was pay a visit to the jail where Weld had served his time. With Liv standing next to him as if she was shackled to him, he sweet-talked the woman in the jail administrator's office into letting him take a peek at the list of Weld's visitors. One of them was Kershaw's mother. Had she been the go-between to set up the escape plans? More and more it looked as if Kershaw had planned every detail of his escape—right down to the murder of the marshals. Other than his lawyer, the only other visitor Weld received was a woman named Kiki Bates.

"Girlfriend?" he asked the secretary.

She didn't look up from her work. "I don't see them."

"What now?" Liv asked when they got back to the SUV.

"Now we call Kingsley and see what he can dig up on Kiki Bates."

"And then?"

"We play her."

Kingsley came up with an address in Nashua. The same one as Nelson Weld. No big surprise. They drove to French Hill and parked in the lot beside an abandoned church. Sebastian called Kiki Bates and got no answer.

"Not home?" Liv asked.

He shook his head.

"So?"

"So we watch and wait." They sandwiched the SUV between two others where they could have a view of the white building time had turned gray. If he'd hoped the long boring wait would have Liv begging to go home, he'd been wrong. He'd met her attempts at conversation with grunts. Lunchtime came and went. He'd offered her no food. And still Liv didn't complain.

Finally at three, a woman appeared, balancing a plastic grocery bag in each hand. She wore a leather coat trimmed with fur and high-heeled boots that allowed her only baby steps. When she started to climb the rickety stairs to the second-story apartment Bates shared with Weld, Liv grabbed his forearm and shook it. "She's here."

Sebastian dialed Kiki Bates's number. "Mrs. Weld?"

"There's no Mrs. Weld here."

"Oh, well, I'm sorry," he said, knowing she and Weld weren't married. "I found this number in Nelson Weld's wallet—"

"Nelson's wallet?" Suspicion spiced her voice.

"Yes, I found it, and I was hoping to get hold of him so I could return it. There's about two hundred bucks in here."

She wasn't buying, and he couldn't really blame her. If she knew anything about Nelson's situation, she probably suspected a squeeze. The question was, from which side?

"Why don't you just mail it to the address on the driver's license? When he gets it, I'll have him pay you back for postage."

"Well, I kinda wanted to give it straight to him, you know. With all that money and all."

"He'll get it." Her voice was tight.

"Okay, well, I'll just turn it in to the police, and he can pick it up there."

"That's not going to work." A note of desperation now. She knew Nelson was in a heap of trouble. So he boxed her in.

"It's the safest thing to do." Before she could add anything, he hung up.

Liv gaped at him. "You just let her go like that?"

He'd worked the game before. He knew how it would play out. "We'll get her back."

"How?"

"I'll give her time to think it through and call back."

Liv leaned against the door. He didn't like the new gleam in her eyes. "She'll recognize your voice."

"You're not giving me enough credit."

She tipped her head and the glints of gold in her brown

hair caught the edge of the sun. He let the liquid shimmer distract him.

"What if I call?" She sucked in a breath and waited expectantly.

He shook his head. "Out of the question."

"Why not?"

"You're not a deputy. You have no authority to act."

"As I recall, neither do you. You're supposed to be on vacation. Spending time with your wife who's recovering from a head injury."

"I still have the badge." That was so lame even he couldn't quite swallow it.

She dug into her purse, took out a pen and ripped a piece of paper from a notepad. With a shaky hand, she sketched a quick facsimile of his badge and affixed it to her chest. "There, so do I."

"Liv—"

She leaned forward and put two fingers over his lips. The piece of paper fluttered between them. Color blazed her cheeks and fire burned in her eyes. And all he could think of was how much he wanted to kiss her. "No, Sebastian, listen. Put yourself in her shoes. You're a man—"

"Last time I checked," he mumbled through her fingers. The taste of her chiseled off another chip from the stone of his best intentions. How could he keep her safe if he allowed his mind to wander to the bedroom with each bob of her hair, with each touch of her finger, with each glance, instead of keeping it firmly focused on his goal?

"She's a woman who knows her lover is on the run," Liv insisted. "She knows he's in trouble. She's got you pegged as a cop."

He grasped her warm fingers from his lips and placed her hand into her lap. "I didn't talk to her like a cop."

But those restless fingers didn't stay still. They crept to

his collar and brushed much too softly against his neck. "Now if a woman calls, she might be more receptive."

"No." Pulling on her wrists, he unhooked her hands from his collar. Her palms pressed, one into his knee, the other on his thigh. Was she doing this on purpose? He snapped the heat dial to low.

"It makes sense, Sebastian. I'm not a threat to her."

Only to me. "No."

Her fingers were dancing now, and he could barely keep attention to the snake charm of her voice. "The faster you catch this guy, the faster he'll talk, the faster you'll get to close your case. It's just common sense."

The scary part was that her argument *was* starting to make sense. Either that or his mind had migrated so far south that he'd lost common sense along the way. He jerked the car into gear and drove off.

Martha's Exchange offered microbrewed beer and homemade candy. In the lull between the lunch rush and before the after-work happy hour, it also offered quiet. He asked for a booth and talked Liv through the call she wanted to make while they munched on club sandwiches.

"Ready?" he asked an hour later. He wasn't sure he was and still couldn't figure out how she'd maneuvered him into this corner.

She nodded.

He switched sides so that he was sitting next to her instead of across. He punched in Kiki's number, handed her the phone and leaned into her so he could listen in. Liv's pad of paper stretched out in front of them. Her fingers sketched absently as she screwed her face in concentration. When Kiki answered, Liv's back straightened and she drew back her shoulders.

"Mrs. Weld, my name is Olivia Spence. I'm with the U.S. Marshals Service. A law enforcement officer handed me your husband's wallet. Based on where the wallet was found, we have reason to believe your husband may have witnessed a crime. We'd like to speak with him. Do you know where we could find him?''

"No, he's out of town on business right now."

"It's important we talk to him. Do you have a number where we can reach him?"

"We've had a few problems lately and he left without leaving me any information."

She was lying. He gave Liv the sign they'd agreed on. She nodded.

"Mrs. Weld, we know your husband was involved in this crime. We have his tag number. We're closing in on him."

"Then what do you need me for?"

"I'm going to tell you something that, if I'm asked later, I'll deny." She lowered her voice, letting the secret she was spilling ride like fog into the phone. "When we catch Nelson, and we will, he's a dead man. I overheard a conversation with the FBI officers in charge of the case. They said the only way to stop a cop killer is to kill him. That's what's going to happen to your husband, Mrs. Weld. You have the power to save him."

"He didn't kill anyone." Interesting answer.

"I hear you. And personally, I don't believe he did. From theft to murder is a big step, and he just doesn't seem like that kind of guy. But you know how men are. They shoot first and ask questions later."

Kiki snorted her agreement. "Isn't that the truth!"

"Ma'am," Liv said with so much assurance that Sebastian had to wonder when she'd turned into such a good liar. "Do you know any police officers?"

Kiki hesitated. "Yes."

"Call that officer and ask him, just hypothetically now,

'Do cop killers ever get killed by cops?' You ask him, see what he says, then you'll know I'm on your side. I want him back alive. Dead, he can't answer my questions. I'm not interested in small fish, Mrs. Weld. I want the big shark.''

Reeled and hung. As arranged, Liv left the number of Sebastian's cell phone.

It was a gamble. Maybe Kiki really did know a cop. Maybe that cop would deny the truth. But Sebastian knew that the beauty parlor where Kiki worked was busted on a regular basis by vice for their special massages. She wasn't about to call one of them—not even for Nelson. And there was that two hundred dollars she thought was in the wallet.

She'd call. And for a price, she'd flip.

Chapter Eleven

At ten that evening, Kiki phoned back. "He called."

Sebastian sat close to Liv on the bed. His arm pressed across her back, and his fist dipped the mattress at her hip. His head tipped into hers as he listened in on the phone call. His proximity was a comfort she relaxed into. Putting herself into his skin, Liv focused on her role as Deputy Marshal Olivia Spence.

"Did he say where he was?" Since Cincinnati, Weld hadn't used the credit card and had ditched his car. Before playing good citizen, Kiki had probably warned her boyfriend the cops were on his tail.

"N-no."

The metallic catch of fear rasped through her voice, so Liv pretended to be Kiki's best friend. "He's going to be okay. If we find him first, we'll make sure he's not hurt. You have any kids?"

"No. We're talking about starting a family, but he wanted to find a good job first, you know. Get some money in the bank."

Given the length of Weld's rap sheet, Liv didn't think such a drastic change in outlook was likely. But then, look at her. Her life was all turned around. She'd once been content to wait. Now she couldn't bear all the loss that could fill each pause. A thin ribbon of sadness rippled through her. She reached for Sebastian's hand and squeezed it tight. His thumb stroked the tops of her fingers, and she relaxed once more. "Yeah, those diapers don't come cheap."

Sirens screamed from the TV drama blaring in the background of Kiki's apartment. "He's a good man, you know. He's made a couple of bad choices, but deep down, he's a good man."

"Yeah, I hear you." Her gaze sought Sebastian. His eyes were dark, a combination of midnight and stars that seemed to hold all of eternity, yet cradled her like a precious pearl. A good man. But a knight chasing the wrong dragon.

"He's trying to protect you, that's why he won't tell you where he is." She spoke as much to Sebastian as to Kiki. Did he understand that she needed all of him more than the protection that cut off access to parts of him? "I want you to agree to let me put a trap-and-trace on your phone."

The flare of TV gunshots stuttered. "You're not going to hurt him?"

"No, he just has information that can help me find the guy we're really looking for. Nelson doesn't seem like the kind of man who would cut up two marshals and just leave them to die."

There was a watery edge to Kiki's laugh that made Liv think she was crying. "He won't even let me kill spiders."

A weight pressed Liv's chest. She was sorry she couldn't make a promise to this woman who wanted a better life, even if it was with the wrong man. But then, who was she to judge? She was clinging to Sebastian as much as Kiki was hanging her frayed hopes on Nelson. "I'll do what I can."

When she got off the phone, Liv sat still. "We got her."

She handed Sebastian the phone and just sat on the edge of the bed, her empty hands dangling between her legs. The carpet's light-blue fibers blended into a blur and the room seemed to rock gently like a mother cradling a child.

He called Kingsley and arranged for him to install the trace-and-trap in the morning, then sat next to her, his pose mirroring hers. "It's a good thing."

"I know. I just feel sorry for her. She didn't do anything, and she's going to lose no matter what."

"Or maybe this'll be the thing that gets her looking to take charge of her life."

"Maybe."

He kissed the nape of her neck, raining a shiver of pleasure down her spine. "You did good."

She tilted her head back until his lips brushed her jaw, trailing a watercolor wash of warmth. Her whole body sang, and she craved the music. Had Sebastian always been able to play so well? When their lips met, the crescendo of yearning knocked them both off balance and tumbled them back onto the bed.

His kiss was soft and tender, but the backbeat of his need pulsed against her palms splayed over his chest, becoming hers.

When she was with him, the world seemed brighter, more colorful. She could see the end of darkness, believe that one day she could look back and find the trail of herself. All she had to do was take his hand and trust.

Doubts tripped over the melody, grinding out sour notes. Was he kissing Olivia? Was he remembering how love was between them? Did she remember how to love?

His touch raised a symphony of pleasure, mellowing the doubts.

He was a man, and she was a woman who was tired of

watching her color fade to nothing. She'd had too much of darkness and death since the accident. On this cold night in February, she wanted warmth. She wanted to feel alive. She wanted him.

She would trust.

He had the power and passion of a hurricane, but he wasn't going to meet a flimsy house that would fold under his force. She could sway and she could bend. She was not going to break.

He would have to trust, too.

She turned in his arms until they lay face to face. In the soft light, she was struck by the pieces of him—the breadth of his shoulders against the white of his shirt and the navy paisley of the comforter, the sharp attention of his dark eyes as he drank her in, the masculine chisel of his fingers as he reached toward her. When he touched her, she understood why Olivia had waited, why she'd fought her subtle battles to hold on to him. His hold was as gentle as sea foam, yet strong enough that she thought he could pull her out of any eddy.

His kiss coursed through her like the warmed brandy he'd offered her after dinner, twining shades of amber into a heat that was all-encompassing. Her heart jumped all out of rhythm. Her thoughts splashed with daubs of colors until they canceled each other out and all that was left was feeling. The dark taste of him. The spicy smell of him. The hard warmth of his body stretched out alongside hers.

Then she stumbled over the holes in her memory, and she couldn't help wondering if her bone-deep attraction to the tall, dark and handsome stranger who was her husband was simply a need for a secure anchor in the darkness, or a true calling of her heart.

But when his tongue traced the seam of her mouth, she yielded to its request like paper to paint, opening to him, taking him in. And in the helpless surrender of his groan, she realized he was as lost as she was.

HE COULD FEEL EVERY INCH of the skin he occupied, from the tingle of his scalp to the curl of his toes. He could feel the rush of blood flowing through his veins, the drum of his heart, the pulse of his life force. And he felt strong. It was weeks since he'd been so in control of himself.

Here, in this bed, she was the woman he'd fallen in love with a lifetime ago, warm and familiar. The sweet scent of her that reminded him of flowers on slow summer breezes. The honeyed taste of her that would linger long after a kiss. The softness of her that tamed all his hard edges.

Until she straddled him. Then the heat in the blue of her eyes became that of the inside of a flame. It consumed him.

Who are you?

A month ago, he could have predicted every stroke of her hands, the texture of every kiss, the tides of her climax. Now he didn't know exactly what to expect. The Olivia he remembered, the Olivia he married, would not have met him thrust for thrust. She would not have demanded her turn to torture him exquisitely with her tongue and her hands. She would not have challenged him to meet her soul to soul with eyes wide open.

Liv did.

And the skin-to-skin contact with this woman whose mind he couldn't predict seemed to open lines of current that were too much to handle. He was crashing. Hard. And he didn't care if there was a net waiting for him. He fit himself to her, around her, in her. The give of flesh cushioned him. Safe. He was safe. The soft sounds deep in her throat echoed his heartbeat. Her sigh became his next breath. Then madness bolted through him. He rode this edge of insanity until he felt her explode around him. The quake of her climax sent him tumbling again, stripping away the grip of his control, leaving him bared from the inside out. Empty, yet strangely full.

They held on to each other, two lost souls, as their breaths struggled to catch up to them.

He had wanted roots. Olivia had given them to him. But for all the roots he'd found with her in their home over the past ten years, part of him had lived in fear of what would happen if his obsessions collided.

Now they had.

He loved her more than he'd thought possible.

And someone still wanted to take her away from him.

If he wasn't careful, this divided attention would knock him right off the tightrope he was walking, and he would lose everything.

As if sensing the treacherous course of his thoughts, she kissed him softly on the stubble of his jaw, then met his gaze, straight and direct. "I can't give you what you want."

"What's that?"

"Everything back to normal."

His hand fingered the chopped lengths of her hair. He buried his nose in the scented curls. Familiar and different. "I'm not sure what's normal anymore."

Olivia before? Liv now? Letting the chase for scum eat up his soul? This mess they were in that seemed to have no doors or windows, only fun house mirrors and carnival lights?

She was no longer trailing behind him, waiting for him safe in the heart of their home. She was insisting on standing on her own, on her terms.

"I like you this way." He liked her strong and assured.

He liked the soft iron of her will. But in the wake of that heady aura of self-confidence he had to wonder, did she still find anything of value in him? And when he'd made the world safe for her again, would she be there when he returned?

SEBASTIAN MADE THE MISTAKE of seeking coffee in the kitchen and telling Liv he'd meet her there. He found himself eye to eye with Paula. After the emotional wringer of last night, the last thing he needed was more drama from his sister in law.

Kingsley was loading the SUV with the equipment they'd need for Kiki's phone. Liv was dressing the part of deputy marshal. And Paula, who had somehow transformed the comfort of his kitchen into alien territory, was doing her best impression of a leech as she followed him so closely he could smell the salt of her fear. With muffins, coffee and sisterly concern, she'd wrung the day's plans out of Kingsley and, surprise, she didn't agree with them.

"You can't do this. You can't have Olivia run all over the state. She's supposed to be healing."

Sebastian grabbed a mug and reached for the coffeepot. He didn't like Liv's participation in this operation anymore than Paula did, but he wasn't about to admit it to her. "This is how she's chosen to heal."

Paula snatched the coffeepot off the machine and poured the dark brew into his mug. "She doesn't know better. We're—*I'm*—responsible for her well-being. You're being completely irresponsible as usual."

He headed for the table, hoping the shield of it would keep Paula at a distance. It didn't. She dropped down into the chair beside his and tried to stare him down. He put the newspaper up. "I'll be right there. I won't let her get hurt."

"That's not the point." With a fork, she crinkled the paper down until she could spear him with her gaze once more. "The point is that she shouldn't be there in the first place." Her hands were flying like debris now, and he leaned back to avoid an errant stab of the fork. "I don't get you. You say you love her. You say you want the best for her. And then you put her in this kind of situation."

"I do love her." So much it actually burned his chest. So much he couldn't think straight. So much the very thought of losing her made him shiver. He shook the paper and the crease unfolded. "I do want to keep her safe. I don't have to explain—"

"Yes, you do." Paula snapped up like a jack-in-the box, hands on hips. "She's my sister. I raised her. I'm responsible for her."

With more patience than he felt, Sebastian folded the paper and placed it on the table. "Paula, listen. I understand that you're worried. I understand that you want Liv to act like the little sister you dressed and played with like a doll—" Paula sputtered, but Sebastian shut her up with a look. "But she's her own person. We have to let her make her own decisions." As much as it scared the hell out of him.

She was pacing now—no zipping—like a crank-up car. "You're putting all these ideas in her head. She would never have thought to try something like this."

He softened his voice, knowing that he, too, had underestimated Olivia. "She did. She signed up for a criminology class *before* the accident. We were growing apart, and she was trying to find a way to bring us back together."

"That doesn't mean you have to play on her weakness."

He laughed. Weakness? What weakness? She'd handled Kiki like a pro. She'd handled him even more expertly, taking everything he had, then giving him back even more.

"Your sister is the strongest person I know. She doesn't need me. She doesn't need you. We'll be lucky if she wants either of us in her life when she realizes how strong she is." He jerked the paper open, seeing nothing but wavy lines of print.

Paula's jaw dropped. "How can you say something like that? She needs us—"

"To give her room to find herself."

And that, he decided, was the scariest thing of all.

SHE FELT THE UNDERCURRENT eddying in the kitchen before she walked in. It was strong and acrid like brush cleaner, sharp and cutting like scissors. Her husband and her sister were yellow and violet causing afterimages with their opposing hues, even if they both claimed to want the best for her. She loved them both. Paula for her loyalty and care, even though Liv had given her nothing but grief. Sebastian for his willingness to allow Olivia to find her footing.

"Are we ready?" Liv asked, nerves jittering like popping corn.

Paula flitted to the counter. "You haven't eaten breakfast yet."

"I had fruit and a muffin earlier." Her cheeks colored at the memory of Sebastian offering her the plate of cantaloupe slices and blueberry muffins. Breakfast in bed was definitely something she wanted to do again. The smoky look in his eyes told her he would, too.

"That's not enough." Paula slammed a bowl of oatmeal studded with diced kiwi, banana slices, dried cranberries and chopped cashews on the table. "Sit."

"We have to go."

Paula blinked at her, making her feel as if her cheeks were on fire. Liv glanced at Sebastian. Paula followed her gaze, looked back at Liv and seemed to sense the new intimacy to their relationship. She wrinkled her nose. "I suppose *that* was inevitable. How could you take advantage of her like that?"

Before Sebastian could defend himself, Liv said, "Maybe I took advantage of him."

Paula processed that, then turned to the counter and twirled amber prescription bottles. "Did you take your medicine?"

"Yes. And I'll be fine." Liv patted her sister on the shoulder, felt it give. A pinch of guilt pricked her for the worry she caused her sister. "We're not doing anything dangerous."

Pale blue eyes shimmering with tears, Paula aimed her anger at Sebastian. "What kind of man asks his wife to take his place and do his job?"

"The kind who trusts her to do the job right," Liv said. "Besides, I volunteered."

"What's going on?" A sleepy Cari flopped at the table and rubbed her eyes. "I can hear you all the way upstairs."

"Nothing." Paula rushed to construct another breakfast. To comfort, her sister seemed to feed. And as she watched Paula's stick-thin figure dart across the kitchen, she wondered where her sister found her nourishment.

"Oh, you mean you're not getting your way, so you're bitching about it." Cari reached across the table and snatched a muffin from the basket.

"Carolina Woodruff!"

"That's no way to talk to your mother." Liv wished she could weave all these soft threads of conflict and bind together all the people she cared for. "She's doing her best."

"Whatever." Cari propped her book on the table and

scrunched down, chin on her folded arm. "I'm just saying what everyone is thinking."

Paula snagged a sponge from the sink and scoured the countertop. "What do I tell Cecilia when she gets here?"

"That I'll be home soon."

"Well, I can see I'm not needed here." Paula launched her sponge into the sink and huffed out of the room.

"I should go after her," Liv said with a sigh. Paula's help had been a godsend after the accident. She needed to know her efforts, if not her interference, were appreciated.

"We need to get going." Sebastian drained the last of his coffee. "Paula will be okay. She's one tough bird."

Not as tough as everyone assumed, Liv thought.

"If you go after her, it'll just drag out the soap opera. I should know. I've been through it enough times." Cari looked up and down at the severe cut of Liv's suit. "Where are you going?"

Liv shared a look across the table with Sebastian. "Out to run an errand. We'll be back by lunch."

"I'm sure it'll be there waiting for you." Cari gave an absent wave. "Have fun."

With one last look through the door where her sister had disappeared, Liv followed her husband.

HE WATCHED THEM LEAVE. Falconer, his wife and the electronics guru. Giddiness fizzed through him. He could not believe his luck. With the gizmo wizard out of his lair, now was the time to strike. He dropped the binoculars and the cord around his neck caught them. Balancing on the branch, he reached for the phone in his pocket.

"It's time," he said. No introductions were necessary.

"I don't know."

"You want him to feel what you felt, don't you?"

"I'm thinking that—"

"There's no time." The last thing he needed was a loose cannon blowing up his careful plans. "If you get there soon, you can get the information we need and this can all be over. We'll both have what we want."

"I'm not sure."

Smoke rose from the chimney at the Aerie. So close. Maybe he should handle this himself. He'd trusted too much already. Except that he couldn't risk being seen by the witch in the kitchen. Not when he could smell the sweet scent of success. So he tightened the clamp. "Not sure about what? That he didn't screw you over? That he wouldn't do it again in a second?"

"You're right."

The words defused a grenade of fury and hot shrapnel peppered his brain. "Like you said. Too late now. You can get what you want or you can lose it all. The choice is yours."

Not that there really was a choice. They both had too much to lose. And he wouldn't hesitate to sacrifice this dupe to get his new life. Bernie owed it to him.

"But—"

"Your secret won't be safe…"

A beat of silence, then resignation. "Okay, but it's the last thing."

For now. He smiled. "Here's what I want you to do."

Chapter Twelve

Kiki's entire apartment could have fit inside the kitchen at the Aerie. The interior was surprisingly cozy, given the neglected state of the exterior. A lace doily and a glass bowl of rose-scented potpourri sat on top of the thirty-six-inch television set that crowded the corner. Covered with floral slipcovers and accented with peach-and-powder-blue pillows, the sofa and chair looked comfortable enough to hug whoever sat on them. The cream-colored afghan, the braided rug and the plants made the small area inviting.

Dressed in black stretch pants that had black daisies embroidered along the sides and a black crochet lace-up tunic that showed off her push-up bra, Kiki invited them in. Her hair, a froth of pale apricot, was piled into a brittle cloud on top of her head. Her face, even with its artful makeup, looked as if it had seen many miles of rough road. A rose quartz butterfly on a suede string fluttered madly at her neck as she offered them coffee and a piece of grocery-store cinnamon pastry. Sebastian and Kingsley refused, opting instead to get down to work. Liv accepted and sat down with Kiki to try to alleviate her fears.

Kiki watched Kingsley and Sebastian work, paying only scant attention to the conversation Liv tried to keep moving forward.

"How does it work?" Kiki asked, flicking the short painted nails of one hand against those of the other.

"When someone calls, the machine traces the place of origin of the call."

Kiki glanced from Sebastian to Kingsley. "They'll have to be here?"

"No, the information'll go straight to a computer at our local office." Technically not a lie. She had said "our", not the USMS's, office.

"Every call?"

Liv nodded.

Kiki cleared her throat and studied her coral nails. "For how long?"

"Just until Nelson calls."

She nodded slowly, her mouth becoming a thin line.

Kingsley pointed at the closed door Liv assumed was a bedroom. "I'm going to need to get in that room to run some wires."

The click of Kiki's nails suddenly sounded like insects eating their way through a closet. "That's Nelson's office. I'm not allowed in there."

"I won't touch anything. I just need to run some wire."

"It's locked." She squeezed her legs tighter together. "I don't have a key."

Kingsley smiled, showing his boyish dimples. "No problem."

He turned and bent over the doorknob. Kiki sprang up. Her high-heeled shoes clacked on the beige linoleum separating the living room from the rest of the apartment. "I don't think that's a good idea."

By the time she reached Kingsley, the door was open. She stopped and stood so still that Liv held her own breath in sympathy.

Kingsley whistled. Sebastian looked up from his huddled position on the floor and unfolded himself like a hawk riding a thermal. He looked over Kingsley's shoulder. Liv followed, drawn to the spectacle that had them all so entranced.

The room held one battered black metal desk. On the desk sat a phone with enough lines to serve a telemarketing firm. The rest of the room was filled with so many boxes that she couldn't tell what color the walls were painted or where the window was located. And each of the boxes was stamped ''USMS.''

''Where did those come from?'' The hard edge of Sebastian's voice shredded the tension in the room like talons across a yard of silk. When he was working, he seemed to have no give.

''I—I don't know.'' Eyes round, Kiki stepped back. Like Bluebeard's curious wife, she seemed afraid of her inevitable punishment.

Liv took her elbow and led her to the sofa where she sat her down. ''It's okay.''

Sebastian leaned over the side of the sofa and spoke directly into Kiki's ear. ''Where did those boxes come from?''

Kiki flinched as if he'd hit her.

Liv punched his shoulder, pushing him off. ''You're scaring her.''

Sebastian leaned in again. ''You know. I know you know. If you don't tell me, I'll take you in as an accessory to theft.''

Kiki's hands snapped into fists and she banged them against her thighs. ''I don't know. I don't know where the boxes came from. I don't know who brought them here. I don't know where they're going.''

''Not good enough.''

Kiki's eyes narrowed. ''I *don't* know.''

Liv moved too fast and the room swam for a moment. She stepped between Sebastian and the sofa's edge, half-twisting her ankle in the process. The glacial cold of his eyes made her shiver. As close as they had been last night, this facet of her husband reminded her that he was still a stranger. She could not guess at the chaos rioting in his mind, but this state was not conducive to getting Kiki to talk. "Why don't you go see exactly what's in those boxes while I talk to Mrs. Weld?"

His nostrils flared as he glared at her. She didn't like the thinness of the line that separated predator and prey, how it wavered so gray against the sharp contrast of what she'd thought of as black and white. Right now, it seemed that only a flick of that thread would turn him into one of the outlaws he hunted.

"Sebastian, please," she whispered, her heart full of a heaviness she couldn't explain.

A splinter of life returned to the dead of his eyes, and she let out her caged breath. With a sharp nod, he relented and strode back to the office.

"Mrs. Weld." Liv crouched next to Kiki. She took Kiki's hands in hers and gave an encouraging squeeze. Here was a woman who dreamed of a better life and so had turned a blind eye to what she didn't want to see—as if what she didn't acknowledge couldn't hurt her. "Where did those boxes come from?"

"I don't know."

"Did you see Nelson bring them in?" Only six months out of jail. He'd worked fast.

Kiki took in a shaky breath and studied the ceiling as if the water stains would spell out the right answer. "I work at the shop five days a week. He could have brought them in when I'm at work." She shrugged, unwilling, it seemed, to admit she'd seen the contents of the office before Kingsley opened the forbidden door. ''That door's always locked.''

''Did he bring people home?''

She shrugged. ''All the time. I don't pay much attention to them. They're messy and rude. I usually go out when he brings his clients home.''

''Did you hear him mention any names?''

Kiki let her head fall to her chest. ''I try not to listen, you know. It's his business, and he doesn't want me involved.''

''But even when you don't try, sometimes something slips through.'' How else could she have stepped so easily into Sebastian's role?

Kiki shook her head. Her amber eyes swam with tears. ''I don't know. I really don't know.''

''It's okay.''

Sebastian came out of Nelson's office with determined strides. He sat on the glass-and-chrome coffee table and faced Kiki. His control was leashed, but the predator's purposefulness shimmered through the superficial calm. ''Do you know anyone named Sean Greco?''

Kiki shrank back from the force of Sebastian's voice and shook her head.

''Built like a heavyweight boxer, crew cut, wears gray ostrich cowboy boots.''

Kiki perked up. ''Yeah. He's got a bulldog named Buster. I take Buster for walks when he comes over.''

''When was the last time he was here?''

As she tapped a coral nail on a front tooth, her forehead wrinkled in concentration. ''I guess it was almost two weeks ago. I was pissed because it was freezing cold and Nelson made me take Buster out anyway.''

''Did you see any of those boxes that day?''

''No. He didn't stay long. But Nelson was gone the next

day. He came back while I was at work and tracked mud all over the place.'' Her hand drew an imaginary line from the front door to the office door.

"Thanks," he said. "You've been a great help." He turned to Kingsley. "Are we set?"

"Give me a test buzz." While he dialed Kiki's number on his cell phone, he explained to her how the machine worked. Five minutes later, they were out the door and back in the SUV.

"What was that all about?" she asked as Sebastian roared down the quiet residential road. A headache took up residence at her temple and seemed determined to hammer itself a home.

"Crooked cop." He ground out the words as if they weren't worth their weight in spit. "No wonder Sutton wanted this boxed."

"I don't understand."

"The investigation officially belonged to the FBI. If they found out the dead marshal was dirty, they'd make sure the news hit the media. That would *not* make Sutton's day. The Service has a hard enough time getting the respect it deserves without having a dirty marshal paraded all over the media. Case closed. No exposure."

"How do you know he's dirty?"

"I don't. Yet."

"We found Greco's name in Weld's computer," Kingsley said. "I copied his hard drive. I should have more information soon."

Could be nothing. Could be everything. "So what do we do now?"

Sebastian merged onto the highway. "*We* don't do anything."

"You're not going to follow through?"

"I didn't say that."

She was smart enough to realize he was planning to leave her behind as he tracked the next piece of evidence. And she was also smart enough not to mention that she wasn't planning on playing the meek and mild wife and obeying him blindly. She concentrated on the snowy scenery that seemed to turn Route 101 into a postcard, and tried not to dwell on the strange tremor in her right hand.

When they reached the Aerie, Sebastian caught Kingsley's eye in the rearview mirror. "Find me everything you can on Greco. And get me the paperwork I need to make this legal."

"Make what legal?" Liv asked, caught in the crosscurrent of his and Kingsley's common ground. Kingsley gathered his equipment and hurried inside without answering.

The engine revved under Sebastian's impatient foot. "Why don't you go in? I'll be back in a couple of hours."

Her headache pounded in answer, and she massaged one temple. "I don't think so."

He was looking for an excuse to cut her loose—just as he'd done with Olivia.

"Liv—"

"You don't scare me."

He closed his eyes and swallowed hard. "I should."

"You don't have to become one of them to do your job."

His gaze found hers and held it, showing her all the hard edges his work had sculpted. "How else am I going to find them?"

Deep in the dark of his eyes, she spied the flicker of vulnerability, a scrap of fear so raw she wanted to reach for him, hold him and tell him everything would be all right. "You can't catch them all."

His gaze snapped back to the windshield. "I have to try."

Loss hummed between them.

"You don't have to do it alone."

Though she yearned to touch him, the new bond they'd started to forge last night was too fragile. She didn't want to risk breaking it. Hands folded primly in her lap, she looked ahead as if the car were already moving. She could not let him shut her out. She'd already given up too many parts of herself. "So where are we going?"

Sebastian growled out a curse, but threw the transmission in gear. "A small town with the appropriate name of Hemlock, Massachusetts."

NESTLED IN A RING of evergreens, Greco's home outside the small town of Hemlock had Sebastian whistling in appreciation. The brown contemporary sat on 2.5 acres—far enough from town to shield Greco from curious onlookers, but close enough to get a six-pack of beer at the convenience store should he run low. A curving lane offered privacy and protection. Peeking through the garage window, Sebastian saw a screaming red 'vette and space for the Blazer Greco had died in. A snow thrower and a ride-on lawn mower shared another bay with a speedboat tarped for winter, a couple of Wave Runners, a couple of dirt bikes and a couple of snowmobiles.

"Lots of expensive toys," Liv said beside him.

"Even for a bachelor with no dependents, these add up to more than he can afford on a marshal's salary." Just like all the scum he chased, Greco must have thought himself invincible. He'd died intestate, making his list of assets a public record.

"Maybe he was independently wealthy."

"Not according to his file. His father drives a truck. His mother works on a factory assembly line." The parents stood to inherit their son's assets, but the court had placed an interesting notation on Greco's probate paperwork. An Alan Verani claimed that he should inherit Greco's goods because of an oral contract they had. Sebastian headed toward the house.

Liv caught up to him. "Maybe the roommate is wealthy."

"According to Kingsley, Mr. Verani is currently unemployed and his bank account doesn't have enough to keep a dog in kibbles."

As they reached the ornate front door, she looked at him and smiled. "Should I play the bad cop this time?"

He couldn't help it; he laughed. "You couldn't play a bad cop if you tried."

"Is that a dare?"

He gave her a quick kiss. "No, it's the truth. Let's see if Mr. Verani is home."

Knowing the world at its worst hurt. Having Liv share this evil with him hurt even more. He'd done everything he could to make her world as safe and as beautiful as he could by keeping work and home completely apart. Out in the field, he wanted results and took plenty of legal latitude when he tracked his targets. Because he'd always put the Service ahead of himself, he'd never had to worry about the consequences of breaking the law to catch a fugitive.

He'd done a lot of good. More than most people dreamed of.

Now, having violated both the Service's unspoken code and his own, he would have to bear whatever fallout came of this alone. He was doing what he had to do. But if Liv got hurt because of him, he'd never forgive himself. Having her grow a stubborn streak was not making the situation any easier for him.

"You're to stay behind me. Is that understood?"

Placing both hands together, she gave a small bow. "Yes, Sebastian-san, two steps behind."

"This isn't a joking matter, Liv. I don't want you hurt." He crushed the doorbell with his thumb. Inside the chimes jingled a melody. Low barks exploded somewhere at the back of the house and grew closer.

"I'm not planning on letting myself get hurt."

"You don't have any experience with this type of people. They go by their own laws." His knowledge had come at a price—one he didn't want her to pay.

"You're right. I have no experience. It's all been wiped from my memory. I need to understand why."

She was like this because of him. He owed her answers. He just wished she'd let him find them on his own. "Stay behind me."

The barks vibrated against the stained-glass panel on the front door. Nails scratched at the wood. A bass voice yelled at the dog to shut up.

The door opened a crack. Dog slobber splotched the toe of Sebastian's boot. Five feet higher, a dark eye glared at him. "What do you want?"

"A look inside Sean Greco's home." He held up the warrant on which he'd forged a judge's signature. Kingsley was at work getting him the real thing, but right now, time was of the essence. If the bluff worked, it would buy them a couple of hours.

The dark eye narrowed. "Sean's dead." Verani then told Sebastian exactly what he could do with his request and tried to slam shut the door.

Sebastian's steel-toed boot held it open. "We can do this my way or the hard way. Either way, I get to take a peek inside. Want me to call in the local cops?"

The dark eye became a slit oozing with disdain.

"There's no reason why he should've been tortured like that. No reason why you should torture me now."

"I'm trying to find out why he was killed. I'm going to make sure whoever did this to him pays for it."

The door jerked open. With a vicious growl, the bulldog sank its teeth into Sebastian's pant leg, tearing holes in the wool blend. Sebastian ignored the beast and walked in as if a fifty-five pound, brown and buff, muscle-bound miniature weight lifter didn't impair him.

With Verani—who was a human version of the dog—on one side, Liv on the other and the dog still attached to his leg, Sebastian made his way through the house. With its vaulted ceiling, fully equipped kitchen, top-of-the-line game room, fireplace in the master suite and sunken, oversized whirlpool tub in the bath, this was definitely a showplace. Someone had dropped big bucks to decorate the place, turning it into a designer's idea of what macho should look like. Interesting, too, was the fact that, of all the nine rooms in the house, only one was a bedroom. How close were Greco and Verani?

He walked into a room decorated with hunter-green plaid wallpaper and burgundy hunting prints. "Is this Sean's office?"

"It *was*." The short, squat man got a little teary. Sebastian silently swore.

"How close were you and Sean?"

The round black eyes gleamed with tears. "As close as brothers. I loved him."

No wonder Sutton was passing bricks. Not only did he have two dead marshals to worry about, he had to deal with the fact that one of the dead agents was possibly dirty *and* gay. The Feebs would love nothing better than to tag the Service with something like this. Blowback of the worst kind.

The dog lost his taste for wool and went to sniff Olivia's shoes. When she scratched him behind the ears, he turned into a pathetic mooch, begging for more.

Sebastian looked over the desk, the drawers and the open agenda book. He saw nothing out of the ordinary—calculator, pens, rubber bands, a pad of Post-it notes, a handful of matchbooks. He flipped through the files in the wood cabinet—bills, mortgage papers, bank statements, investment statements, insurance records. Then he opened the closet door. "Bingo!"

Crammed into the space were boxes of folders, tape, pencils, paper clips, ink cartridges, reams of paper—enough stuff to last Greco a lifetime. And all the boxes were labeled "USMS."

"Just like Kiki's apartment," Liv said, still petting the dog.

"Yeah." Sebastian turned to Verani. "Why don't you have a seat, Mr. Verani?"

"What for?" Verani's tone of voice had the bulldog scrabbling away from Liv and setting his sights on Sebastian. The dog seemed to choke on his own tongue as he tried for a cross between a growl and a bark.

"We need to have a little talk." Sebastian patted the wing chair, but Verani ignored him.

"I don't have to say anything to you." Verani started to leave. Sebastian blocked his way. "We can do it here or I can haul you in for obstructing justice."

Bared teeth aimed at Sebastian's leg, the bulldog snarled. So did Verani. "Then haul."

Sebastian had to keep the whole situation cool and calm. The last thing he wanted was to have the incident turn. Watching Liv out of the corner of his eye, he speared Verani with his most cutting glare and reached for handcuffs. The bulldog snagged the pants and tugged, growling all the while.

"We're on your side," Liv, ever the good cop, said. "We're trying to find out who murdered your friend."

Verani studied her, then shifted his gaze to the nails of one of his hands. "Right."

"How did you meet Greco?" Following Liv's lead and ignoring the dog shredding his pants, Sebastian adopted a more relaxed pose.

Verani crossed his arms, beefing up his torso to appear bigger than he was. "At a club where we both go." *Make something of it,* his attitude said. The dog's growl seconded the scorn.

Sebastian didn't care which way Greco bent. What he wanted to understand was why a good cop had turned bad.

"Tell me about it." Liv sat on the desk's corner. When Verani saw no judgment on her face, he opened like a spigot. The story of love and betrayal seemed to tranquilize the dog. He let go of Sebastian's pant leg, plopped on top of his boots and snored.

"It's your own kind that turned him," Verani said, spearing Sebastian with a narrowed gaze. "If you hadn't made life so difficult for him, then he wouldn't have had to get his payback."

During a raid, one of the fugitives had recognized Greco from the club and fingered him as gay. From that time on, being part of any USMS operation had turned to hell on earth for Greco. As if his choice of lifestyle was a threat to their masculinity. Anger led to skimming part of the take on a bust involving drugs. During one of his investigations, Greco had come in contact with Weld, a petty thief into fencing. Stealing from the USMS, Greco had discovered, was easy. And he'd soothed his wounds—real and imagined—in the balm of the luxuries the goods he stole from them bought him.

"Let's go," Sebastian said.

"Where?"

"If you're telling the truth, then you have nothing to worry about."

Sebastian took Verani to a private polygraph analyst and paid cash for the test. It wasn't that polys were reliable, but Sutton would want some corroboration of Verani's story. Doing the poly back channel gave Sutton the option of burying it.

Verani passed the test with flying colors.

Somehow all this—Olivia's accident, Kershaw's escape, Greco and Carmichael's murders, Greco's greed and anger—all fit together. But Sebastian still wasn't sure how. There were too many blanks between the chunks of evidence.

Sebastian dropped Verani back home. He had barely gotten on the highway to head to the Aerie when he noticed that Liv had fallen asleep. He shrugged out of his coat and draped it over her. Paula would cut him to pieces for tiring her out. But he'd seen the thrill glow in Liv's eyes. He'd felt the adrenaline flow through her blood as they uncovered evidence. She'd tasted a bit of his life. Even swimming in this cesspool hadn't seemed to detract her. He hadn't expected such strength in her.

And he could not deny her this discovery of her strength, even if he knew it meant she would outgrow her need for him. He'd already taken too much from her.

They were crossing into New Hampshire when the first hit came in on the trap-and-trace.

Chapter Thirteen

The first time Nelson Weld called home, he used his cell phone. All Kingsley could tell Sebastian was that Weld was west of the Mississippi. Sebastian had the number disconnected.

The next evening, Weld called from a pay phone and reversed the charges. Kingsley located him at a bar in Denver.

Denver—Grand Central Station for fugitives. From there, he could head to the northwest, California, Canada or Mexico. All options were open—depending on which way the wind blew and how skittish he got.

"We've got a visual on him," Skyralov said after Sebastian had passed on the information. Music drummed a pagan beat in the background. "He's crying in his beer at the bar. Want us to have a little talk with him?"

"Better coordinate with the local office." Sebastian didn't want to jeopardize Reed and Skyralov's careers just because his own gut couldn't digest the meal of sugared lies placed in front of him. "And the Feebs."

"I could have him singing in no time."

Sebastian had no doubt Skyralov could deliver on that promise, but he didn't want to burn all his bridges with

Sutton. When all this was over, Sebastian still needed his job. So did Skyralov. "Let's go by the book on this one."

THE USUALLY GRACEFUL and confident Liv seemed to turn into a klutz overnight. She'd dropped both her glass of orange juice and her teacup at breakfast. Her hand had missed her fork several times. Her right foot seemed to catch on shadows, and she'd tripped down the stairs as they'd gone to the office. If Sebastian hadn't caught her, he hated to think how she might have hurt herself. And her memory seemed to grow fuzzier by the hour. How often had he caught her rubbing an invisible ache at her temple since they'd woken up? Had he allowed her to do too much? Was his weakness in giving in to her responsible for her worsening condition? While Cari had Liv distracted upstairs, Sebastian called Dr. Iverson, her neurologist.

"Slow, jerky or uncontrolled movements are normal for the type of injury your wife sustained," Dr. Iverson said.

Sebastian frowned. "But she seems to have no muscle strength on the right side."

"The hemiparesis should improve with time."

Sebastian picked up the pen on the desk and doodled question marks across the blotter. "She seems to be getting headaches more frequently, too."

"It's only been ten days since her accident. You can't expect her brain injury to heal completely in such a short time. She may look normal, but her brain took quite a beating."

In those ten days—was it only ten days? It felt like a lifetime since her car had run off the road—she'd become a whole different person. Strong. Independent. Courageous. She was handling adversity like a winner. In the process, he'd forgotten how truly fragile her situation was.

He'd gotten used to the changes in her. To the soft steel of her strength. Liked it, even. And he hated himself for wanting Olivia to retain Liv's boldness. He flicked the pen away. "She was doing so well."

"Is she still taking her medication?"

"Every day."

"If you're worried," Dr. Iverson said grudgingly, "I can take a look at her."

Sebastian heaved a sigh of relief. "Yes, I'd like that."

"Bring her in tomorrow and we'll run some tests." Sebastian heard the flip of pages. "I have a cancellation at 10:15."

"We'll be there."

BALANCING THE COMPUTER on his knees in a fast food can, the stench of a urinal cake assaulting his nose, he pounded the keys, looking for Okie. He didn't like being played. Didn't Okie think he'd find out? All this for nothing? No, he refused to accept the game ended here.

Sk8Thor: The info U gave me is no good.
Okie: What do U mean?
Sk8Thor: There's nothing there.
Okie: What did U want?
Sk8Thor: U can't b that stupid.
Okie: Up yours!
Sk8Thor: Where's the rest?
Okie: The rest of what?
Sk8Thor: The $.
Okie: U didn't tell me U were looking for $.
Sk8Thor: What did U think I wanted the @%*&! acct. #s for?
Okie: Scramble.

He swore. That's what he got for trusting. He kept having to learn that lesson over and over again. First Nadine. Then Bernie. All the way down to this piece of worthless flesh. Everyone, *everyone,* had cheated him out of his due. *Maybe you're the one who's stupid,* he thought. He dismissed the notion with a jerk of his shoulder. Well, he'd show them he wasn't out for the count yet. He cracked his knuckles and typed.

Sk8Thor: Where is it stashed?
Okie: He doesn't have much.
Sk8Thor: What about the house?
Okie: A wedding gift.
Sk8Thor: The rest?
Okie: Hers.

Swerving as he swore, he punched the flimsy wall of the bathroom stall. Pieces of plaster pinged on the dirty tiles of the floor. He signed off the stolen laptop and paced the confines of the room.

Someone knocked at the door.

"Get lost!"

Just as he was about to take his frustration out on the hapless customer waiting to take a leak, an idea came to him. "Of course."

If he couldn't get it one way, he'd get it another. He'd aimed right the first time. Now all he had to do was see it through. It didn't matter much how he got where he wanted to go—as long as he got there.

As he yanked open the restroom door, he saw himself sipping beer from an open bar. Palms trees swaying in the background. Bikini-clad girls promenading on the beach with the eye-hurting blue of the ocean behind them. *That's the ticket.* Key West. A nice place to start over. He'd heard a man could be himself there and no one would bother him.

LIV AWOKE IN A SWIRL of black and nausea that coated her like dry black acrylic on white pine. She could not move her right arm. She could not move her right leg. She could not feel anything except the hammer pounding at her temples. Lost and alone, she was flaking to pieces, and she didn't know how to hold herself together.

Then arms embraced her, held her tight. Sebastian's sure voice lifted the veil of darkness and dizziness and brought her back to the nest of quilts and flannel sheets that was their bed, back to her body. "Shh, it's okay. You're all right, Liv. I'm here."

She hung on to him, afraid of losing what she'd found since Olivia had died and Liv was born. If she kept looking for the tracks Olivia had left behind, she would get stuck in the dark. And she didn't want to end up alone in the blackness of her own mind. She needed a home to belong to. She needed the security Sebastian offered her. She needed him.

This skin-to-skin connection was real. Everything else was illusion. This relationship, this marriage, was more important than finding the things that were dead anyway.

With the steady beat of Sebastian's heart beneath her hand, with his body warm against hers, she relaxed. She would put the past away for good and look only forward.

This was her home.

This was her husband.

This was the life she chose.

Nothing else mattered.

AT SIX THE NEXT MORNING, Sutton called, a frantic edge to his voice. "What the hell's going on? Why are Reed and Skyralov in Denver? Why are they getting our guys out there involved in a bust? Why are they talking to the FBI?''

Wiping the sleep from his eyes, Sebastian sat on the edge of the bed. He'd spent the night analyzing Liv's every movement after the nightmare that left her quaking against him like a scared rabbit. She was getting worse, and he'd never felt so helpless. "I sent them there."

"I told you to stay out of this."

Sebastian felt Liv stir beside him, her hand clasped the notch between his hips and thigh. He groaned silently as her touch had the inevitable result. Hot and heavy, he slid out of bed, tucked the quilt around her shoulders, and mouthed, "Go back to sleep." To Sutton he said, "I couldn't ignore a good lead. Greco was dirty. That's what you were trying to bury."

Sutton swore. "We've got to talk about damage control. I don't need a scandal like this right now."

Not with D.C. as his next stop. Sebastian reached for jeans and stepped into them. "You can bury everything I've found."

"I want you down here now."

He glanced at Liv. She'd been clingy all night. He'd felt her fear, sensed her subtle fight to regain control of her body. There was no way he could miss their appointment with Dr. Iverson this morning. "I can't—"

"You're already on my bad side, Falconer. Don't dig yourself in deeper. I want you here now."

"My wife—"

"I told you this would happen. You started this. You finish it."

"I'll be there after her appointment."

"You'll get here *now* or I'll have your badge."

Sebastian scrubbed a hand over his face. It always came

down to this—a choice between Olivia and work. He needed them both, and each demanded he sacrifice the other. "Right."

The line went dead as Sutton slammed down his receiver.

He sat on the edge of the bed and watched Liv sleep. Her face was pale. Too pale. The bruise along the left side was still a reminder of how he'd failed her. He fingered one of the soft curls of hair that couldn't quite hide the damage. She turned her cheek to meet his palm, and a small smile curved her lips. With a satisfied sigh, she buried deeper into the pillow, taking his hand in hers and holding it to her heart.

"I love you," he whispered, then kissed her temple and slowly slipped his hand free.

One last time, Liv. He had to leave her one last time. He needed the protection of his badge until whoever had killed Kershaw was caught. It was the only way to keep her safe.

After that.... He shook his head.

At least this time, he wasn't leaving her alone. Kingsley was here. He could call Mercer back from surveillance. Paula and Cari would take her to her appointment. She wouldn't be alone. Not for a minute.

And he'd return in time to hear the results.

BY THE TIME SEBASTIAN reached Sutton's office in Boston, Weld was in custody and Sutton was wearing a groove in the industrial carpet of his office.

Unlike most paper pushers, Sutton hadn't given up his membership at the gym when he was promoted. He believed physical fitness made for a sharp mind. And he believed that a marshal was a symbol. The way he presented himself at all times was a reflection not only of himself, but of the Service. More than that, he lived what he believed. Dressed in a custom-made charcoal suit, square-faced, square-shouldered, with just enough gray at the temples to look distinguished, he was a poster boy for what a marshal should look like.

"Do you know what those Bureau pricks did?" Sutton asked before Sebastian had closed the door.

Sebastian knew better than to answer. He stood at ease, a brick wall ready to bear the bluster of Sutton's anger.

"They agreed to meet our guys across the street from the bar where Weld was," Sutton said. The vein at his temple throbbed purple. His neck was an unhealthy shade of red. "Our guys waited. But the Bureau guys never showed up. Do you know why they didn't show up?"

Sebastian shook his head, but Sutton, caught up in the steam of his fury, didn't notice.

"The Feebs went straight to the bar and popped him."

"And took the credit for the arrest," Sebastian said. "At least we got him."

Sutton stopped and pinned him with a look. "You understand we can't have him talk." His steps were slow now, deliberate. "I want something done fast. Before everything hits the fan." His eyes blazed. "I want you to do the transport. It's a short drive from jail to the airport. One man is enough. No follow car. This mutt doesn't have any friends out here to help him. Stay out of traffic." Sutton balled his fists on his desk and leaned into them, spearing Sebastian with the fervor of his intention. "I want Weld to make a break."

What Sutton left unsaid turned Sebastian's insides to ice. Sutton wanted him to kill a man in restraints to preserve the image of the Service.

When Sebastian said nothing, Sutton added, "I'll make

it right with Internal Affairs. And we can put your disciplinary action behind us.''

Sebastian opened his mouth to answer, but Sutton put up a hand. ''Don't say anything now. Sleep on it. I'll have my secretary make the arrangements.''

As he made his way back to his SUV, an oily nausea settled in his stomach. The less afraid you were to kill, the less afraid you were to die, the better chance you had to survive. That all went toward longevity. He'd killed before. But only when there was no other alternative. Only when he'd explored all other options. Survival this time meant going against instinct.

As he drove along Route 3, he felt as if he were watching himself on a wide screen. All his flaws showed up magnified. Some dark part of him didn't care whether Weld made it to court alive or not. Some part of him only cared about himself—his self-appointed mission in life, his future with the Service, his future with Liv.

He'd made a lot of sacrifices for the Service, but it seemed the more he gave, the more they wanted. Now they were asking for his soul.

And the worst part was that he was even considering it. A man like Weld had no future. He'd be in and out of the system for the rest of his life. Society would be better off without the likes of him staining its face.

But for all his faults, Weld wasn't violent. He was a nuisance, but not a killer.

The road was a blur in his window. His body responded to the rubber band push-and-pull of traffic automatically. The flap of windshield wipers flicking snow from the glass became a backbeat to the pounding of his thoughts.

All of his life he'd sought justice for the innocent. He'd wanted to do the greatest good for the greatest number.

He'd wanted to make the world safe for people like his parents. For Olivia. For the family he'd once planned.

If he did as he was asked, what did that make him?

No better than the scum he hunted.

If he didn't?

Then he'd be as lost as Olivia.

As he crossed into New Hampshire, the snowfall lightened. The Everett Turnpike curved near exit 4. Snowcovered mountains, white and granite gray against the steel of the sky, came into view. He thought of Liv. He thought of the Aerie. He thought of all he'd done to protect them. And something inside him settled.

He picked up his phone. Skyralov answered. "Sutton's sending orders for a transport. You and Reed are on it. Make sure nothing happens to Weld on the way home."

When he got to the Aerie, no welcoming light greeted him from the front porch. The kitchen windows were dark. So were all the others.

Sebastian frowned as he pressed the remote to open the garage door. Were they still at the hospital? Was something wrong? He glanced at his watch. Why weren't they back? *There's no point panicking before you know the facts,* he told himself as he parked the SUV.

A smiling Kingsley greeted him when he entered the office. "How did it go?"

Sebastian grumbled. "Where are the girls?"

"Cari called and said they were going out for an early dinner before coming home. They'll bring back take-out."

A snake of apprehension wound itself around his guts. He didn't like the idea of Liv being out there, open and vulnerable. Paula and Cari were no protection against whoever had killed Kershaw. Why had he thought she would be? For someone like that, life held no meaning.

"I've got the lowdown on Weld." Kingsley passed over

a sheaf of papers. "According to him, all he did was bring a car to the rendezvous point. He says he didn't do any of the killings."

"Weld's greedy, but he doesn't have the stomach for blood."

Kingsley nodded. "He passed the polys. He didn't want to talk, but he finally cut a deal. He says Greco was in on Kershaw's escape, that Greco was being paid for his co-operation."

"How about Carmichael? Was he in on it, too?" That was more manure than even Sutton could bury.

"Wrong place, wrong time." Kingsley leaned back in his chair and hooked both thumbs around his red suspenders.

Sebastian couldn't believe Greco had sacrificed one of his own men to feed his greed. *It's your own kind that turned on him.* "Pull up Carmichael's jacket. And I want to take a look at the pictures taken at the scene of the murders."

"What's up?"

"A hunch."

"Going to let me in on it?"

"I think Greco chose Carmichael for a reason. What he didn't count on was that Kershaw would do to him what he was doing to Carmichael." Felon loyalty didn't stretch far. And Kershaw had good reasons to hate everyone associated with the Service—even someone on his team.

Sebastian grabbed his keys. "There's still something missing. Has Mercer checked in yet?"

"No." Kingsley glanced at his watch, then double-checked the time on the computer. "I don't like it."

"Neither do I." Sebastian headed for the door. Mercer wasn't much on procedures, but he understood the value of having someone know where you were. If he hadn't checked in, something was wrong. "Pull up the jail phone records we have in Kershaw's file, the phone records for his mother's house and Weld's phone records."

"Where are you going?" Kingsley asked.

"To check on the take-out. Olivia always forgets to order Ma La Lamb. Golden Pagoda?"

Kingsley nodded and eyed Sebastian's run through his equipment. "Need back-up?"

"I need you here. Try to locate Mercer. Pull up those records."

Once more, Sebastian had let the job win over Liv. Once more, he'd made the wrong decision. He should never have let her out of his sight.

Chapter Fourteen

Liv sipped green tea from a small white cup without a handle and ignored the moo shu vegetables on her plate, even though she was told the dish was her favorite. Cari ate her chicken fried rice as if she hadn't seen food for a month. Paula mostly stirred her shrimp lo mein around her plate with chopsticks as if doing so would prevent anyone from noticing she wasn't actually putting anything in her mouth.

The tinny music playing in the background picked at Liv's headache like a hen at crushed corn. The scent of grease and soy sauce stirred the cauldron of nausea in her stomach. All the tests they'd put her through at the hospital seemed to have sapped what little energy she had, leaving her disconnected from the world as if she were halfway to being a ghost.

She didn't look impaired—even her bruises were fading fast—so everyone expected her to act as she had before the accident. It was as if she was living a secret. But Liv couldn't let anyone see how close to disappearing she really was. Fear was shaking the small sense of self she'd recently discovered, making everything seem uncertain.

You are more than your pain. She tried to remember Cecilia's words of wisdom, but they were getting harder and harder to believe. Six to eight weeks, Dr. Iverson had told her, for the bruised tissues in her brain to heal. Six to eight more weeks of this subtle but constant pain. It seemed such an impossibly long time to wait for the dizziness, headaches and weakness to ebb.

She wanted Sebastian here, now. She wanted to see the dark of his eyes shine at the sight of her—the way they had last night when she'd come out of the shower. She wanted the solid feel of him to anchor her before she floated away. What had happened in Boston? Why had she told him not to worry about her, to concentrate on his business? She should have gone with him. If he had found something new, would he leave her out just as he'd left Olivia in the dark?

"We should go shopping," Cari helped herself to a shrimp from her mother's plate. "There's a quasi mall in Keene, isn't there?"

Paula sighed wearily. "Olivia needs to rest."

"I am tired," Liv agreed. The day had been long for all of them. Cari had tried to keep them entertained with a monologue of her job search, but Liv couldn't quite recall any of it. Paula had remembered to ask the doctor, nurses and technicians all the questions Liv forgot. And Liv had begun to see that her sister's tough crust was an act of self-protection. She hurt easily, adding the wounds of the people she loved to her own as if her sacrifice would lessen their burdens and thicken her skin.

Paula shooed away a fly that wasn't there. "Sebastian will worry if he gets home before we do."

"Since when do you care what he thinks?" Cari stabbed at the chicken in her fried rice as if it wasn't quite dead yet.

Paula sighed again. "He loves her."

"Like that's news."

And in the downcast resignation of Paula's shoulders, Liv saw that it *was* a new realization. Did Paula feel as if she'd lost whatever tug-of-war for her affection she and Sebastian were playing?

"We've been cooped up forever in that stuffy house." Cari signaled the waiter for a refill of her Coke. "And we need to get the hospital smell out of our noses."

"Bubble bath." Liv thought of sinking into a tubful of bubbles and could imagine the tightness in her muscles unwinding. Peppermint and rosemary. Or maybe lavender for a good night's sleep.

"Yes," Paula agreed with a long draw of breath.

They both smiled over their cups of tea. Cari looked at one then the other, then settled on Liv. Her forehead wrinkled and her eyes narrowed, accusing. "You're turning into an old lady."

"I'm just tired," Liv said, feeling as if she'd somehow disappointed her niece. "We'll do something tomorrow."

"Yeah." Cari stabbed at her food. "Hey, remember that gallery I told you about?"

"The one in the pink Victorian?"

"Yeah." Cari rolled the thick leather of her watchband over her thin wrist. "I checked my messages in the car. They offered me a job framing."

"That's great, Cari." Liv meant to add more encouragement and ask more questions, but just then the restaurant door opened, blowing in a cold slap of air. Sebastian walked in, and her whole insides seemed to light up.

"Hi! What are you doing here?" Maybe the new drug the doctor had given her was finally kicking in, or maybe it was just the sight of worry slipping out of Sebastian's eyes, but the tingling in her hand and foot abated and the headache seemed to lift.

He kissed her and slid into the empty chair next to hers.

Wanting to hang on to the solid feel of him, she reached for his hand. He squeezed her fingers and didn't let go. And his dark and endless gaze seemed wide enough to hold only her. "I wanted to be sure you brought home some Ma La Lamb. It's too spicy for you, so you usually forget."

Even before. Liv smiled. "Paula thought of it."

Without looking at Paula, he said, "Thanks. I appreciate it." And Liv knew he meant more than the Ma La Lamb. Asking Paula to take her to her appointment had seemed to cut the heart right out of him this morning. He'd called three times in the space of an hour. Finally, Paula had grabbed the phone and told him that the hospital personnel were asking her to shut the phone off for the duration of the tests. She'd bet anything Paula had forgotten to turn it back on and that was why Sebastian was here.

"Funny how you can make time for lamb, but not for Liv." Cari pushed away her plate. Liv wondered at the anger threading through her voice.

"That's enough, Cari," Paula said wearily.

Cari scraped her chair back. "I know. My opinion doesn't count. I'm going to the ladies' room." The thick heels of her black boots left scuff marks on the linoleum aisle.

"What's with her?" Sebastian asked.

"Teenager," Paula said.

"Long, boring day," Liv said.

A long day that suddenly seemed to spread longer. There were too many inches separating her from Sebastian, too many people around them, too much noise against the beat of their pulses trying to find each other's rhythm. Then, as if something was unleashed by their need to touch the other, their words spilled and wound around each other.

"How did it go?" he asked.

"What happened?" she asked at the same time. Then she smiled and pulled him up. "Let's go home."

She wanted to draw that bubble bath and share it with him while they exchanged the separate tracks of their day. She wanted to fall asleep wrapped in the glow of their lovemaking and wake up with him spooned around her. She wanted him so desperately it charged her with new energy. With unknown danger hovering at the edge of their lives, squeezing every drop of good out of the present seemed more important than ever. After all, yesterday was nothing but black, and tomorrow was only a gray ghost.

The heat in Sebastian's eyes and in the spread of his smile seemed to agree. Leaving Paula and Cari to catch up, he paid for their bill and grabbed their take-out order. All the while, he held on fiercely to Liv's hand, making her feel as if nothing bad could ever touch her again.

WITH THE CHINESE TAKE-OUT getting cold on the conference table in the office, Sebastian, with Liv at his side, went over everything the team had found. Reed and Skyralov would transport Weld in the morning. Kingsley was out trying to locate the missing Mercer.

Sebastian rubbed his eyes as he reached once more for the phone records from the prison, Kershaw's mother, Greco and Weld. "According to Weld, Greco was in on the escape. Weld was to have a car waiting in Connecticut. And Weld passed the polys. What I don't see is any communication between Weld, Greco or Kershaw."

"Third party," Liv said. Her shoulder rubbed his as she ran a finger down each of the pages. Instinctively, Sebastian wrapped his arm around her shoulder and the frustration stringing him tight loosened its grip.

"I thought of that," he said. "But the mother had no contact with Weld or with Greco."

"Unless they used pay phones."

Sebastian rubbed the nape of his neck. "Jail records show incoming calls and Kershaw had none from Greco or Weld." He reached for the phone. "There's one way to shed one ray of light on this."

It took some wheeling and dealing, but he finally got Weld on the line. "How did you make the arrangements with Greco and Kershaw?"

Thinking singing was going to get him away scot-free, Weld became a canary. "Phone."

"It doesn't show in the records."

"I don't know who he was. He'd call, pay and I'd deliver. That's what I do. I fill needs."

Yeah, a real upstanding guy. "How'd you know he was real? A job like that, he could've been setting you up."

"The code." Smugness tainted Weld's voice.

"The code?" Sebastian frowned.

"Yeah, he gave me the code, so I knew it was coming from Bernie."

"What code?"

The chains around Weld's wrists rattled. "We had a deal. If one of us needed something, we'd use a code word."

"So this guy calls you and gives you the code, and you get him a car."

"Yeah, that's right." Weld's relief sounded like a balloon losing air.

"And you have no idea who this guy is?"

"Never saw him. No name. No nothing."

And that's how business was done, Sebastian thought as he disconnected. The answer was here, he just couldn't see it yet.

To keep himself sane, he punched in Kingsley's number. "Anything on Mercer yet?"

"He bought groceries at Gus's Market on 101. Looked like he was heading off on a hike."

"We'll follow in the morning. I don't need to go rescue two of you."

"Give me a little credit here, Falconer. I grew up in these mountains. I know my way around."

"Safety first."

"Always."

Even though the case was technically closed. Even though the team was technically not a team anymore. Even though Mercer was pursuing his own lead on his own time, he was doing Sebastian a favor, and that made Sebastian responsible for his well-being. Always, officer survival came first. Where the hell was he, and what was he up to? Sebastian hoped Mercer wasn't leading Kingsley into more trouble. Eagle Scout or not, these mountains demanded respect.

"What happened?" Liv spooned Ma La lamb onto a plate.

Sebastian raked a hand through his hair, ignoring the food she pressed on him. "Damned if I know."

"Not to Mercer." She pushed the plate toward him. "To you. Why are you so afraid for the people around you?"

He dragged a hand over his face. "I'm not. The house is full. I'm fine."

"But it puts you on edge."

Ankles crossed in front of her, she rocked the executive chair from side to side with one heel. She reached out a hand and the tips of her fingers connected with the back of his hand. He didn't want to melt under that soft warmth. Now more than ever, he needed to stay strong. Against his will, his hand turned and his palm accepted the link she offered.

"Murder puts me on edge," he said. "Scum who refuse to take responsibility for their actions put me on edge. Fugitives who put innocent people in danger put me on edge."

She cocked her head. "Why do you feel responsible, though?"

He leaned back in his chair and shook his head against the bloody memories creeping in. "It's my job."

"It's more than that." She rolled her chair until their knees touched, then leaned forward. "Olivia knew."

He studied her as if, for the first time, he was seeing how all the pieces of her fit together. He did not recognize Olivia's patience in the face so eagerly awaiting answers. He did not meet Olivia's quiet in the blue eyes seeking to understand. He did not feel Olivia's restraint in the soft steel of her fingers. Olivia was gone, and in her place was a stranger who took up too much room in his heart. He loved her as much as he'd ever loved Olivia. He didn't want to dwell on the weakness of character that could have him switch his allegiance so easily.

"Olivia knew," he admitted.

"Tell me. I need to know, too."

He spun the chair toward the bank of electronics, skimming over the data they offered. Mercer, where are you? What are you doing? What have you found? The digital readouts blurred.

Grabbing one of the arms of his chair, Liv wheeled him back to face her. For a moment, Sebastian could almost read all the thoughts jumbling in her mind, and it scared him. He didn't want to revisit the past and see it play in her eyes. Then she sat on the floor next to him and put her head on his lap, offering the reassurance of closeness without the hardship of eye-to-eye contact.

"Tell me," she said, "please."

Tension wound his muscles into aching bundles. Silently, he stroked his fingers through the silk of her hair and tried to find his voice.

"My parents were professors at Keene State College," he said and cleared his throat. "My father's world was made up of mathematical equations." A short sharp laugh rumbled through him as dinnertime conversations played through his mind. Watching the heat spark through his parents' eyes, their smiles grow wider, as they volleyed banter back and forth had often made him feel he was at a tennis match. Once he'd even worn a whistle at the table and had them exploding with laughter when he'd called one of their shots out-of-bounds. "It's not that there wasn't any room for anything else. It's just that you could tell numbers were his passion."

"And your mother?"

"Her passion was poetry. Words were like colors are to you. She painted pictures with them. She plucked out feelings with them. She created whole new universes."

His heart grew heavy as he saw them again in his mind, alive and radiating with energy. "They were good for each other." *Like we are. If this situation ever ends, things are going to be different. I promise.* "He kept her grounded. She taught him to fly."

"And you? How did you fit in?"

The softness of her hair, her warmth draped over his knees both relaxed him. "I was their pivot point."

"That couldn't have been an easy role for a child."

He shrugged. "They were good parents."

"What happened?"

How could he explain insanity and make sense out of it? After all these years, he still did not understand how such good people found such a violent end.

"They got distracted easily." He half wished he could

blank out the pictures of the past from his memory as Olivia's accident had done for her. "Once, when I was eleven, my dad left the backdoor wide open after he took out the garbage. They went up to bed never noticing, and a deer came in." Sebastian could feel Liv's smile against his knee.

"A deer? In the house?"

"A deer in the house. The commotion in the kitchen woke us up. Dad came into my room, looking for my baseball bat. He ordered Mom and me to stay in our rooms, but of course, we didn't. Mom and Dad were inseparable. Wherever he went, so did she and vice versa. If he was going to get mugged by an intruder, she was going to be right there with him."

He shifted uncomfortably in the chair. Liv kissed his palm and her touch eased the black tide rushing at him. He tried to hold on to the sound of their laughter and not the screams he'd imagined as their last breaths, the imagined screams that had haunted his dreams for years.

"I don't know who was more surprised when he got to the kitchen, him or the doe," Sebastian said. "But she couldn't find the backdoor again and ended up sprinting through the living room. Dad tried to calculate possible paths, and Mom raved about her beauty. Neither was helping much with the situation. It took us an hour to lead her out again."

Liv craned her neck and smiled up at him. "What solution did you come up with?"

Sebastian laughed. "A clear path and potato peelings."

He became silent, and she didn't press him.

"After that," he said, "I always made sure the doors were locked."

"That was too much responsibility for a child."

"I chose it." He'd known even then his parents needed a keeper.

"Still."

He'd failed them. Closing his eyes, he let the memory of that day inch forward. "It was my best friend's birthday. We turned thirteen within weeks of each other. We always watched a marathon of movies at each other's houses on our birthdays. Tradition. We were big on that. Cam was into slapstick comedies, and we must've watched six in a row before we fell asleep." Sebastian swallowed hard. "And sometime while we were splitting our sides laughing, someone came into my parents' home."

Liv's arm stretched up and tucked itself around his waist. Suddenly, he needed her close, so he reached for her, lifted her into his lap, wrapped his arms around her as if she would fly away. Or maybe he was afraid he would—right back into the bloody mess he'd walked into that long-ago morning. He leaned his head against hers. Her scent and her warmth calmed the wild beating of his heart.

"They were sleeping. Someone woke them up and asked for their money. All they had between them was seventy-six dollars."

Liv's hand cupped his cheek. "It's okay. I'm sorry. You don't have to tell me."

"No, I want to." Sebastian closed his eyes. "He killed them. Stabbed them with a knife from their own kitchen."

"If you'd been there, you would have died, too."

He'd tried to believe that, but no matter how much he wanted to absolve himself, the conclusion he came to was always the same. "If I'd been there, the door would've been locked, and he couldn't have gotten in."

She looked at him and shook her head. "Sebastian, no. You were a child."

A child who'd understood that his parents didn't quite belong in this world. "I know."

"Sebastian…"

He kissed her bruised temple, reminding himself what happened to the people he cared for. "He was a fugitive."

"So you became a hunter."

"Yes." Something inside him gave. She understood.

"And then?"

He frowned. "Then what?"

Liv tilted her head as if she saw into the dark folds of his soul. "Well, you have whole teams of people to work with. That should make you feel secure. The power of the many to catch the few. What happened to make you turn away from them, too?"

He stared into the clear sky of her eyes. "You were always too observant."

Her grin was mischievous. "So I haven't lost all of myself."

No, the best parts were still there. The loyalty. The courage. The grounding earnestness. And he wanted to find that settled feeling again.

He kissed her softly, deeply. As her hands wound around his neck, he pushed away all thoughts of evil and violence. As good as that fuzzy teal sweater looked on her, it had to go. His hands slid up her back, taking the sweater with them. He kissed the hollow behind her ear and reveled in her gasp. He kissed the curve of her shoulder and gloried in the catch in her breath and the widening of her pupils. He unhitched the clasp of her bra, slipped the silky straps down her arms and filled his hands with her breasts. His reward—the peaking of her nipples and his own rock-hard readiness.

"I was a rookie cop," he whispered into her ear. Why

was he going there when he could plunge into her and forget all about the past?

She knuckled his cheek gently and tucked her head into the cradle of his shoulder. ''Tell me.''

He fished for her sweater and draped it around her shoulders. His fingers continued the slow exploration of the bumpy curve of her spine as the past slinked back to the present. ''Nothing ever happens in a small town. Drunk drivers. Domestic disturbances. The occasional bank robbery.''

Failure made him itch, and he tried to push Liv away. She looked at him with those sure blue eyes and shook her head. ''I'm not going anywhere.''

He swallowed around the lump in his throat and hooked his fingers in the belt loops of her jeans, holding her close. ''One night, we got a call of a domestic disturbance. By the time we got there, it had turned into a murder-suicide. We were securing the scene when we heard a noise upstairs. Mike was lead. I was watching his back. A six-year-old kid was standing there with a gun. Shot Mike right between the eyes before I had time to even react.''

She stroked a hand through his hair. ''How were you supposed to know a six-year-old was going to shoot?''

''It was in his eyes.''

''He was a child. Probably terrified.''

That didn't alter the end result. He was supposed to protect Mike. And failed. ''Mike died.''

Liv rubbed her cheek against his. ''That's why you let Olivia go.''

Silence. It bumped to the rhythm of their pulses.

''Pushing people away just because something might happen to them isn't going to stop bad things from happening,'' Liv said.

''I know.''

"People aren't meant to live as islands."

"I know."

"Sebastian…"

"Mmm."

"What happened to Olivia wasn't your fault."

He didn't say anything, but his guilt made itself tangible in the stiffening of his muscles.

"I won't let you push me away because you're afraid."

His arms tightened around her waist. "I'm not sure I could let you go."

And the confession seemed like an admission of weakness. He could not give her up anymore than he could stop breathing. She anchored him. She reminded him that the whole world wasn't the cesspool where he worked. She made him believe there was still a scrap of good inside him. He wanted her. Always.

The sweater slipped from her shoulders. He slid his hands up her bare back. She bent her head to meet his kiss and took his breath away with her fervor.

She was unfastening the buttons of his shirt and he was reaching for her zipper when the phone rang.

"Let it ring," she said, running her tongue over his lips.

"Mercer," Sebastian mumbled as he scooped up the receiver. "Falconer."

"I got a lead on Mercer," Kingsley said.

Holding on to Liv, Sebastian punched up the GPS ID beamed from Kingsley's phone. "Where are you?"

"I'm at the Spiltoir campsite near Harrisville. I found his backpack."

"And?" Sebastian asked, waiting for the other shoe to drop.

"Blood. I found blood."

Sebastian swore. Another soul on his conscience.

HE'D HAD A CLOSE CALL with the sneaky one. By the time they found that green-eyed hunter, his bones would be picked clean. While they were scrambling to find his body, he'd take away everything Falconer owned. And by the time Falconer figured it all out, he'd be in Key West sipping margaritas while bikini-clad girls pleasured him.

Sk8Thor: Tomorrow.
Okie: When?
Sk8Thor: As early as U can. He'll b busy.
Okie: OK. C U in the a.m.
Sk8Thor: Don't forget the Thermos.

Chapter Fifteen

Loose ends drove him crazy. Sebastian liked to tidy things quickly and efficiently so that he could put them behind him and move on to the next case. But these loose ends seemed to fray even more every time he tried to tie them. And every time the knot got away from him, Kershaw's mother was right there in the thick of it. He pushed away from his desk. "I have to go see her."

Liv got up, neatening the papers he'd scattered over the conference table. "I'll go with you."

"No, I need you here." Safe and sound behind these secured walls. Too many of the people under his responsibility were already spread out all over the place. He had no control over them or what happened to them. He wanted this case over. He wanted to go back to hunting alone. He wanted this one measure of peace where Liv was concerned. Besides, this would all go faster if he wasn't distracted.

She cocked her head. "Did I get in the way before?"

"No, you were a great help," he said, twining his arms around her waist. And a great distraction. Focus would fill that one last hole in the puzzle. "But I need someone here in case Kingsley calls."

She wound her arms around his neck. "He has your number."

"Skyralov and Reed should be back by lunch, and they'll need an update of what's happened to Mercer."

"They've got your number."

He pressed his forehead against hers, trying not to get lost in the blue of her eyes. "But this is where the information is, and you're the one who filed it all away."

"I did, didn't I?" A satisfied smile curled her lips. "You need me."

"I need you." *More than you know.*

THE AFTERGLOW OF SEBASTIAN'S confidence in her didn't last long. After an hour, she'd run out of things to neaten in the office and boredom set in. Padding her estimates generously, Liv gave him an hour to get to Nashua, an hour with Kershaw's mother and an hour to get back. She had at least two more hours to wait for Sebastian's return.

She wasn't feeling useful.

He'd used her need to be part of his life to finesse her into staying at the Aerie, she decided as she put away the label maker. He'd done it as smoothly as if he was an artist and she were clay. Worse, she'd let him. Was that how he'd manipulated Olivia into obedience? Sweet-talked her until she glowed, then left her behind, a pampered prisoner in an ivory tower?

No wonder she'd grown frustrated.

"I am not Olivia." She slammed the door of the supply cabinet. He needed to see that in a real way—not just in the changes in her, but in a way he could separate the two instead of superimposing them.

Liv cranked up the bell tone on the office phones and headed up the stairs to Olivia's studio. The promise of snow hung on the eerie yellow light that pooled on the oak floor. In every corner of the room, Liv sensed Olivia's spirit. But there was also a stillness that spoke of death.

The finished trunk that had once stood on the black iron stand was gone. On the bottom shelf of the ceiling-to-floor unit that spanned the whole of the back wall were stacked several other trunks. One was half painted. Another sported only a white coating. Several more were still in their unfinished state of naked pine.

She took down the half-painted one and touched each detail—the maples with red-gold leaves, the calm blue water of the lake, the tiny people picnicking on a red, white and blue windmill quilt. She lifted the brass clasp. Inside were sketches on onionskin paper that showed a Victorian house, a barn and three horses out at pasture. Looking over the supplies stuffed into the shelf unit, Liv found a series of spiral-bound books filled with sketches. She plucked several that reminded her of Olivia from their pages.

Liv placed the half-finished trunk on the iron stand. With a paintbrush and glue, she layered the sketches with their bold, confident, graphite strokes, making the colored landscape on the trunk appear to fade away—just as Olivia had.

She grasped tubes of paint and several more brushes from Olivia's supplies. With red and blue and yellow and green and violet, she painted swirls of rainbows on the bottom-inside half of the trunk. The domed top half, she painted black.

"What are you doing?" Cari's voice startled Liv from her concentration.

"Burying Olivia."

"What?"

Liv shook her head. "It's just an idea."

"Oh." Cari plunked down the plate she carried on the flat utility table and circled around Liv's project.

Cari's protective layers of dark makeup were painted on thick. The dog collar was back at her throat. Chains jangled from her black leather jacket. The thick soles of her boots made her appear to move like an astronaut on a moonwalk. "Mom sent me to feed you. I'm supposed to make sure you have at least one of those fruit bars."

"Later." Her mind could barely stay in the room now that she'd entered willingly again into the folds of Olivia's life. A frantic need pulsed in her. *Do it, do it, do it.* Do what? Bury her. Bury Olivia. Olivia's dead.

Liv's gaze swept across those full shelves, each holding a piece of Olivia—her paints, her brushes, her treasures. She chose a tube of gold paint, a brush with fine bristles that came to a perfect point, a fresh pad of paper and a sharpened pencil. She grabbed the brass looking glass, a fat nut shaped like a crooked heart, a snow globe that housed Cinderella's blue-and-white castle on top of a snow-covered mountain.

"Liv?"

"Mmm." A ribbon caught Liv's attention, and she pulled it from its hiding place—violet with silver speckles. Sky and stars. She imagined those were Olivia's last sight on the night of her accident.

"Don't you think maybe you should wait?" Cari asked.

"For what?"

"For Sebastian."

"This is for Sebastian."

"What do you say we take a break? Go outside? I never did show you the sugar house."

"Can't." Liv stirred a finger in a pewter candy dish filled with coins and a Canadian quarter with the word "creativity" stamped on one side fell out. The branches of the tree etched on the coin whipped about a boatload of people in a canoe. The mountains in the background made the trunk of the tree appear to become a totem pole. Were totems for the living or the dead? Liv couldn't remember—or maybe she never knew. She added the quarter to her growing pile.

Cari stood in Liv's path, forcing her to look up. "Why not? Why can't you go?"

Liv slid around Cari, her gaze already focused on a small silver frame on a high shelf. "I have to stay here in case Kingsley calls."

"Mom'll get the phone."

"I know where the information is filed." That suddenly seemed silly and she laughed. She of the blank mind could find the needle in the haystack of files in Sebastian's office. Crazy.

With fingertips, she swept at the frame until it fell on top of the pile in her arm. The frame held the print of a wild horse galloping across an open prairie, making the words "Dreams need hope to run free" seem as if they were part of the wind. Liv started to add it to her stack, then placed it back on the shelf. Dreams still needed hope. And, if nothing else, Liv was filled with hope. Hopes for herself, for Sebastian, for the life they could create together. She may not have a past, but she definitely could make a future.

Cari grabbed Liv's arms and the load they held fell to the polished oak floor. "Okay, that's enough, Liv."

"No, I need to fill the trunk with all the pieces that made her." Liv crouched to the floor and picked up the fallen fragments of Olivia, plucking the castle out of the shattered shell of its glass globe.

"A change of scenery. That's what you need." Cari tugged on Liv's sleeve.

"Later." Liv's gaze swept the room, but nothing else

caught her eye. As she rushed out of the studio, she said, "Listen for the phones, will you?"

"This is crazy."

"This is necessary. You're all hanging on to Olivia as if she was coming back. I don't want her back."

"What?" Cari trotted behind Liv. "What are you talking about? Where are you going?"

Liv climbed the stairs. "Closet."

Cari followed, shifting from side to side as if trying to find a way to divert Liv's straight track. "Are you leaving?"

"No. I'm just making room for me." The master bedroom door bounced against the wall, but Liv didn't notice. She headed straight for the closet. She pulled a suitcase from the top shelf and filled it with all the navy pants and pastel sweaters she would never wear.

"Sebastian isn't going to like this." Cari glanced nervously at the clothes crammed into the suitcase. "You know how he is."

Liv moved on to the dresser. "I know that he wants what's best for me."

"You're wrong." Cari rubbed the wide band of her watch back and forth across her wrist. "He wants what's best, what's easiest for him. He likes the way things are. Can't you tell how hard this is on him?"

Liv knew this situation was hard on Sebastian. This would help. She plucked out a sheer scarf from a drawer. The swirls in shades of blue were so Olivia, soft and ephemeral. Liv placed it on the bed. "He can adapt, Cari. That's what he does."

"No, don't you see?" One arm waved as if Cari were a wounded bird trying to take off. "He can adapt out there because things stay the same here."

Liv added the teal vase from the dresser's top and the

oval sapphire from the jewelry box to the growing pile on the bed. "But they aren't the same. They were changing anyway."

"He would've found a way to bring her back and make things the same."

Liv dropped the last of Olivia's silk T-shirts in the suitcase and zipped it shut. "Now, I'm not giving him the chance. We're going to bury Olivia. We'll hold a memorial service, have a funeral. Then he'll see that things have changed."

"And if he doesn't accept your view?"

"Then things will change anyway, won't they?" Liv fiddled with the wedding band on her finger. It slipped easily over her knuckle. She glanced at the gold circle and noticed the inscription, "SEF to OAS—Forever."

Forever, the ring said. Till death do you part, they'd vowed on their wedding day. She didn't even know what the A stood for—Anne? Alexandra? Abigail?

Liv dropped the wedding band on top of the pile on the bed. She would not honor Olivia's promises. She would make her own.

One arm wrapped around her middle and chewing the thumbnail of her other hand, Cari suddenly looked like a small child as she slouched against the door frame. "Why can't things stay the same?"

"You're afraid." Liv walked over to her niece and hugged her.

Cari's shoulders shook, and she dropped her head onto Liv's shoulder. "I—I…"

"You don't like change."

Tears exploded out of Cari. Black streaks of mascara ran down the red shoulder of Liv's sweater. "I'm scared, too," Liv said. "I love Sebastian, and I'm not sure he can ever love me the way he loved Olivia."

Forcing him to face his fears was a risk. He could just as easily reject her as he could embrace her. Olivia was a part of him. Liv didn't want to take that away from him. But she wanted a clean start for herself. She wanted him to want *her,* not just the Olivia in her. She wanted to feel as if she had a solid footing in her home. To have both on her terms, she needed to take that scary step into the unknown. And it was like jumping out a high window. Would she break or would she land on her feet?

"You've been so good to me, Cari. I really appreciate the way you've stood up for me with Paula and Sebastian. It's not like our friendship will change just because I choose to stand on my own."

"I know, but…"

"But what?"

Cari shook her head.

"It's okay." Liv was touched that Cari cared.

"I think I made a mistake."

"We can fix it."

"Why are guys such jerks?" Cari wailed. "Why do we always have to change for them? Why can't they change for us? Why aren't we good enough the way we are?"

"We are." Liv wiped Cari's tears with her thumb. "We just have to believe it first."

Cari pushed away from Liv, took both of her hands and grasped them so tightly Liv whimpered. "I'm sorry, Liv. I'm so sorry. I didn't mean to screw everything up. I thought, I thought—"

"Cari?"

"Liv, if I tell you something, do you promise not to ask questions?"

The fiery look in Cari's pale blue eyes frightened her. "Cari…"

"It's important, Liv. Please trust me."

Reluctantly, Liv nodded.

"If you want to help Sebastian, you have to help me find your account numbers. Now."

"I promised Se—"

"He's going to kill you. Unless I bring him the account numbers, he's going to kill you." Cari tugged on Liv's hand. Liv resisted. "Sebastian won't hurt me."

"Not Sebastian, Thor."

"Who's Thor? What account numbers?"

Cari shook her head. "I thought if I did what he asked, then Sebastian would see what it's like. He could've helped Dad, but he refused."

"Wait. Stop." Liv pulled Cari down at the foot of the bed. "Now tell me what you're talking about."

Cari popped right back up. "A mistake. I made a mistake. I gave him Sebastian's accounts, but there's not much there. Now he wants yours. And I can't find them. They're not on the computer."

"Sebastian keeps Olivia's and his financial things separate."

Cari's eyes widened and she reached for Liv's hands, squeezing them tight. "You know where they are?"

"Of course. I filed them."

Cari heaved a loud sigh of relief. "Oh, I'm so glad. I never, ever, meant to hurt you. Only Sebastian, and I never meant it to end like this. Let's go."

"I don't understand."

"It's okay. As soon as I give him the account numbers, everything'll be fine." She led Liv down the stairs at breakneck pace.

THE FUMES OF CHEAP RED WINE in Nadine Kershaw's apartment were so thick, a lit match could have blown the whole thing to the moon. Her body conformed to the faded orange recliner's contours as if she'd been poured into it— a soft white pudding of a woman draped in black stretch pants and a dizzying yellow-and-black vertical-striped top. The television flickered images from *The John Walsh Show,* but the sound was muted to white noise. Was she expecting Walsh to run a segment to find her son's killer? Sebastian could almost understand how that would make sense to her.

He patted Nadine's fleshy hand to regain her straying attention. "I need to know who helped you."

"No good," she slurred. "I tried, you know. I did the best I could."

"I'm sure you did. But to find who killed Bernie, I need to know who was the contact between him and Weld."

"No good." Her sausage fingers reached for the bottle on the end table covered with cigarette butts. She tipped the bottle back to her open mouth and found it empty. Her head dropped forward and her whole body shook as she cradled the empty bottle between her huge breasts.

"Whoever was helping Bernie after he escaped is the one who killed your son."

Her bloodshot eyes connected with his. "Jealous. He was always so jealous." Tears magnified the tired brown of her eyes.

"Who?" Sebastian prodded. "Who was jealous?"

"I tried."

"I know. I can understand how a mother would want to keep her son out of prison. You gave birth to him. You raised him. Sacrificed for him."

"Damn right. Gave everything to him."

Sebastian sought eye contact with Nadine. This was taking too long. He needed to get back to Liv. "That makes you an accessory, Nadine. You realize that, don't you? It means you could go to prison." He scooped a half-empty bottle of wine from the shag carpet so filthy he couldn't tell what color it was. "They don't serve booze in prison."

She made a grab for the bottle. He swung it out of reach. "You can have this, Nadine. Just as soon as you tell me who made all the calls from the disposable cell phone you bought."

She stared at the bottle and swallowed hard. He sloshed the liquid to whet her thirst. She licked her thick lips.

"I'm not going to make this easy for you, Nadine. You can talk to me and fix your pain, or I can take you in and we can wait you out. Either way, we're going to find out who you gave that phone to."

She looked away, out the window where some kid had scrawled "Wash me" in the dirt. "Why should I help you? You never helped me."

"I'm helping you now, Nadine. You don't want to go to jail."

She snuffled. "I tried. But he made it so hard to love him."

"Bernie?" Sebastian asked, confused.

"Bernie was a good boy. He always took care of his mother."

"So you took care of him."

She nodded. "The other one, it was always, I want, I want, I want. A mother can only give so much."

Sebastian's pulse jumped. The other? The brother? "Nathan helped Bernie set up the escape?"

"I said I'd take care of him. I got a settlement check coming. He could go to his fancy school and get his fancy degree. Don't know why he needs it. It's not like he's got any brains in his head. Special needs, they said. He was always slow.'' She shook her head, jiggling her jowls. ''Bernie would take care of me. He always did.''

''What happened?'' Sebastian prodded, biting back impatience.

''He said five years was enough. I owed him. Bernie owed him.'' She swatted at the tears streaming from her eyes. ''If he'd kept his mouth shut, he'd have gotten probation. But no, he had to show how smart he was.''

Something clicked in Sebastian's mind. ''Nathan went to jail for Bernie?''

''Cops.'' She spat out the word. ''They're always picking on Bernie.''

Yeah, poor Bernie. It's not his fault he had to rape and kill and steal. ''So what happened to Nathan?''

''I had to use the money for the funeral. Bernie needed a good funeral. He was a good boy.''

The picture Nadine painted was turning into a horror flick. A son sent to prison to save his brother from a harsher sentence. A brother helping a brother for money. Brother betraying brother, leaving a trail of broken promises behind. ''Where's Nathan now?''

One of her hands shot out and Sebastian jerked away from its orbit just in time. ''Good riddance. He was always more trouble than he was worth.''

Sebastian swirled the wine in the bottle. ''Where is Nathan now?''

''Burning in hell.'' She reached for the bottle. ''If there's any justice in this world, he's burning in hell.''

Sebastian suddenly felt the hairs on the back of his neck bristle. He'd been so focused on one detail, he'd forgotten the big picture.

Footsteps in the snow after Bernie died minutes away from the Aerie. Mercer's blood at a campsite half an hour from the house. And Olivia was home alone an hour away.

BUNDLED IN WINTER CLOTHES, Liv followed Cari's footsteps as her niece led her farther and farther into the
woods. Cari was determined to go on this fool's errand
and Liv could not let her go alone, not when she seemed
so unstable.

Watery light softened the harsh lines of granite in boulders. Pine boughs scented the air. Even the atmosphere had
a soft, expectant quality to it—as if the world were pre-
paring for magic. There was nothing sinister about the
chirp of nuthatches, the scamper of squirrels up and down
tree trunks or the lazy twirl of scattered snowflakes.

Still, she could not get her heart to stop beating as if a
monster lay in wait just around the corner. She wanted
Sebastian's solid weight behind her. He would know what
to do. She was sketching blind, not quite sure where this
maze of lines was going. The pines gave way to maples
so thick they could hide a man as big as Skyralov, and
Liv's sense of unease snowballed.

"Cari, slow down." Liv needed time to think. This isolated rendezvous could not be good. Why ask Cari to meet
him in such a place if his intentions were honorable? The
only reason for such a play was to harm Cari. Liv didn't
see a happy ending to this script.

Sebastian would look for her, of that she was sure. But
what if he found them too late?

"Cari, *stop.*"

Cari's backpack slipped from her shoulder. She shoved
it back up without missing a step, driving forward as if
she were metal being pulled by a powerful magnet.
"We're almost there."

"Let's wait for Sebastian."

"No, I can't." Cari shrugged. "I thought..." She shook
her head. "Never mind. Once I give him these numbers,
it'll all be over."

"Cari, I don't think he—"

"I never meant to hurt you. I just wanted..." She stopped. In the clearing ahead, thin smoke writhed against the gray clouds. The scent of maple syrup invited closer inspection. The door of the dark cabin opened and a young man smiled at them. His body was sapling thin. A black knit cap covered a shaggy growth of brown hair. His fisherman's sweater was stained and looked all stretched out. Bony knees poked through holes in his jeans.

"Okie, you made it," he said, without looking at Cari. His feral gaze ate Liv and gave her the creeps. How could Cari have trusted him?

"I got 'em." Cari let the pack slip to her feet. She crouched next to it and started digging through the front pocket.

"Yeah, whatever." The amber of his eyes made Liv think of a caged wolf thirsty for blood. She wanted to run, but wasn't quite sure how to get back to the Aerie.

She should have stopped Cari. She should have asked Paula for help. She should have left Sebastian a note. Anything but follow an upset girl blindly into a storm.

Now they were prey for someone out for murder.

Liv looked back at the trail of their boots. Falling snow already softened their edges. If it snowed much longer, their tracks would disappear. And no one would find them.

Chapter Sixteen

"Tie her up." Once they were in the sugar house, he thrust a length of rope into Okie's hands.

She jerked her arms as if the rope was on fire. "No! I gave you the numbers. It's over now. You have to go."

Bitch! "Fine."

If you wanted something done, you had to do it yourself. He grasped the princess's arm and twisted it back. She gasped, but she didn't fight. Almost took the fun out of it. He'd love to stamp the print of his hand on that flawless skin. Time enough for that later. Maybe not so flawless skin, he thought, as he caught sight of the puke-green bruise along the side of her face.

"Hey!" Okie clawed at him like a cat on a catnip high. "Leave her alone. You have what you wanted."

"And more."

He shoved the princess onto a pile of burlap feed sacks. Then he whipped around and caught Okie's wrist as she tried to help the princess up.

"She's not Olivia," Okie said. "He won't lift a hand to save her."

"Nice try. He'd follow tracks even for you. Not that you're worth saving."

"Hey, what are you doing?" Okie kicked at him as he

wrapped the rope around her wrists, then she head-butted him. But he was strong. Jail did that. Living on the edge did that. Made steel out of muscles and mind. Made him as powerful as Thor.

"Taking care of loose ends." He twisted the rope tight against her wrists.

"Ouch! You're such a jerk. This isn't going to work. You don't understand—"

Holding Okie by both shoulders, he brought her face close to his. "You think they'll forgive you once they find out how you betrayed them."

"Betray? But you said—"

"Anything and everything that would get you to cooperate."

"But it's over. I gave you the numbers."

He backhanded her. "Shut up. You've served your purpose."

He threw her on the ground next to the princess.

"I'm sorry, Liv." Tears streamed down Okie's face. "I thought…I thought—"

"I said shut up." He withdrew the Glock pistol he'd stolen from Bernie from his waistband and pointed it at her. His finger tightened around the trigger. He wanted to shoot her. He wanted to watch her face explode—just like Bernie's. But the noise might attract attention, and he still had one thing to set up before he left a trail of crumbs for Falconer to follow.

He got out the Thermos of hot chocolate Cari had so thoughtfully provided—to warm him up, he'd told her. He laughed as he added the powder he'd guarded for the past few weeks to the Thermos. "Drink up."

"Up yours!" Okie spat at him.

He shoved the Thermos cap at her. It bumped against her teeth, splitting her lip. "Drink."

Her knee struck his elbow, tingling his funny bone. Hot chocolate sloshed over the sides of the cup, burning the back of his hand. He threw what remained of the hot liquid in her face. She squealed like the pig she was. "Do that again and next time I won't be so kind."

He hog-tied the squirming sow with duct tape, then re-filled the cap.

"Cari," the princess said, "don't make him angry."

At least one of them had an ounce of intelligence.

"You don't understand. He's not going to let us walk out of here."

"Drink up, sweetheart." He was eyeball to eyeball with Okie and took pleasure in the lightning of fear crackling in those pale blue eyes. With a hard swallow, she surrendered and opened her mouth. He poured the hot chocolate in the pink cave he'd fantasized about over the past months and rubbed her throat to make sure she swallowed. He grew hard at the thought of how differently he'd seen this scene played out in his dreams. Too bad.

When he got to the princess, she didn't bat an eyelash, just meekly complied. He liked that in a woman.

When he was sure they were both asleep—a pinch here, a kick there—he gathered his equipment and stole into the storm.

All he needed was Falconer and his revenge would be complete. He wanted the high-and-mighty marshal to see everything he loved destroyed—first his wife, then his home, and, if he was lucky, the clues he'd left behind would cost Falconer his career, too.

He'd used Falconer's own measly savings to make it look as if Falconer had been the one to finance Bernie's jailbreak. How would the Marshals Service deal with someone who'd free a felon for his own personal vengeance? And, by the time everything got unraveled, Thor would no longer exist and a new man would be living high on Olivia's money.

THROUGH THE VEIL of her lashes, Liv watched Cari's friend gather a pillowcase heavy with something lumpy. He added rolls of duct tape and bits and pieces she couldn't quite make out. On the way out, he plucked her gloves from the ground. The door creaked as he shut it.

She strained to listen to the quiet outside the sugar house. The patter of snow on the metal roof sounded like mice skittering in an attic. A blue jay warbled a reedy gurgle. A squirrel squeaked a tirade.

He was gone, but he would be back. How long did she have to get out of here with Cari?

Slowly, Liv dribbled the hot chocolate she'd held in her mouth. It left a brown track on the light blue of her parka. Her one small swallow to show him good faith had loosened her muscles, making them feel thick. Her mind was fuzzy on the edges, but she was used to functioning at less than a hundred percent these days.

In the gray light as opaque as wet decoupage glue coming through the dirty windows, Liv studied her surroundings. Plastic and metal buckets, syrup taps, drill bits, boxes of bottles and cans with a snowy maple tree design waiting for this spring's crop of syrup, and loops of green-and-purple plastic tubing littered shelves and the workbench. She spied a pair of pliers near the evaporating pans. But that wouldn't help. She needed something sharp. Then she spotted the ax near the woodpile along the back wall.

"Cari, wake up!"

Liv struggled to her duct-taped feet and wavered. With her elbows propped against the wall, she regained her balance, then hopped to the woodpile. Groping blindly with her hands tied behind her back, she tried to locate the ax.

She wedged it between two pieces of wood in the pile, then positioned her wrists above it.

"Cari, come on, sweetie. You have to wake up."

Sawing the rope as fast as she could against the dull edge of the ax, Liv planned her next step. They couldn't fight against hatred and determination. Her body was too weak to stand a chance to win; Cari would be too groggy from the drug. Liv would have to get out of this with her wits. A short sharp laugh escaped her. What wits? They, along with her memory, were trapped in the black hole that was her mind.

They had to be gone before he returned. Before Sebastian came looking for them. She'd feel safer if Sebastian was here, but she could not let him walk into this death trap.

"Cari! Come on. Wake up!"

Sweat broke out as she sawed at the rope. She could do this. She could. All she needed to do was free her hands. Then she could free her ankles. Then she could free Cari. Then they could walk to safety. One step at a time. She could do this. And when they got to the Aerie, they would have a whole team of law enforcement to pounce on Cari's misguided friend.

Piece of cake.

All she had to do was keep herself from falling into the black pit of panic.

"WHERE'S LIV?" Sebastian asked as he bulldozed his way into the kitchen.

Paula spun around startled and dripped dishwater over the tile. "Cari said she was with you."

"I left Liv here under your care."

Face pinched, Paula returned to the dishes in the sink.

"Look, there's a lot going on in Cari's life right now, but she doesn't lie."

"I left Liv here."

Paula looked at him over her shoulder, then frowned as she wiped her hands on her apron. "I don't understand."

"Where's Cari now?" Liv's fine, Sebastian tried to convince himself. Cari was impulsive, but she wouldn't hurt Liv.

Paula shrugged. "In her room, pouting. As usual."

Taking the stairs two at a time, Sebastian raced up to Cari's room. It was empty. Puffing hard, Paula caught up to him.

"Check if her coat's still in the mudroom," he said, remembering the last time Cari lured Liv outside. Maybe they'd just gone for a walk. But the hair on the back of his neck wouldn't stop bristling.

With a glance at the empty bed, Paula nodded and left.

He circled the room, willing himself to see through the mess of clothes piled on the floor. Half-opened drawers spilled sweaters, bras and T-shirts. The closet door hung open. Black boots and thick-soled shoes boxed each other for space. Only her bedside table was neat. He pulled open the drawer, saw a diary with black pages sitting at an odd angle and half a dozen pens with pastel ink. As he lifted the book, the dispersing pens rattled like bones. Beneath the diary was a piece of paper with familiar numbers. A chill zigzagged through him. The numbers to his bank accounts. How had she gotten them? Why?

Swearing, he started down the stairs toward his office, nearly crashing into Paula.

"Their coats are gone," she stammered, flattening herself against the wall to let him by. "Liv's and Cari's."

"Was Cari in my office today?"

"I don't know."

The force of his expletive had Paula cowering.

"How could she do this?" He crumpled the piece of paper in his hands. "Why would she need access to my bank accounts?"

Without waiting for a reply, he raced back up the stairs and zeroed in on the laptop on Cari's bed. Paula walked into the room like a prisoner on her way to execution.

"What's her password?" he asked, trying for the easy way.

"How should I know?"

With a growl, he tapped a few commands, then a few more, and finally accessed Cari's e-mail account. What he read made his heart sink. Sk8Thor was Nathan Kershaw, Bernie's brother, and he'd enlisted Cari to do his dirty work. The evidence was all laid out in black and white. He'd shown her step-by-step how to change the fuse in Olivia's car to cause the electrical fire. He'd told her step-by-step how to neutralize the security system for his forays around the Aerie. He'd described step-by-step how to get into the computer system to retrieve Sebastian's financial information.

"What did she do?" Paula asked in a thready voice as she wrung her hands.

"Your daughter," he said through gritted teeth, "is responsible for your sister's accident. For all of this mess."

"No." Paula sank to the mattress like a lead weight.

He shoved the laptop at her. With trembling hands, Paula turned the screen toward her and read. Tears streamed down her cheeks. "I didn't know."

"Where did she meet him?"

Paula's hands fluttered like drunken butterflies. "She's been volunteering with this church group. They write to convicts. I thought... I thought the correspondence was innocent enough. I thought it was helping her see that her problems are small compared to the troubles of others.''

Sebastian grasped Paula's shoulders and shook them. ''Think, Paula, where would Cari have taken Liv?''

Her pale blue eyes were rounded with fear. ''I don't know.''

Sebastian paced the room, trying to order his thoughts. This was his fault. He'd brought Cari here. He was the one who'd insisted she and Paula help him out with Olivia. How could he have been so blind? How could he have made it so easy for her and Kershaw to tear his world apart?

Time for blame later. He needed to concentrate on Liv.

With her blank slate of a mind, Liv was a trusting creature. She would have thought nothing about following Cari. And Cari, he knew, could put on quite a convincing act. Because of a misplaced need for love, Cari was leading Liv straight to Nathan Kershaw. Cari had no car. Paula's was still in the garage. Mario's was still parked next to the gatehouse.

They had to be near. He glanced out the window to the snow-misted view of the mountains. Somewhere out there.

Boxing away his fears for Liv, he bolted to his office. He forced himself to check his equipment meticulously. There'd be no room for error. He scribbled a note for Skyralov and Reed and rushed up the stairs. Just as he was about to leave the house, the phone rang.

''I found Mercer,'' Kingsley said when Sebastian answered. ''He doesn't look good.''

Sebastian swore. ''See he's taken care of, then head back here. Kershaw's brother has Olivia.''

''Wait for backup.''

''I'll track and let you know what I find.'' Without waiting for an answer, Sebastian headed into the fast-dimming afternoon light. With dusk approaching, there was no time to lose.

Snowflakes ticking against the nylon of his parka, he bent to the task of finding Liv. Using the tracking skills he'd honed over the years, he followed the fast-disappearing trail Liv and Cari's boots had left behind.

As he focused on the depressions in the snow, he tried to separate emotions from responsibility, but they were meshed as tight as chicken wire. This time, he could not separate Liv and work. He could not leave one to find the other. A failure now would cost him more than his life— it would cost him his soul. He shivered, hunched his shoulders and forced his mind back to the tracks in the snow.

Liv, where are you?

He'd find her. He'd protect her. He didn't want to think beyond that.

As he entered the woods, he spied a navy glove sugared with snow.

Chapter Seventeen

"Cari," Liv said as she tried to lift her niece's unconscious weight. "Wake up."

Cari moaned, twisted her head from side to side and gagged. "Sick."

Great, Liv thought, just what we don't need. They had to get out of here now. She'd had to spend too much time resting while she freed their hands and legs. On the other hand, throwing up would get the poison out of Cari's system and maybe they could move faster. Liv reached for one of the sap buckets and supported Cari as she vomited into it. Sympathetic waves of nausea swirled in Liv's stomach. She patted her niece's back. "You're doing fine, Cari."

Cari whimpered. "I told you to stay home."

"I couldn't let you go alone."

"I didn't mean—"

"We'll talk later. Right now we have to go."

Cari clung to the sides of the bucket as her stomach heaved more of its contents. "He said he understood. He knew what it was like to be accused of doing something you hadn't done. Just like Daddy." Her voice hitched. "He said he loved me."

"It's okay." Liv felt sorry for Cari, so young and trusting. An easy recipe for a broken heart. "We need to get out of here before he comes back."

Panting, Cari nodded and tried to get up. Her feet slid from underneath her. She sobbed. "I can't. You go."

Liv tugged at Cari, attempting to find a hold on the slippery jacket. But Liv was too weak. Her muscles refused to clasp strongly enough to heft Cari. Had Olivia been this helpless before her accident? "Help me, Cari."

"You weren't supposed to get hurt."

"I'm fine." Liv shifted her weight, bracing. "Put your arm around my shoulders."

Cari whipped a slack arm. It slid right off Liv's shoulders. "Sebastian. He was the one who was supposed to feel what it was like to be scared for someone you love."

"Come on, Cari, help me." Liv braced her legs and pushed herself up, dragging Cari up with her.

"He wouldn't help Dad, Liv."

How could someone as slight as Cari feel as if she weighed a ton? Liv adjusted her hold. "Well, people like your friend don't seem to help anyone but themselves."

"Sebastian. If he'd helped him, Dad would still be alive. Said it was too late. Dad had to face his mistakes."

Liv attempted to move forward only to have Cari list backwards. "Well, then, I'm sure that's true."

"Daddy was a good man." Cari grabbed on to the collar of Liv's jacket. "It was just money, Liv. Sebastian should've helped him. He said he didn't have access to your money. But he never asked you. You would've helped. Daddy died because Sebastian wouldn't help him."

Liv used Cari's tight hold to propel them forward. "Even good men can make mistakes."

"I miss him."

"I know you do, sweetie." Liv prodded another step out of Cari. "Losing someone you love hurts."

"My fault." Cari bent at the waist, nearly taking Liv with her as she dry heaved.

"We can sort it out later. Let's try to make it out the door. Just a couple more steps. Come on. There you go."

"I told Thor what Sebastian found. I tricked the security system like he told me. I let him in."

"That's all in the past now, Cari. What's important is that we get out of here."

"I can't, Liv. The walls are spinning." Cari slid right down the side of Liv's body and landed in a heap at her feet, unconscious once more.

The door of the sugar house squealed. Gasping, Liv turned from her pretzeled position as she tried to lift Cari and faced Cari's friend. He leaned against the door frame, a dark silhouette against the gray haze of the storm. Her stomach pitched, surging a wave of acid up her throat.

"Well, well, what have we here?"

He uncurled himself from the door frame like a snake from a warm rock and struck her before she had time to react. She fell onto her back, as helpless as a turtle turned over on its shell.

He smiled down at her. A flat, mean smile. "I leave for a few minutes and come back to this." He wound a fresh length of rope around her wrists. Interlacing her fingers, she pressed against the cruel pull of the rope, creating a pocket of space between her wrists, yet letting him think the knot was tight.

"It won't be long now," he said. "I saw your husband coming home. He'll join us in no time." His cold smile widened. "He won't be able to miss the crumbs I left behind."

He pulled the rusty card chair from its position against

the evaporator pans and plunked it before the front window. From the corner, he watched the trail. ''I expect he'll try to circle around to catch me unaware. But I didn't leave him a choice. He'll have to come out front.''

''Why are you doing this?'' Liv struggled to find a way to keep her heart from jumping right out of her chest.

He shrugged. ''They owe me.''

''What does Sebastian owe you?'' She flattened her hands and tried to wriggle out of the loosened rope, hoping the sound of her voice would mask her activity.

With narrowed eyes, he turned on her. A gun appeared in his hands—a black, unblinking eye pointed right at her head. ''Shut up!''

''I'm just trying to understand.'' Her knees rattled one against the other. She draped the rope over her freed wrists and held the loose ends in her fists.

He waved the gun. ''And I said shut up.''

She ought to fight. She ought to do something, not just sit there like a lump. But her heart was thundering, her pulse was all out of kilter and her muscles felt like overcooked noodles. And he was armed. What could she do against a gun? Dead, she wouldn't do Cari any good. Dead, she couldn't warn Sebastian. Tears burned her eyes. She blinked them back. *Stay alert. Stay alive.* Whatever it took. She would not let him hurt the people she loved. She'd lost too much of herself already.

Minutes later, Cari's friend rose from the chair and lifted the gun in a shooting stance, aiming it at the door.

''Right on cue.'' He smiled a jackal's smile. He pulled on the rope he'd rigged to the door handle.

Sebastian. A spurt of joy gushed through her, quickly replaced with a bloom of dread. ''He has a gun,'' Liv yelled and dropped the rope from her wrists.

"Come on in, Deputy Marshal. We've been waiting for you."

"Put the gun down, Nathan. You're surrounded."

Sebastian's voice came from outside, but Liv couldn't see him. "He's going to kill you." She glanced at the ax near the woodpile. Could she get to it before Nathan turned his gun on her? She inched sideways. "No matter what you do, he's going to kill you. Run!"

"I know you're alone." Nathan whipped his arm around and pointed it at Liv, stopping her in her tracks. He stood sideways, invisible to Sebastian on the other side of the door. "Drop your gun or your wife dies."

Liv did not want to die. She didn't want Sebastian to die. She didn't even want this hard-hearted man to die. Springing up with energy she didn't know she possessed, she lunged at Nathan's legs. But he anticipated her clumsy effort. His steel-toed boot connected solidly with her rib cage. Cari's unconscious body broke her fall. Dust rose from the feed bags, making her cough and blinding her for a second.

"Next time," Nathan said, eyes narrowed and gaze lethal. "Straight to the heart."

Liv heard the clatter of Sebastian's gun hitting the wood floor. "No, Sebastian, don't listen to him!" Holding her aching ribs, she scrambled up.

"Kick it toward me," Nathan said. The gun slid into view. He picked it up and tucked it in the small of his back. "Now hands up and come on in. It's not polite to stand outside when you've been invited in. Even white trash has some manners."

Sebastian walked in, and her heart sank. Fear was a live fire in her blood. All the hope she'd held close to her heart evaporated.

Liv watched Sebastian pick out shades of possibilities.

He was all muscle, adrenaline and determination. He was Atlas, shoulders bent and curbed, against the weight of the world. He was Zeus with the lightning of judgment in his hands. And just as she'd known that day in the parking lot in the hospital, he would die to see her safe. She couldn't let him. Nathan had no intentions of letting any of them live.

"Sit." Nathan waved the gun in the direction of the rusty card chair in the corner.

Sebastian took a backward step toward the chair.

Liv coughed to get Sebastian's attention. When their gazes connected, she silently drew it down her arm to her hand. Slowly, she reached her hand toward the burlap bag wedged beneath a box of bottles on the workbench.

Sebastian took another step back.

"Let's hurry it up," Nathan growled. "I don't have all night for this."

Sebastian reached the chair, but didn't sit. Every muscle was poised for action. With eye movements, Liv communicated her intentions to him. Nothing in him moved. He gave her no acknowledgment except a flicker of love quickly replaced by a flutter of fear in the dark intensity of his eyes. Each gave her courage.

Nathan waved the gun. "Sit."

Sebastian sat.

"Pull out your handcuffs. Slowly."

While Sebastian reached for the cuffs at his belt, Liv silently counted down from three to one with the fingers of her left hand so Sebastian could see. The look in Sebastian's eyes hardened to a *No* as loud as if he'd shouted it. But she had to keep going. She had to give them a fighting chance before Nathan handcuffed Sebastian to the chair. As her last finger curled back into her fist, she yanked on the burlap.

The box whispered against the wood of the workbench. It hung for an eternity on the edge. Then it bounced against her shoulder and crashed against the floor, spilling shards of glass halfway across the floor.

Instinctively, Nathan jerked his head to look at the commotion.

In a flash, Sebastian was out of the chair and parallel to Nathan's gun. He locked Nathan's wrist with his left hand, grabbed the gun barrel with his right hand.

He was going to get shot. He was going to die. Frantically, she scampered toward the ax on her hands and knees.

Sebastian pushed down on Nathan's wrist with his left hand while pulling up on the gun barrel with his right hand, breaking Nathan's trigger finger.

Liv grasped the ax with both hands and rushed at Nathan.

Folding over at the waist, Nathan screamed. Without wasting a second, Sebastian thrust the gun straight down toward the ground. The gun slipped out of Nathan's hand. With a quick side step, Sebastian scooped up the gun and moved out of Nathan's reach.

Relief seemed to turn her bones to jelly. The ax slid from her hands.

"On the ground," Sebastian yelled, holding Nathan at gunpoint. "Now."

Breathing heavily and holding his limp hand against his waist, Nathan spat in Sebastian's direction. "You think you've won." He laughed with the glee of a hyena. "You can kill me now, and I'll still get the last word."

"I'm not the one looking at the wrong end of a weapon."

"I've got nothing." Nathan was hyperventilating now. "And nothing's what I'm going to leave you with."

"On the ground. Now."

"Five years." Nathan shook his head. "That's what you cost me. Probation. They told me I'd get probation if I said I'd done what Bernie did. I was going to get out of here. Start all over. A fresh new life. She promised. All I had to say was that Bernie was innocent." He sneered. "I believed her. I believed him. I believed that greaseball lawyer." Nathan swore. "Then you caught Bernie, and she spent the money she'd promised me on Bernie's appeals. An example, the judge said when he sentenced me. You have to pay."

Sebastian seemed to have the situation in hand, but Liv wasn't taking any chances. Moving as surreptitiously as she could, she grabbed the metal card chair by the legs. Pinching her lips between her teeth against the pain in her ribs, she heaved the chair up, then brought the chair's back down on Nathan's head.

He crumpled like tissue.

Gun still pointed at Nathan, Sebastian reached for her and drew her close. "Are you okay?" he asked, kissing the top of her head. Nothing had ever felt so good.

"I'm fine." She shook so hard her teeth rattled. "He drugged Cari."

"Reach in my coat pocket and get my phone out. We'll get some help out here."

Just as her hands wrapped around the cold plastic of the phone, Skyralov and Reed burst through the sugar house's front door.

"Figures," Sebastian said, smiling. "The hard work's done, so you guys show up."

"You know Hollywood," Skyralov said, gun drawn, gaze taking in the whole situation. "He doesn't like to get his suit dirty."

"We'd have been here sooner—" Reed whipped handcuffs from his belt and cranked them around Nathan's wrists, "—but Cowboy had to stop for lunch. Two cheeseburgers with fries, a chef's salad and apple pie. And you know what he orders to drink?"

"What?" Liv asked, suddenly feeling so alive the whole world looked bright in spite of the gray skies.

"Green tea." Reed shook his head. "For digestion, he said."

Laughter rumbled through the room, cutting the tension.

"Let's go home." Sebastian held her as if he never intended to let her go. That was just fine with her. She had no intention of letting him out of her sight for a long, long time.

Liv smiled up at him. "Let's."

Skyralov slung a shackled Nathan over his shoulder like a sack of potatoes. Reed hoisted a moaning Cari into his arms. Sebastian closed the door of the sugar house with a decisive click.

Liv sighed as she sunk contentedly into his embracing hold. It was over. Now they could move on. They could bury Olivia and start their new life as a team.

"Where's your wedding ring?" Sebastian asked, frowning as he rubbed his thumb up and down her finger.

She glanced down at her bare finger, thought of the trunk filled with pieces of Olivia. "Long story." She smiled up at him. "But I was hoping we'd renew our vows."

A long sigh escaped him and a smile shone on his face. "I think we can arrange that."

As they stepped onto the trail back home, a boom shook the ground. Then the whole sky lit up in a blaze of orange fire and black smoke.

Liv's grip choked Sebastian's arm. "Paula."

Epilogue

Wind whipped around Sebastian. He welcomed its bite. The bright blue of the sky was insult enough to the blackened wreckage that was his home. The last thing he wanted was the caress of a warm breeze.

It was over. All of it.

Yesterday afternoon, Skyralov and Reed had left Paula in Mario's care at the gatehouse, then followed his tracks to the sugar house. They'd asked Paula to divert Kingsley their way when he got back from the hospital. When Sebastian and the rest of his group had emerged from the woods, they'd found Paula and Mario huddled together outside the gatehouse, staring at the spectacle of the Aerie burning. The local volunteer firemen had done their best but the blast Nathan had set was too strong to salvage any part of the house. Even the stone fireplace lay crumbled on its side as if someone had broken its spine.

Mercer would spend one more day at the hospital. He'd suffered a concussion when Nathan had cracked a branch over his skull. When Nathan had dumped Mercer's body down a narrow crag, Mercer had broken an ankle and a wrist. As he'd fallen, he'd bounced off the granite wall and landed on a ledge. If he hadn't, Kingsley might not have found his body until it was too late. From what

Kingsley had gathered, Nathan had caught Mercer by surprise as he released a deer from a plastic six-pack-ring hobble.

Wiser and sadder, Cari had revived quiet and contrite. She would have to deal with her part in Olivia's accident. Paula would have to deal with her failure toward Cari. They were both back home in Nashua, unable yet to accept Liv's forgiveness. It would come with time. The ties between these women were too strong to snap so easily. He could see that now and was no longer jealous of their shared history. At Liv's urging, Mario had packed his remaining hawk and had gone to watch over Paula and Cari. They were in good hands.

Sebastian and Liv now occupied the gatehouse—until he could decide what came next.

Alone for the first time in weeks, he was feeling adrift, torn between wanting to be here with Liv and the need to put people like the Kershaw brothers in jail where they belonged.

The hiss of snow as a charred supporting beam shifted brought Sebastian back to the ruin of his home.

He was no stranger to the sight of devastation. That was the territory he entered when he hunted. The lowest of the low. The baddest of the bad. The filthiest of the filth. But he hadn't stood by and watched life pass him. He'd done *something*. He'd made a difference. Being idle, that was something new.

The Aerie had made it possible to seek out evil and remain sane. The Aerie and Olivia.

They were both gone now. The Aerie lay in smoking ruins. Olivia was locked in some broken place of Liv's brain.

And his career was finished.

He could no longer pretend that things would go back to the way they were before.

If he'd bent the rules and regulations to further an investigation, Sutton would have stood behind him. But Sutton had warned him off, ordered him to close the case, and given him a directive to silence Weld. And Sebastian had kept pushing—strictly for personal reasons—and he'd chosen to disregard orders. He'd put his duty to the Service second to his own. Not only that, he'd involved a whole team of good men and jeopardized their careers. They would all have to face an internal investigation.

Shoving his hands deep into the pockets of his parka, Sebastian sneered. He'd thought he could do anything as long as his motives were good. What had that gotten him?

A rising plume of smoke made the summit of the mountain appear to dance.

He'd filed his report. Sutton hadn't called. Instead, he'd grasped every lie Kershaw told and used them to cover his own mistakes and to end Sebastian's career. The truth would come out. Eventually.

In the meantime, he was finished.

Mittened hands wrapped around his waist, taking him by surprise. Where had all his instincts gone that he hadn't even heard Liv's approach?

"We can rebuild," she said. He hooked one arm around her and cuddled her against his heart, shielding her from the sight of the burnt shell of their home.

The insurance would cover the cost of reconstruction. But he wasn't sure that was the best course of action. Especially now that he was out of a job. "The house was a wedding present from your father. I chose the spot. You chose the design. Your father paid for the construction."

"We can rebuild, Sebastian. We can start new. Your

own specialized Special Operations Group. Your own seekers. Your own rules.''

"I wouldn't have all the access I have now.'' The badge had opened doors that were now forever closed.

"You would if you surrounded yourself with the right people.''

He chuckled at her optimism. No one with the right skills would want to associate himself with someone with a tarnished reputation. Not a good career move.

Self-absorbed. Self-righteous. Self-important. That's what he'd been, and he was now paying the price. "And who would you get to pay for those services?''

She ticked off the possibilities on her mittened fingers. Red to match her hat and scarf. She looked good in red. Full of life. "You hire yourself out as a consultant to the Service,'' she said, "to other law enforcement agencies or to investigative firms. You charge hefty fees to civilians who can afford you, and that pays for the people who can't. You get to do what you're good at.'' She smiled up at him—a smile so bright, it nearly stopped his heart. "And I get to work with you. I'm good at finding the information in the haystack of your files.''

"You've given this some thought.''

"I've given it a lot of thought. We make a good team, Sebastian. You can't deny that.''

Could he really start over? Determine his own course. The idea was an aphrodisiac. Could he really give up the adrenaline high of the chase and settle down to a quieter life?

"We'd need more space.''

"So?''

"I have no money,'' he said.

"But I do.''

Money he'd carefully invested for her over the years.

He'd refused to let her use it to support them. Providing for her was his job. He shook his head. "No, I can't let you—"

"Why not?"

Olivia had stood by him. She'd endured the possibility that he'd die on the job. She'd endured his long absences. She'd endured the barriers he'd put between them as he sought to keep work and home separate. And she'd died for her loyalty.

He'd always thought of himself as strong, competent, self-reliant. He saw now that Olivia had held the true strength in their marriage. Liv was willing to give him—give them—a second chance. How could he deny her?

He thought about the high closing a time line could rush through him. But the high never lasted. The cuffs went on, then the high rang hollow—until he got home to Olivia. How could he keep forgetting something so important?

"We'll need a bigger office." He closed his eyes to the skeleton of their home. He held Liv close, imprinting the vitality of her spirit into him. She believed in him. He would believe in her.

"I have ideas."

"I'll bet you do." He laughed and, for the first time in a long time, it felt real, rumbling all the way down to his belly. He kissed her long and hard, and she melted into him, opening all the possibilities before them. "I love you."

Smiling, she pushed back in his arms. "You're trying to distract me."

"As I recall, it used to work well." He rubbed his thumb over her ringless finger under her mitten. "We'll need to do something about getting a new ring on your finger."

"I love you, too, but we have a couple of things to

decide on before we make wedding plans.'' She raised an eyebrow and her eyes twinkled with mischief. ''I won't let you dismiss me.''

He held up a hand as if to ward off evil. ''Never!''

She hooked her arm around his elbow. ''I was thinking of a compound.''

''A compound?''

She led him away from their scorched past. ''Yeah, you know, a place not just for strategy, but a base of operations…''

Her voice was a melody that warmed his heart. And as they walked down the snow-covered path back to the gatehouse, he knew he was heading into the best part of his life.

* * * * *

Look for the next installment
in THE SEEKERS,
the thrilling new miniseries by Sylvie Kurtz:
MASK OF A HUNTER
Coming in May 2004
From Harlequin Intrigue

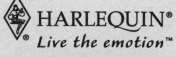

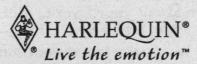